LOVERS KEY

C. F. FRANCIS

To Shirley
Enjoy!
C.F. Francis

For Cathy, who encouraged me to take the leap and has remained my biggest cheerleader

&

*To Neil, who has supported me every step of the way.
Love you...*

PROLOGUE

J ust a few short minutes ago Josie Boussard had foolishly believed her torturous journey had finally come to an end. She'd stood at the door of *Island Images* and stared into the darkened photography studio. Her legs, already weak and unsteady, buckled as she read the *CLOSED* sign hanging above the names of the studio's owners: Gibson McKay and Colton James—Steve's former Special Forces Commander.

Daylight was hours away. Tears stung as they'd channeled down the open wounds on her face. Colton James, was the key to finding Steve. Without Steve, she had no one else she could turn to. Nowhere else to run.

The sound of tires on asphalt invaded her world of self-pity, bringing her back to a place of urgency and fear. She needed to get out of sight. After she'd wiped the tears from her eyes, she'd spotted the patch of utter darkness across the driveway and had painfully made her way toward it. A garden. *Perfect*.

It took every last ounce of Josie's reserves to navigate her battered body over the fence that surrounded the property.

She crawled the last few feet to the massive potting bench she'd spotted once inside the small jungle. She shoved aside the bags of potting soil that rested on the lower shelf of the bench, then slid her long frame onto the rough wooden platform behind the wall she'd just created. Pulling her knees upward in the tight space, Josie clasped them to her chest, shivering against the unusually cool Florida night. Her eyes drifted shut as she said a prayer that no one would find her before morning.

1

Steve Brody had packed his duffel bag in the pre-dawn hours. Now that it was daylight, he scanned the master bedroom for any gear he might have left behind. Colton James and his wife, Cat, had been kind enough to let him bunk at their Sanibel home while they were on their honeymoon. He, along with a few other members of their Special Ops team, had stayed on the island after the wedding to enjoy the tropical November weather.

As Steve made his way through the living room, the sound of Rick Wilcowski's booming voice registered, yanking him from his solemn thoughts. But it was the sharp tone of Gib's response that had Steve dropping his duffel and heading out to the rear deck to find out what the commotion was about. Gibson McKay never raised his voice. Colt's partner was the wise-cracking, easygoing member of their group. For him to be arguing with Rick meant something was up.

"What the hell's going on?" Steve asked as he stepped onto the deck, shielding his eyes against the bright morning sun. As his sight adjusted to the glare, the picture in front of him left him momentarily deaf and dumb.

Rick was holding the door to the neighboring unit open. Gib was halfway through it, the limp frame of a woman was draped across his arms. Steve recognized the dark, cascading curls, despite them being dirty and disheveled.

"Josie?" Steve shot Gib an accusatory look. "What the hell are you doing with my wife?"

"Your wife?" Gib stepped away from the door, his rounded eyes reflecting his confusion.

"That's Josie?" Rick asked, his voice raised in surprise.

Steve ignored both questions as he rushed forward, gently taking Josie from Gib's arms. "What the hell happened to her? Did you call nine-one-one?"

"I don't think that would be a good idea," Gib answered as he followed Steve through Colt's kitchen and into the living room.

"Why the hell not?"

"Because I found her hiding in the garden next door. And I do mean hiding, Steve. She'd crawled under that large potting bench behind stacked bags of potting soil. If her hair hadn't fallen over the end of the shelf, I'd have missed her entirely."

"That doesn't explain why you didn't call for medics," Steve reprimanded as he tenderly placed Josie on the couch and pushed salt-encrusted hair from her brow. Her exposed skin was covered in cuts and bruises. A large knot was forming above her left eye. What were Gib and Rick thinking not calling for paramedics? He pulled his own phone out of his pocket.

"Hold up on that, Lieutenant," Rick said, joining them in the room. He shoved a warm, damp towel and an ice pack toward Steve.

If the statement hadn't been made to sound like an order, Steve would have ignored it. But Rick would not normally give him orders nor would he delay getting assistance for someone who needed it without good reason. His position as a detective with the Sanibel Police Department wouldn't allow him to look the other way.

"Why should I?" Steve asked, taking the items from Rick.

"Because Gib has a point."

Steve's anger momentarily turned to surprise, his eyes narrowing at the statement. For Rick to so easily agree with Gib was telling.

Steve knelt on the floor next to the couch, his eyes on the woman he'd once called his wife. "Either explain or I'm making the call," he said.

A mosaic of black, blue, and purple bruises covered Josie's face. The soft freckles on her nose were no longer visible under the grime. Swelling from a busted lip had diminished but was still distinctive. The bump on her forehead, however, was recent. Dirt and sand were caked under ragged fingernails. Jeans that were ripped, stained, and bloodied in places covered the long legs he remembered in his dreams. Bare, sandy feet were dotted with small cuts on their soles. He placed the ice pack on her forehead then tenderly began to clean her face with the warm cloth.

"Somebody better start talking fast." Steve's voice vibrated with anger.

"You know I've been keeping an eye on the Copeland property," Gib began.

The men were all aware of Gib's morning routine. Cat had a lease on the house and jungle that occupied the lot across the drive. Once she had rezoning approval it would become her garden design center and plant nursery.

5

"I don't need the backstory," Steve barked. "Get on with it."

"This lady—Josie," Gib corrected, "was hiding under Cat's big potting bench. I'm pretty sure she was sleeping, though. Not unconscious. She woke up startled and terrified. I thought she was going to bolt but as soon as I told her my name she immediately began asking for you or Colt."

"Who knows you're here on Sanibel, Steve?" Rick asked.

"Only friends and Josie. I texted her with my location. It's a habit." Legally, they weren't married but he hadn't been able to break the connection.

He rolled up the sleeves of Josie's blouse, only to find more bruises. Defensive wounds. "You need to get to the reason why I shouldn't call the paramedics. We can sort the rest of this out later."

"Because," Gib explained, "she should have been asking for help not two former members of a Special Forces team. Both you and Colt have shit in your backgrounds that will never be public knowledge, so I called Rick. When she saw his badge, she knocked herself out running away from the man wearing it. She does *not* want to be found by any authorities."

Steve gave a curt nod in agreement. If he'd been focused, he would have put it together, too. But this was Josie. He'd never been able to think straight when he was around her.

"What were you planning to do?" Steve asked, returning to his ministrations of Josie's face. While he carefully cleaned the grime from her tender skin, he listened. Gib had the intuition of a trained operative. The team had learned to trust it.

"When she woke up she was very animated—at least until her head hit that tree. The plan was to assess her condition and find you," Gib explained. "Why aren't you fishing?" he asked, suddenly aware Steve wasn't where he was supposed to be.

"I passed on Don and Kevin's invitation." Their friends had booked a morning charter to go deep-sea fishing. Steve had initially agreed to join them but changed his mind after he'd awakened in the middle of the night to find himself once again reaching for the woman who was not there. "Believe it or not, I was on my way to find Josie," he said, indicating the packed duffel bag on the floor of the living room.

"I guess she saved you the trip. I didn't know you were married," Gib added.

"I'm not."

"But you just said…"

"Not now, Gib," Rick warned, placing his hand on Gib's shoulder.

"How long has she been out?" Steve asked, ignoring the question hanging in the air.

"A few minutes," Rick answered.

"I don't like this," Steve rose to his feet and lifted Josie off the couch in one fluid motion. "I'm taking her to the hospital."

The limp body in Steve's arms suddenly stiffened. He looked down to see Josie's dark, violet-blue eyes staring wildly back at him.

"Josie?"

"Steve..." His name came out on a whisper as she buried her face in his chest and began to cry.

Holding her tightly against him, Steve ached at his loss. He'd missed this woman. He'd missed her laughter, her quick wit, as well as her bullheadedness. He'd missed holding her while he wrapped himself around her slim body then loving her until she trembled with desire. But desire and love hadn't been enough. She'd left before he'd had a chance to find out why.

Now she was in his arms again but beaten and crying. The tears were as alarming as her injuries. Josie never cried. He lowered his cheek to her hair and savored her closeness. Then he told her that he was taking her to the hospital.

Every muscle in her body went rigid. "Nooooooo," she said, her voice shaking as she struggled to break free from his arms. "They'll find me!"

2

_____

"Who'll find you?" Steve demanded.

Josie craned her neck so she could look over his shoulder. The man with the badge remained.

"Rick's okay. He's a friend. He was part of the team," Steve told her.

"The James Gang?" That had been the team's handle when they all served under Colton James.

"Yes," he confirmed. "Rick won't do anything that would put you in danger."

"See? I told you calling a real cop was a bad idea." The pony-tailed man took the opportunity to elbow the cop.

Rick's silence and his obvious assessment of Josie had her stomach doing somersaults. "I need to go," she told Steve as she wrestled to break free of his arms. Why had she expected Steve to be alone if she was lucky enough to find him? Now, not only were there others present but one had a direct connection to the system she'd been trying to avoid. They had found her once. She didn't doubt they would do it again. She needed to get out of there. Fast.

"You're not going anywhere until you tell me what's

going on and why I can't take you to a doctor." He tightened his hold, binding her to his chest.

Josie gave up the losing battle. Besides she had enough aches and pains without adding to them. "You don't legally have any say in the matter." The remark was a low blow and undeserved. But Josie was terrified. Her heart was pounding against her breastbone trying its damndest to break free. She pressed a fist to her chest, half expecting it to succeed.

"Can you give us a few minutes?" Steve turned to his friends with Josie still in his arms.

"We'll wait next door," Gib quickly agreed.

"You can have some time, Steve, but I can't walk away from this," Rick warned him. "I'll be back to talk with her."

As soon as they left, Steve returned Josie to the couch.

"Wait here," he said, unsure if she'd listen. But Rick and Gib would be keeping an eye on the exits, so she wouldn't get far if she decided to run. Steve quickly grabbed what he needed from the master bath and returned with a first aid kit and another warm washcloth.

"Put that ice pack back on your forehead," he ordered, then continued the process he'd started earlier. As the dirt and grime disappeared, her injuries became more apparent. She'd been beaten days ago from the look of her bruises. "Who did this to you?"

"It's a long story, Steve." With a groan, Josie attempted to sit up. "God, I hurt all over."

Grasping her shoulders, Steve gently pushed her back into the couch. The possibility of her having been raped quickly crossed his mind and almost made him physically ill. "You weren't....?"

"No," she answered, quickly catching his meaning.

"You should be at a hospital," Steve reiterated as he wiped her arm with the warm cloth. Again, she stiffened. What the hell was going on? He could force her into his car or call the paramedics and hold her there until they arrived but her fear was so palpable he couldn't bring himself to do either. Not yet.

Besides, Kevin and Don would be returning shortly from their fishing trip. Kevin was a Special Operations Combat Medic and he would check her out. If he said that Josie needed medical help, then Steve would get it for her—one way or another. Right now, experience told him that no argument would change her mind. The last thing he wanted was to give her reason not to trust him. They'd knocked heads as often as they'd made love and with the same amount of passion.

Josie had remained quiet as Steve continued to wipe away dirt and crusted saltwater from her pale skin. How had she managed to be covered in both?

Her silence gave him further cause to worry. Josie was rarely silent unless she was working. He glanced up from her battered feet and saw her head resting on the wide arm of the couch. The ice pack was still balanced on her forehead. Her eyes were closed but she wasn't relaxed. Tension vibrated in every muscle he touched as he tended to her injuries. He didn't miss her slight trembling although she'd been doing her best to conceal it. When was the last time she'd eaten? Josie'd always had a thin, athletic body but now she looked almost anorexic.

"Whose place is this?" Josie asked, sitting up with Steve's help.

"It belongs to Colt and his wife, Cat," he told her.

"It's nice," she said, glancing about the room. Her

appraisal of the space gave her time to catch her breath and organize her thoughts. So be it.

He didn't push but followed her gaze. He'd been in the home so often that he rarely noticed the details anymore. Designed and decorated with an artist's eye, it wasn't until Steve had seen this place that he began to think of his former commander as someone other than a soldier. Natural light flowed into the room from the windows that lined one side of the large space, accentuating the furniture upholstered in rich tones that sat on the golden bamboo flooring. Everything in the room reminded the occupant that they were in the tropics, including the stunning photographs that hung on the walls.

"A few of us are bunking here while they're in the Keys on their honeymoon," Steve volunteered.

"When do you deploy?"

She'd asked the question so softly, Steve almost missed it. He didn't miss the sadness, though, reflected in those deep-blue eyes before she dropped her gaze from his. Had it been there the last time she'd asked the question? He thought back to seven months ago when he'd received his orders to deploy. She'd said little when he'd told her. He'd selfishly thought she'd been worried about him but there had been more to her silence.

"Do you know where they're sending you next?" This time, her voice was a little stronger. Still, Steve had to strain to make out the words. Her gaze was trained on the hem of her shirt.

Steve laid a hand over the fingers that picked at bits of dirt embedded in the clothing. With his other hand, he cradled her jaw and gently tilted her head up to look at him. Even battered, she took his breath away.

Looking past the damage to her face, he could still see the passion, intelligence, and spunk reflected in her eyes. He'd lost his heart to her the day they'd met. She'd reluctantly accepted the gift only to return it to him as battered and beaten as she now appeared. The life he'd planned with Josie might not ever happen but before he started down a new path he needed to get her out of his system or tear down the barriers that kept them apart. To do either, he'd have to swallow his bitterness and talk to her, assuming she was willing to do the same.

"Where I go and what I do depends on you."

"I don't understand." She wrinkled her brow then flinched as those tender muscles met the lump on her forehead.

"I've done my last tour, Josie."

"You're what? The army is your life!"

He'd expected the stunned look. He'd never hidden the fact that he was a career man. His plan had been to stay in the military even after being part of the elite Green Berets was no longer an option for him. His family was army. He'd grown up on bases. His dad had served as had his grandfather. Each generation had loving, tight-knit families. Something he wanted too.

Josie had been an army brat, as well, but what little he knew of her background, it was the opposite of his. She blamed the breakup of her family on the military. He'd thought they'd gotten past that but it had become blatantly obvious that he'd been wrong. The day he'd received the news she was leaving would forever be ingrained in his memory. A bullet to the gut would have been easier to take.

It had been a dumb move on his part but Steve had given Josie the time she'd asked for to think things through when the life-changing error had been discovered. He'd commended himself for being understanding and unselfish. But he, too, had needed time to adjust to the news that they had never legally been man and wife. Not legally.

Anger and resentment had filled the first few months after she had moved out of their apartment near the base. There were times when he thought it was best not to resurrect the issue. If Josie could so easily walk away from their future, they'd never had one to begin with. Had he mistaken lust for love? He hadn't thought so at the time. And he didn't believe it now. Seeing her again proved to him that his heart had been engaged from the beginning. The break was real.

After the news, he'd done his best to compartmentalize his personal life, to set aside thoughts of their non-marriage, while he'd fought a never-ending battle in the mountains of Afghanistan. But unlike before, the camaraderie of his team had not been enough to fill the void—a void he hadn't realized existed until he'd met Josie. The days were long and the nights had been eternal. His lack of focus had been shot to hell. His Afghani interpreter was still recovering at an Air Force hospital in Germany due to that lack of focus.

Watching Colt and Cat together this past summer had opened his eyes. His happiness and future did not have to be tied to the army. He was proud of his service but after returning to the base from Sanibel that summer, he'd notified his superiors that he was retiring. The next step was determining whether his new life would include the woman he hadn't been able to purge from his system.

Yeah, giving Josie the space to "figure things out" had definitely been a mistake. The break had torn them both apart and the wounds wouldn't heal as long as they were allowed to fester. The two of them needed closure but that would have to wait.

"Josie, I need to know what's going on before Rick runs out of patience. He'll only wait so long, so start talking, Josie. Who did this to you and why?"

As a JOURNALIST, Josie had learned to read people. She didn't doubt Steve's statement about the cop but how did she explain what she didn't understand?

"It's a long story. I don't know where else to start but at the beginning." She took a breath and let it out.

"Try the beginning," Steve told her.

"Did I ever tell you about Erica?"

"I don't remember the name."

"No reason you should. We hadn't been in touch for years." The familiar tinge of guilt settled on her shoulders for letting her relationship with Erica slide.

"With all the base transfers, she was my only childhood friend that kept in touch. We even roomed together in college for a while but then she was in a terrible car accident. After she was released from the hospital, I never saw her again. I assumed she went home to her family. I reached out but never got a response. After a while, I stopped trying. Then a couple of months ago I got a Facebook friend request from her."

"Josie, what's this got to do with you being beaten?" Steve interrupted, a little snap to his voice.

Steve had never been a patient man, at least when it came to Josie.

"I told you it was a long story." She took a breath. "Erica and I exchanged contact information but neither of us used it —until a few days ago. An email arrived from her. She asked me to save the document she'd attached to the email—to put it some place safe. She was specific, though, that I not look at the attachment. I knew from her Facebook page that she did research for Political Action Committees. Her email said that she had gotten ahold of some very hot stuff but she didn't elaborate. She wanted someone to have a copy as backup."

"Why would she ask you? You hadn't talked in years."

"I asked the same question. She said that was exactly the reason she'd sent it to me. Since we hadn't spoken in ages, no one would look to me for a copy. She told me again not to look at the attachment unless something happened to her."

"She sent you information for safekeeping that was potentially dangerous? And you accepted it?" Steve didn't have to raise his voice for Josie to know he was pissed. His teeth were clenched, accentuating the granite line of his jaw. His eyes had narrowed as he'd shot the question her way.

"First of all, I already had it so it wasn't like I could write 'refused' across an envelope and send it back. Besides, that was before this shit happened," Josie said, indicating her injuries and torn clothing. "I figured she was being overly dramatic. She'd been a bit of a drama queen growing up."

"Did you look at the attachment?"

"No."

"You weren't curious?" Steve asked, watching her closely.

"Actually, I wasn't. Do you have any idea what type of crap PACs go after? I wanted nothing to do with any opposition research." Most PAC researchers mucked around in places Josie didn't care to know existed. Naïve thinking for a journalist, but she worked freelance because she never had the heart—or lack of one—to dig up the kind of dirt others would gleefully go after. It just wasn't necessary to destroy others in pursuit of a story. Freelancing gave her the option to pick and choose her topics.

"Okay. What happened next? Obviously, something did." Steve didn't bark but it had been a close call. His fists were clenched as tight as his jaw. His eyes bore into hers as if he wanted to reach into her head and pull out the information.

"A few days later, I received a text from Erica." Josie

looked at her hands to confirm what she already knew. They were trembling. She willed them to stop. They didn't.

Steve reached over and, for a second time, covered her hands with one of his. "What did the text say, Josie?"

She raised her face to look at him. Her eyes welled up and her lips quivered. "It said *run*!"

3

"Why didn't you call me?" Steve squeezed Josie's hands tighter trying to ignore the ache in his chest. She hadn't reached out to him and that hurt. But now was not the time to dwell on it. His focus needed to be on Josie and not the wound to his heart. Her fingers still trembled in spite of his touch. Her lips quivered but calmed after she took a deep breath.

"I thought Erica was pulling some sort of joke," Josie explained. "This was right out of a movie. I told myself this sort of shit didn't happen in real life. It didn't sink in that it was for real until later."

"When did you realize it wasn't a joke?" Steve's grip on her lessened.

"I was angry after I got the text. Joke or no joke, I wanted Erica to know I didn't think it was funny. But she didn't respond to my texts, calls or emails. I didn't sleep much that night. By sunrise, my concern had morphed into fear that something had happened to her. I contacted the Tallahassee Police Department. That's where she lives. I'm sure they thought I was crazy but they still put me through to someone who took my report. I didn't expect to hear from them again."

"But you did?" Steve prodded her.

"Not exactly."

"What do you mean?" he snapped but quickly reigned in his impatience. He needed to forget that they'd briefly shared a last name. You never argued with a victim. And whether he liked it or not, Josie was obviously a victim.

"Sorry, Josie," he said, apologizing for his outburst. "Just tell me what happened."

"My gut told me something was wrong. It ate at me until I couldn't ignore it any longer. I'd made up my mind to head over to Tallahassee to look into it myself. I didn't make it out the door, though, before a man showed up identifying himself as a detective with the St. Johns County Sheriff's office. He said he was following up on the report I filed about Erica."

The hairs on the back of Steve's neck slowly rose to attention. The most he would have expected from the authorities was a follow-up call from the Tallahassee PD. Why would the sheriff's office in St. Augustine be interested in a request for a wellness check on the other side of the state? There were very few options and Steve didn't like any of them.

"Initially, he asked a couple of general questions about Erica but he quickly turned his focus to the email. That made me nervous."

About time. "Why did that make you nervous?" The whole situation had alarms going off in his head.

"At the time I filed the report, I'd only mentioned the email in passing so the police would have a timeline. It shouldn't have raised any flags. I'd never mentioned the contents. For all I knew, Erica might have been looking into police corruption. After he demanded I produce the email, I told him I'd deleted it along with the attachment. It never occurred to me that he would go bat shit crazy. But he did."

Steve had known this was coming but that didn't help to contain his anger. He launched himself off the couch and glared at Josie.

"A cop did this to you?" It explained why she was spooked when she saw Rick's badge. It also explained her fear of being taken to the hospital. Once they saw her condition, they would have to call in the authorities to report the beating.

"I'm not sure…"

"What do you mean you're not sure? Either that man hit you or he didn't."

"Yes, Steve, he hit me. As you can see, he beat the shit out of me." She raised her hands, a signal for him to remain quiet. "But what if he wasn't a cop? He was in plain clothes but since he said he was a detective, I didn't question the lack of a uniform at the time."

"How did you get away?" Steve managed to keep his tone even despite the rage that pulsed through his veins. He wanted to find the bastard and do things to him most people have never heard of. Nobody touched Josie—not while he still had a breath left in him.

"His last hit was so hard he couldn't maintain his grip," she continued.

Steve hadn't missed the band of bruising encircling her upper right arm. Fury welled up inside him as he pictured the man backhanding Josie with so much force that the blow sent her flying to the floor. He'd seen his share of violence, although Josie had no idea of the atrocities he'd witnessed. But none of that had been directed at someone who had touched his heart. He was having a difficult time concentrating on her words while fighting a rage directed at a man he couldn't reach.

"When my head hit the floor, I was stunned. He must have thought I was unconscious because he left me lying on the kitchen floor and began tearing up my place. I'm not sure what he'd thought he'd find but as soon as I heard him thrashing around in my office, I grabbed my purse off the counter and ran out the back."

"Why the hell didn't you call me then?" he asked, no longer attempting to hide his frustration. She had to have known he would do anything to help her.

"I was scared, Steve. He knew about the report I'd filed on Erica. If he had access to that information I figured he could trace me through my phone. I didn't want your number to be the last one I called. They can figure that stuff out, can't they?"

If someone did hack into the police department and track Josie, then she could be right about their ability to tap into her cell. Normally, it wouldn't be all that easy but considering the speed at which this guy had moved, she had reason to be scared.

"Where's your phone now?"

"At the bottom of the Matanzas River."

"Good." It was smart to rid herself of the tracking device but it also showed how terrified she was.

"How'd you get here? Where's your car?"

"After I tossed my cell into the river, I drove as far as Daytona Beach before I figured I'd pushed my luck far enough. I left my car in the parking lot of a Walmart there."

Steve's forehead wrinkled in confusion. "Then how did you get here?" Any other form of transportation would leave a trail unless she...

"I hitchhiked the rest of the way."

"Holy shit!" He ran his fingers through his hair in fear and frustration. A single woman hitching her way the length of Florida was begging for trouble. "Jeezus, Josie. Do you have any idea what you did?"

"I was careful. I never stayed with anyone very long. As soon as we hit the next city or truck stop, I'd get out and find another ride. I did my best to make myself harder to track. Was that a mistake?" Her voice was, once again, trembling.

She'd flinched at his angry tone. Yes, he was angry. He was angry at the chances she took. Angry that she hadn't called him. Angry that he hadn't been there to protect her. But his strongest emotion was fear. Her story scared the living crap out of him. He wanted to rail at her. He wanted to pull her close and thank God that she was safe. How in hell had she made it this far without someone taking notice? Any one of her rides could have taken advantage of her—especially in her current condition. How had she made it to him alive? "Didn't anyone question the shape you're in? God, Josie, look at you!"

"You should have seen me a couple of days ago."

"There's nothing funny about this."

"I know," she sighed in agreement. "I told everyone who asked that I was running from an abusive relationship and that he had friends in law enforcement. That put an end to the suggestions to call the police. I explained to them I was headed to someone who would help. Someone I trusted."

Their gazes locked. Her eyes were brimming with tears. "There is no one I trust more than you," she choked out.

The admission cut at him. He didn't point out that she hadn't trusted him enough to wait for him to come home and resolve the problems between them. Still, Steve gathered her into his embrace and held her close to his heart.

Tall and thin, she had the body of a ballet dancer and after getting her into bed, he could attest to the fact that she had the agility of one. Blue eyes so deep they were almost as black as her hair; hair that used to slip through his fingers like silk. He'd thought she was his future—that they would build a life together. Then she was gone.

And now she was here. She trusted him enough to find him when she needed help, which was good because it sounded like she'd been dragged into the middle of an ugly firefight. Once she was safe, though, he would get her to face the issues that drove them apart. It wasn't fair to either of them to continue on without closing old wounds.

He'd taken a lot for granted in their short relationship. He'd never brought up her past even though he knew it had played heavily in her hesitation to become his wife. Hell, he'd never asked what would make her happy. That thought would have to be saved for later.

"I'm going to ask Rick and Gib to come back," Steve told her. "I promise, Josie, Rick won't put you in any kind of danger."

4

S teve intercepted Gib and Rick as they entered the kitchen. Josie was in the master bath taking some time to gather herself. Understandable. She'd spent days running from the authorities and now he was asking her to trust not a police officer but also one who was a close friend of his. Josie wasn't stupid. Hell, she was wickedly smart. Apart from Gib, the team knew what had happened between Steve and Josie. So she would, most likely, expect to be facing some hostility. He should have set Josie straight before she'd retreated. Rick wouldn't let personal feelings get in the way of an investigation. None of his friends would do less than their best to help someone in need regardless of their personal feelings.

"Is she okay?" Gib asked.

Of course, Gib's first question was about Josie's well-being. Gib had a soft spot where women were concerned. He was the consummate lady's man. He was also a good man.

"She could use some medical attention," Steve said, "but I can't be sure how much. She refuses to go to a doctor or hospital." He turned to address Rick, specifically. "She doesn't want to talk to the authorities at all. A police detective, or someone posing as one, beat her. There's good reason to believe that once her name is entered into any public database, she'll be traced."

Rick's eyes narrowed and the corner of his mouth shot up. "That sounds pretty farfetched, Steve. And if she needs medical help," he added, shooting a worried look down the hall, "you know I can't walk away from this."

"Just hear her out. Then we can make some decisions. And I'll ask Kevin to look at her when he and Don return."

Rick hesitated. Steve couldn't remember a time when Rick had second-guessed his judgment but his former teammate would be concerned that his judgment was skewed when it came to Josie. The entire team was aware that Steve had never gotten over her.

Steve waited while Rick wrestled between duty and friendship. Rick had walked that thin line just this past summer when Cat was in trouble. He should have been done with that balancing act.

"I'll listen to what she has to say prior to making any calls," Rick agreed.

Before Steve could silently revel in the small victory, they were distracted by the woman inching her way down the hall. She was barefoot, and each step she took was visibly painful. A battle of pure determination.

Rick leaned closer to Steve, softening his tone so that his voice wouldn't carry. "Are you sure she doesn't need a hospital?"

"For the moment." Steve muttered, though he wasn't actually all that sure. Josie's clothes, filthy and tattered, hung loosely on her frame. Her face, hands, and feet had been cleaned revealing the damage that the dirt and grime had hidden. Bruises, cuts, and scrapes covered most of her exposed flesh. The injuries had looked superficial. But if he was wrong, he'd have a hell of a time getting her to the ER willingly. When she dug in, it was just about impossible to move her.

GOOD GOD, Josie thought, as she gingerly made her way toward the living room. Was there a size requirement for this group? Steve was a big man but these two were his equals. A grin briefly flashed across each of the three faces and she realized she must have given voice to the thought. She'd gotten into the habit of talking to herself to break the silence that engulfed most of her days and nights since Steve had left. She'd have to remember to keep her thoughts contained.

Spoken or not, the question remained. She'd been too terrified to notice anything during their initial meeting but the three men standing shoulder to shoulder, looked like half the defensive line of a football team.

Rick was broad-shouldered and rugged, and possessed silver-blond hair that looked amazingly like Legolas from *Lord of the Rings* except for the military short cut.

The second guy must be Gib. She'd recognized the name from the door of the photography business. The attractive man sported the long hair that Rick was missing. His thick honey-blond mane was pulled back into a rawhide tie allowing the ruby stud in his left ear to shine. With his gray eyes and long lashes, the man was stunning. There wasn't another word to describe him. Why was this man behind a camera instead of in front of one?

Somber faces soon replaced their quick smiles. Concern etched the features of each man. She didn't like it. Not one bit. Yes, she'd been at the losing end of a fist fight but she was not weak.

A single heartbeat passed before Steve extended a hand to her. The roughness and strength of his grasp was a tactile reminder to Josie of his years spent protecting and defending others. He was offering her both those gifts. She didn't deserve them but she'd come to him for help. She would not insult him by refusing.

"Tell them what you told me," Steve instructed Josie as he steered her toward the couch. "Rick isn't going to report any of this unless you agree." When Rick's nod confirmed Steve's statement, Josie achingly lowered herself to the cushion. She wasn't prepared when Steve settled on the couch next to her instead of joining his friends. His weight had her leaning into him. He wrapped his arm around her shoulder and put his hand on her thigh. Buoyed by his show of support, she began to retell the nightmare.

"She 'friends' you on Facebook then suddenly sends you an email? Nothing else from her in years?" Rick questioned her after she'd finished.

"Yes. I can't explain it." She felt that twinge of embarrassment again. She should have made more of an effort to stay in touch with Erica after the accident.

Gib appeared in front of her with a small tray of coffee and toast. When had he left the room? God, she was tired. Her stomach growled. Obviously, she was more hungry than tired.

"Thank you," she said after taking the tray. "Were you part of the team, too?"

"Honorary," Gib announced, flashing a dazzling smile.

"You don't know what was in the attachment?" Rick asked, bringing Josie back to the problem at hand.

"No."

"Can you guess?"

"She worked for political action committees doing opposition research. My guess it was some dirt she dug up on a political figure or organization. Whatever it is, it must be something juicy. I've never known a PAC researcher to look for positive information. And for her to hand it off to me it must be pretty damning."

"What about the guy that showed up at your place. Can you give me a description?" Rick asked.

"He was between thirty-five and forty years old, I'd say. Short, dirty-blond hair. He was about six-foot. Other than needing a shave he was presentable." She closed her eyes envisioning the man. "He was wearing a polo shirt and khaki pants."

"He had to identify himself. Do you remember his name?" Rick asked.

"His first name was simple. Ron, John, something like that. His last name was Watson. I remember thinking of Sherlock Holmes and Dr. Watson."

"You didn't check the name against his ID?" Steve asked.

"He showed me a badge but I didn't look at it closely," she admitted.

"Don't beat yourself up over it," Rick assured her. "Most people don't."

Rick started tapping keys on his phone. Josie came up off the couch. No one had to tell her what he was searching for. She attempted to swat the phone from his hands. "I'm checking public records," he told her. "No one knows we're looking," he assured her, dodging her outstretched arm.

Steve placed his hand on Josie's neck after she returned to her spot on the couch and began to massage the corded muscles. He leaned over and whispered in her ear, "Breathe."

She hadn't realized she was holding her breath. She took a gulp of air and let it out slowly.

"No detective with the St. Johns County Sheriff's office

or St. Augustine PD by that last name. A couple of uniforms but they don't match your description," Rick said, clipping the phone into the holder on his belt.

"Then who the hell is this guy and what does he want with that email?" Steve asked.

5

"I need to know all you can tell me about Erica," Rick said to her, all business now. "How did the two of you meet?"

Steve had warned Josie that she would have to revisit, in detail, everything she'd shared with him about the incident and that Rick would want to know the history behind her relationship with Erica.

"We met in grade school. Both our dads were in the army, so we naturally gravitated toward each other. The inevitable transfer came but she kept in touch. Email, regular mail—whatever was available. I'd gotten used to losing friends as time passed, but Erica stuck. When it was time for college we decided on the same school. The same course of study. We were roommates until her accident in our junior year."

"She now lives in Tallahassee?" Rick asked.

"Yes. I don't know much about what she's done or where she's been since she left college but from what I've seen on Facebook and that email, she's been freelancing her research skills to political action committees." Josie had no idea why Erica went that route instead of sticking to journalism. The lack of information punctuated the break between the two friends.

"Do you know what she was working on or who she was researching?" Steve asked, pushing her for answers

"I have no idea." Josie told them as she dipped her head to take another sip from the cup of coffee.

"And she gave you no hint as to what was in the attachment?" Rick asked.

"None. But if you've got a computer I can use, we can find out."

The complete silence in response to her statement had the coffee in her stomach rolling over in waves. "What is it?" she asked Steve. "What's wrong?"

"You said you deleted it." His stare was intense. He wasn't going to like her response.

"I did, but not before I saved it to my Cloud."

GIB LEFT to get the required computer. Steve's brow furrowed once again as anger seared the back of his eyes. The significance of what Josie related had him laser focused on her. Unlike most people, she was unfazed by his piercing stare.

"Are you telling me," he said trying, but failing, to reign in his temper, "that you let a man beat the crap out of you when you could have given him what he wanted?" The end of his sentence lashed out at her like a whip.

"I'd be dead if he'd gotten what he wanted." Josie's back was once again ramrod straight. Her eyes dueled with Steve's icy stare.

This was the first time since her arrival that he'd gotten a peek at the Josie he remembered. He blew out a breath in relief. In their time together he'd never pegged her as someone who would walk away from a fight—which was why leaving him had come as such a shock.

"Could Watson have found your passwords when he searched your place?" Steve asked. She'd never listened to his endless warnings about keeping a written record of her passwords. She'd tuck them away someplace she considered safe. But for a man on a mission that wouldn't be much of a deterrent.

"I'm sure he found all my passwords," she admitted, grudgingly.

"Then he could have the email. It may already have been deleted from your Cloud."

"No. That password isn't written down anywhere."

What made this particular password so special that she didn't have to write it down? His curiosity regarding the password was forgotten when he saw Josie's hand tremble over the keypad of the tablet Gib had given her. He was about to snatch the computer from her but Josie found her inner strength and opened the file.

"Josie," she began reading, "if you felt it necessary to open this attachment then there is a good chance I'm talking to you from the grave." Josie's voice was barely audible. It killed Steve to watch her painful reaction to the news. They hadn't been close recently but she and Erica had been friends. Of course, his own opinion of Erica wasn't very high at the moment. What sort of friend dragged another into a minefield?

Josie's fingers were now shaking so badly she couldn't control them enough to scroll down the message. Steve was tempted to toss the device across the room as if that act would banish her pain. If it were just that simple. Instead, he took the tablet from her lap. She didn't fight him. Another sign she'd reached her limit. Rather than bluster at him for taking charge, she closed her eyes, steeling herself against the rest of the message.

Steve took one of her hands in his. She didn't pull away so he gave her a supportive squeeze then began reading Erica's message.

"I kicked open a hornet's nest following up a big lead—a lead that would have given me the story of a lifetime. There isn't a network out there that wouldn't have wanted it. This was my chance to leapfrog straight to the networks from this piss-ass research job. I knew I was sticking my nose into dangerous territory but I didn't know how dangerous until my source disappeared. I realized I could be next."

Steve stole a quick look at Josie. She was frozen, her expression unreadable. He returned to the email.

"We were best friends once. I owe you so much, Josie. Consider this a small repayment. You have the KEY. Use it."

Steve braced himself before he looked at Josie again. The sadness and fear he had expected was reflected in her expression. But for the first time he saw something else. Vulnerability. Tough, irritating, intelligent, beautiful, sexy... He could list a host of adjectives to describe Josie but she had never let down this shield. Not until today. What else had he missed?

Josie reached for the device in Steve's hand. Stubbornness. If the situation wasn't so serious, he might have smiled. That was definitely one trait to which he needed no introduction. The woman could dig in when she wanted to. Her pigheadedness had also been one of the biggest roadblocks to their union. Whenever Steve pressed her about a sullen mood, she would clam up. Rather than push, he'd let it drop. He'd been afraid of what he might discover if he'd pushed. When it came to getting to tie the knot, though, he'd bested her in the stubbornness category and gotten the wife he'd wanted—or so he'd thought.

Again, this wasn't the time or place. She was hurting. He set the tablet aside and pulled her close. As he did, she let her tears flow freely.

JOSIE MELTED into Steve's arms. For the first time since she'd received the text from Erica, she felt safe. If only she could stay in his embrace, protected from whatever, or whomever, had chased her here.

Coward! The accusation echoed through her head as if someone was shouting it in her ear. She'd run from Steve and now she was running to him. She had used him to build a world around her where she was safe, secure, and loved only to abandon him when the feeling of security waned. Now she was using him again.

He deserved so much better. At the very least, he deserved someone he could trust.

Josie pulled away from Steve and brushed the tears from her cheeks. The salty moisture caused her scraped knuckles to sting, giving her a jolt back to reality.

Retrieving the small computer, Josie composed herself and looked at the attachment. Numbers. The remaining portion of the email was nothing but numbers. She stared at them, perplexed.

"Why would she send me a bunch of numbers?" She studied the screen again. Lottery numbers? No. That couldn't be. They were separated by lines and spaces. The answer niggled in the back of her brain but couldn't make its way forward. "I don't understand," she confessed to the others in the room.

Steve took the computer from Josie, glanced at it again then handed it to Rick. "Is this what I think it is?" he asked.

"Don't keep it a secret. What is it?" Gib asked, speaking up for the first time since the questioning began.

"A code," Rick answered. "It's some sort of a code."

"What key is she talking about, Josie?" Steve asked.

A key. Josie massaged the lump on her forehead as she struggled with the question. Erica thought she had a key. What key and why did Josie feel like she should know the answer?

The backdoor slammed shut tearing her thoughts away from the thread she was mentally following. Seconds later two men entered the living room. *Jeezus!* She was now convinced there had to be a minimum size requirement for this group. Josie felt like *Alice in Wonderland*, shrinking in size as the room filled with two more giant men.

6

S teve introduced Don and Kevin then he'd added that
Kevin would be assessing her injuries.

Josie had stared at Steve for a few seconds then turned to
address Kevin. "Thank you. I appreciate the offer but
I'm fine."

"You were out cold! You damn well need to be checked
out." Steve was seething. She needed to be examined and he
was going to get his way. "You're not going to win this argument, Josie," Steve warned, gearing up for a fight.

"Josie?" Gib said, stepping between the warring factions.
"There isn't a man in this room who isn't concerned about
your injuries. You would be doing us all a favor if you'd
allow Kevin to take a look at you."

Josie quickly dismissed Steve. Instead she was solely
focused on the man who Cat jokingly referred to as a combination between Magic Mike and Thor. While Gib's face
wasn't visible from where he stood, Steve could see Josie's
face clearly. Her features had softened as Gib spoke and the
flame in her eyes had dimmed.

"Fine," she huffed in resignation.

Leave it to Gib to get Josie to agree to the exam. The man could charm the habit off a nun. But even Gib's charisma hadn't been able to soothe Josie's temper completely. She was still pissed at Steve. She didn't like his hard-handed effort and the silent treatment he was getting was proof of that. He'd take it. Anger was preferable to the sadness that had overwhelmed her earlier.

Knowing Kevin would have a more cooperative patient if Steve wasn't around, he left them and returned to the living room. The men were huddled over the small computer studying the attachment from Erica.

"It's a cypher of some type," Rick said.

"Don?" Steve asked. Don was the computer guru on the team. He was as big and fit as the other members, but when it came to a keyboard, he had the hands of a concert pianist. Don considered hacking a form of entertainment.

"I agree. A book code to be more precise," Don told them. "A simple book code."

"If it's simple, we can break it. Right?" Gib asked.

Don shook his head, "There could be millions of combinations."

"But you just said it was simple." Gib responded, confused.

"He means simple, if you have the key," Steve explained. "A specific book would be the key. Each number would correspond to a page, paragraph, line and word of that book."

"I'm afraid that without the key, we're getting nowhere with these numbers," Don added. "It would take a computer with special programming and a lot of time to crack it—and that isn't even guaranteed. If we can get our hands on the book she used, it should be a relatively simple code to break. Assuming this isn't a joke," he added.

"Did you get a look at her?" Steve's temper flared. "This is no joke."

"Then you'd better hope that she remembers the key. There's no way we're going to crack this without it."

Steve's eyes drifted back to the hallway that ran the length of the home. Colt and Gib had designed and built their two units to be mirror images of one another. The living quarters lined the outside walls of the second floor above the photography studio to maximize natural light for each room. The hallways ran through the interiors, shotgun style. The corridors served two purposes, connecting the front with the rear of each unit but also acting as an additional sound barrier between them.

The minute Kevin stepped out of the master bedroom, Steve turned toward him. "Is she okay?" he asked.

"She's pretty banged up," Kevin answered as he reached them. "But there's not much the ER can do for her that we can't. I told her to get in that whirlpool tub with the water as hot as she can stand it. I'll clean and treat her cuts when she's done."

"She hit her head pretty hard," Gib said. All signs of the charming Lothario disappeared as he glanced at the hallway.

"I saw the lump. She claims she's not dizzy or nauseated. Having her checked out would be ideal but the minute I suggested it, her blood pressure soared. There is no way in hell she's going to the hospital without a struggle and her condition doesn't warrant the battle right now."

"You're sure?" Steve asked.

"As I can be. She doesn't need stitches. A couple of butterfly bandages will take care of the larger cuts. I'll keep a close eye on her."

"So, will I," Steve said, looking in the direction of the bathroom.

"She's going to need some clothes to put on after she gets out of that tub," Kevin told him. "Hers are crusted with salt not to mention filthy. There's not a piece of clothing Cat owns that would fit her."

Hardly, Steve thought. The men referred to Cat as petite but even that was being generous. Josie was a good six inches taller. About the only thing the two women might have in common was their panty size—and no man here would risk rifling through Cat's underwear drawer. Colt would have them drawn and quartered.

"I'll find something," Steve said.

"Has anyone but me thought about Gravestone?" Gib asked. "Erica did use the word *grave* in her email. They're still out there, you know."

No one in the room would ever forget the murder-for-hire organization that had accepted a contract to kill Cat and a State Senator earlier that year. Even though the organization no longer had a reason to target Cat, the team remained on alert. When they found the sons of bitches, there would be some payback coming for the hell they'd put Cat and Colt through.

"This doesn't smell like a professional job," Rick said. "And I doubt that Gravestone is doing any subcontracting after the last time."

Steve thanked God for that favor. If Gravestone was involved in this she wouldn't have made it out the door, let alone to Sanibel.

"Once you've got Josie patched up," Don said to Steve, "we need to focus on the key to those numbers. Without it, we're not going to know what we're up against until it hits us right between the eyes."

"She's sharp," Steve assured them. "It's what makes her good at her job." Josie was able to take bits of information she'd gathered and assimilate them into a coherent story that any number of news services would pick up. "It will come to her. She needs a little time." Then again, he'd said that about their relationship not that long ago and look what happened.

HEATED water rushed over Josie's beaten body. Normally, a whirlpool bath would rank high on her personal relaxation scale and she would have allowed herself the mental escape it offered but she couldn't give into that temptation. She slipped deeper into the tub. As the water raced through the jets, her mind raced through the multitude of problems she faced. Who was after the information in the email? Why did Erica want her to have it? And what the hell was the key that Josie was supposed to have?

As big as those problems were, they didn't compare to the one that currently waited for her in the living room. Why did the man of her dreams also have to be the man from her childhood nightmares?

She'd long ago made up her mind not to fall for someone in the military yet she had stayed in North Carolina after college because of the beauty of the area. Her apartment had been an hour north of Fort Bragg. It was only a matter of time before she met someone from the base. Just her luck he would turn out to be the love of her life. She should have walked away the second he'd told her he was army. Run, when she'd discovered he was Special Forces. Instead, she'd fallen head over heels for the sexy soldier and married him in a hastily arranged ceremony.

He'd pushed, cajoled, and loved her until she'd said yes. When he'd deployed, she worried about him day and night. She had no idea what he faced while overseas; he never talked about his deployments. Steve enjoyed telling tales about his current and former teammates but never once had he talked about what he'd experienced. She knew his work was important and dangerous but that was it. He didn't fear his deployments but they terrified her.

In his absence, the memories of the childhood she'd swore she would never replicate returned. A mother, lonely and bitter. A father, all too happy to deploy. A child resented by one and forgotten by the other. It wasn't fair to compare Steve to her father, yet it was the only yardstick she possessed.

The day the notice arrived informing them the marriage wasn't legal in the eyes of the State of North Carolina, she'd taken off like a jackrabbit escaping a trap. Their split was for the best but that was no excuse for how she'd broken the news to Steve. No one deserved to find out their marriage was over via an email especially while they were deployed. She was pond scum.

7

Josie was sitting on the edge of the tub, wrapped in an oversized bath towel when Steve strode into the room, handed her a t-shirt then told her to meet him and Kevin in the bedroom after she was dressed. She didn't miss his quick assessment. Black and blue from head to toe, she resembled a specimen growing in a petri dish. She'd expected the concern in Steve's eyes but there'd also been heat. The old pull, the same physical attraction still existed. Spontaneous combustion, Steve used to call it.

Had she made another mistake in coming here? How could she ask him to help her and at the same time want him out of her life? She should leave. Being here was just rubbing salt into a wound she'd created.

Her palms began to ache as she wrung the life out of the piece of material Steve had given her. She unfurled the shirt, staring at it until her eyes welled up and she could no longer see past the tears. The t-shirt was a memento of a long weekend they'd spent in Charleston. She had its mate.

The original idea behind the trip had been to explore the beautiful, old city. Instead, they'd spent their time exploring each other's bodies. On one of the rare occasions they had ventured out of the bed and breakfast, they'd stumbled upon an out-of-the way dive that served good beer and great sandwiches, and had a local band that played classic rock 'n' roll. Steve had been in heaven and she'd been right there beside him. Josie had insisted they buy matching t-shirts to commemorate the evening. Steve had winced at the idea— as any man would—but he hadn't refused. She still wore hers on nights she missed him so much that it hurt. Josie grasped his soft, worn shirt and pressed it to her heart. He'd kept it.

She managed to compose herself and pulled the shirt over her head. Good thing Steve was such a big man—the t-shirt was generous enough to cover her to mid-thigh. As no under-clothes had accompanied the shirt, she cringed as she stepped into her salt encrusted panties. Steve had seen all she had to offer, but Kevin was waiting for her, as well

Josie sat on the edge of the chair in the corner of the bedroom as Kevin re-examined her injuries and applied oint-ment and bandages. Steve battered her with questions about every cut, bruise, and scrape. Before Kevin had finished, Steve's grilling managed to erode her earlier feelings of guilt.

"I got the shit kicked out of me, Steve. What else would you expect?" she asked.

"Did he take razor blades to your feet, too?" Steve squatted next to the chair and raised her ankle to examine the bottom of her feet. The lines of his jaw were rigid again. His eyes flicked from hers to the foot he'd rested on his knee.

"I lost my shoes," she glowered, reclaiming her foot.

"When? How?"

Josie let out an exasperated sigh. "I don't remember," she lied.

Steve sneered at her response. Kevin appeared to be

enjoying the back-and-forth conversation, if you could call it that.

"Was it at the same time you took a swim?" Steve asked.

Unfortunately, the saltwater in her hair and on her clothing hadn't gone unnoticed. Josie decided it wasbest to remain silent. Wasn't that what attorneys recommended their clients do? She'd left that leg of her journey out of the story she'd told. The single time she'd broken the law during her trek south was last night after she'd reached the marina on the other side of the bridge to the island. The minute she'd seen the long span over the water she'd known she would never make it across on foot. Attempting to hitch a ride in the middle of the night to an island occupied by upscale residents would have sent up flares to the authorities. Besides, the toll booths on the causeway had actual people collecting tolls in addition to the transponder lane. She would have never gotten by unnoticed.

It hadn't taken her long to find a boat with its keys left in the ignition. Following the lights of the causeway bridge, she had steered the small craft toward the Sanibel shoreline. As she'd approached the beach, she'd cut the engine. She didn't know the area but there hadn't been any lights. Considering the time of night, though, that didn't mean there weren't any homes nearby. As soon as the boat had stopped drifting in the direction of the island, she'd jumped into the water. She'd taken off her sandals and tucked them in the waistband of her jeans. At some point during her swim, she'd lost them. By the time she'd made it to shore, she was gasping for breath. Her feet were the least of her worries.

She had no plans to tell Steve about the theft. Not when one of his friends was a cop.

"Drop it, Steve. Please?" Josie asked. "I don't have it in me to argue with you."

Steve, thankfully, stopped interrogating her. Unfortunately, Kevin wasn't spared. "I don't like that bump on her head. Any sign of infection in those cuts?"

Kevin winked at Josie. "Some of the cuts are a little inflamed but the ointment should do the job," he answered. "Is she allergic to any antibiotics?"

"No," Josie answered cutting off Steve's response. "And I'm sitting right here."

Kevin nodded at the rebuke. "She'll need water to take some pills," he said to Steve. While Steve left to get the drink, Kevin quickly pulled a syringe from his bag and thumped it a couple of times with his fingers. "Turn around Josie and do it quick. If Steve catches me looking at your ass, he'll wipe the floor with me."

Josie complied before it crossed her mind to question him.

"It's an antibiotic," he explained.

She winced as he jabbed the needle into her right cheek. He swabbed the injection site again then quickly tugged her shirt over her rear.

"I thought I was getting a pill."

"You are," he explained, "for pain." He stashed the used syringe into his pack and handed her a couple of white tablets.

After Steve returned with the water, Kevin repacked his first aid equipment and both men adjourned to the hall. They spoke in hushed tones, their words too soft for Josie to make out what they were saying. No doubt Steve was grilling the medic again over her condition.

Josie scanned the large bedroom. She was tempted to lay down on the king-sized bed and give in to her exhaustion but it didn't feel right to crawl into a stranger's bed. She'd ask Steve. Hopefully, after she was rested, she'd be able to figure out what to do and where to go. When she'd needed help, she had automatically sought out Steve. It had been selfish, self-preserving, and totally unfair.

Josie heart still skipped a beat when Steve returned to the room. God, he was still the most handsome, sexiest man she'd ever known. Whispers of gray now ran through the temples of his dark-brown hair. Had his mission aged him?

Had she? She'd been so anxious about the future... But that was no excuse for running away or for hurting a good man.

She reached out for him as he approached her. Her heart settled as he took her hand. She'd been half afraid he would refuse her need for his touch.

"I'm sorry, Steve," she whispered.

"For what, Josie?"

"For everything," she expelled on a breath, stumbling over where to start. "For what I did to you. For bringing you into this mess..."

Steve released his grip on her and he turned his back. He jerked the covers down on the bed with such force she slid deeper into the chair. "Get some rest," he ordered. His shoulders were rigid as he walked toward the door. "We'll talk more later."

STEVE STALKED out of the room but took a few minutes for himself before rejoining the group. Seeing Josie again had hit him hard. The sight of her was always enough to take his breath away.

He had a good idea where she was going when she'd started the apology. He'd long imagined her telling him how she'd made a mistake. How wrong she'd been to leave. How sorry she was for the misery she'd caused him.

But during the endless nights since receiving the news, he'd come to realize that the blame was his to share. He'd never forget the look on her face the day he'd told her what he did for a living. She wanted nothing to do with a military man. Her fear couldn't have been any more blatant if he'd announced that he was tossing her off a bridge. Still, he'd taunted her. Dared her into another date. The physical attraction between them had been cosmic. He'd wanted her. He'd pushed and manipulated her like he would have any target. She was the woman he loved and he'd been selfish in wanting her so badly that he hadn't taken the time to understand her fears before practically dragging her to the minister.

Just that morning he'd intended to find her and resurrect the issue. It had been past time to finalize their relationship one way or another. They'd either work together to resolve the issues that stood between them or make a clean cut.

Now the situation had changed—and changed drastically. As much as he would like to, now was not the right time to decide their futures.

"I understand that until we find the key," Steve said, refocusing as he entered the room full of men, "there's not much we can do. But, Don, if you could keep working on that attachment, you might get lucky."

"As for the rest of us," Steve continued, "we've been down this road before. Josie appears to be a target. She can identify her attacker and she has information someone wants very badly—perhaps badly enough to kill. She took precautions to get here. Hopefully, those were enough." His stomach clenched at the thought of her perilous journey south.

"Rick, I know this is murky territory for you—again. What's your next step?"

"I'll check her story out. Under the radar," he added when Steve started to object.

"She's not lying." Steve scowled at his friend.

"I wasn't insinuating she was but her memory could be faulty. She's been through a lot. Trauma can affect a person's take on things. We need to confirm what she told us, Steve, before we go forward. There could be more info available that might help us."

Footsteps on the rear deck had Steve reaching for the sidearm that wasn't there. He needed to start carrying again.

"That will be Troy," Rick told him, heading toward the rear door. "I texted him while you were with Josie.

"What's up?" Steve heard Troy ask as he entered the unit.

"We've got trouble," Rick explained.

"Could it have anything to do with the guy out front pretending to fix his bicycle?"

8

The men in the living room collectively fell in step with Steve as he headed toward the kitchen. The element of surprise would be gone if any of them exited the front door.

Steve grabbed Gib by the shoulder, pulling him aside. "Try to get a picture of him," Steve said pointing toward the street. "And stay with Josie until we get back," he added as he disappeared out the back with the others.

The men silently descended the stairs then quickly dispersed as they hit solid ground. No orders were given as they split into two groups. They knew their roles. There could be only two potential outcomes to this foray. Either an innocent tourist would have a heart attack when he was confronted by half a Special Forces team or the guy would be long gone. The second scenario was the more chilling of the two.

In the first case, they would simply apologize—assuming the man didn't die of fright. The second could mean that Josie hadn't been as successful at losing her pursuers as she'd hoped. It could be that a single male tourist was actually having trouble with his bike but the team trusted each other's instincts. If Troy believed this guy was suspicious, that was good enough for Steve.

As they rounded the corners of the building, the cyclist was already making his way north along the bike path that paralleled Periwinkle Way across the street from the business. Steve was able to make out the single, male rider as he disappeared around a curve in the path. No one was going to catch him on foot and by the time one of them got to a vehicle, the man could be anywhere on the island. Their hunt was over before it began.

"Did you get anything?" Steve asked as they met Gib in the living room.

Gib dropped into one of the two big arm chairs. "He was already too far away. If I had a camera instead of this phone then I might have had some luck."

"It was a long shot," Steve admitted, massaging his brow with his thumb and index finger as he circled the room. While Kevin and Don had deposited themselves on the couch, Rick and Troy remained on their feet. Rick's shoulder rested against the door jamb to the kitchen, one ear cocked toward the rear door. Troy kept an eye trained out the window.

Steve stopped stalking long enough to glance down the hallway. "Is she sleeping?" he asked Gib.

"I haven't checked on her," Gib answered. A mischievous grin crossed his face as he got to his feet. "But I'll take care of that right now."

"No, you won't," Steve scowled. "Sit down."

Until Gib's sly remark, it hadn't crossed Steve's mind that Josie might have moved on. He hadn't wanted to consider it, but what if they had no relationship left to salvage? There'd been no indication she'd been dating but also no reason to believe she hadn't. Until he knew, she was still his to win or lose.

Steve buried the thought for the moment. "Describe the man," he said to Troy.

"White male. I'd say about twenty-five," Troy answered. "Dressed like your typical tourist. Tan shorts, white t-shirt, navy ball cap, and sneakers. My guess is that he's either been on the island for awhile or lives in Florida. Only someone from the tropics has a tan that dark. Height is a little sketchier since he was squatting next to the bike but it's safe to say he wasn't over six foot."

"What put you on alert?" Rick asked him.

"His reaction to me. He was fiddling with the bike, like he had an issue with it, until he saw me make the turn in here. He maintained his position but his eyes locked onto me like heat-seeking missiles."

"He doesn't match the description of Josie's attacker," Steve said. "That man was older by a decade. She doesn't get those sorts of details wrong—not with her journalistic background." And she was a damn good journalist.

"I don't like this. Anybody else's gut saying something different?" Steve surveyed the men in the room.

"We may still have an innocent cyclist out there but I'm with you," Rick agreed.

"We need to assume that Josie is a target. Even more so now." Steve said. "I'll work on a rotation schedule for guard duties but it's going to be tight with only the five of us."

"Do we know when Colt and Cat will be back?" Steve asked Gib.

"If Colt has his way it will be sometime next week but the last time we talked, he said Cat wanted to come back earlier. She's chomping at the bit to get to work. He mustn't be keeping her busy enough," Gib chuckled. "Why?"

"We can't stay here if the newlyweds will be back any day and there's no way to know how long this is going to take to figure out. Besides, even with them gone, it's going to be tight in here." With the Murphy bed in Colt's office and the king size bed in the master bedroom, the place could sleep four if one of them used the couch. If necessary, the guys could bunk on the floor. The team had slept in worse places. But he had Josie to consider and if Cat and Colt came back early, none of them wanted to intrude.

"You're welcome to use my place," Gib volunteered.

"We may have to." Steve appreciated the offer, but Gib's place wasn't any larger than Colt's. Troy was bunking at Rick's. Rick could easily handle another guest but Steve preferred the team members closer than farther away.

"What about next door?" Gib suggested.

"Next door? You talking about the garden center?" Steve asked. The garden where Gib had found Josie had a three-bedroom house on the street side of the property. Cat planned to turn it into an office for her design center.

"Yes. Cat has a lease on the entire property. She can't do any remodeling of the house until the zoning change has been approved. The Copelands left behind a few pieces of furniture Cat was going to donate. It's big and you'd have the bare essentials including a bed, hot running water and electricity. There's no internet or land line, though," he added.

Steve shook his head. "I'm not moving Josie to a place that's not secure."

"It's as secure as Fort Knox," Gib smiled. "We're talking Colt here. Do you honestly think that he would let Cat work over there alone if he hadn't secured it? There's more electronic surveillance and built in security there than we have up here."

Colt's overly protective instincts with regard to Cat were well known within the group. Obsessive, was a better description of Colt's concern for her safety.

"Get me the keys," Steve said, relaxing a bit. "We'll check it out."

∽

STEVE OPTED to stay in the unit with Josie while the others went next door to determine if using it as a safe place for Josie was feasible and what they would need if it suited their purpose. Gib had remained behind, as well. Steve waited for the question.

"Are you going to share the story behind the two of you?" Gib asked, no shame in his voice for the prying question. He charmed the ladies and enjoyed a good prank but when he wanted answers, he could shoot straight from the hip.

Gib had proven his mettle and loyalty this past summer. He'd put himself between Cat and a bullet. It didn't matter that he'd never worn a green beret. The entire team thought of him as an equal. He was a brother.

But Gib hadn't been there when Steve met and fell for Josie. Or when things fell apart. Steve's team knew the ugly story and there'd been no point discussing it with anyone outside the unit. But if Gib was going to help protect Josie, he had the right to know.

"I'd say it was a long story but it isn't. We met at a classic car show." Steve managed a grin as Gib stared at him in disbelief.

"Yeah, not the usual place you'd expect to pick up a single woman and that hadn't been my intent. It was a charity event. I'd entered my Mustang." Steve's primary means of transportation was his '68 Ford Mustang Fastback GT that he'd fully restored. Steve McQueen would be proud of the results.

"Josie was there taking pictures. It's her hobby. What you

see in nature, she sees in the lines of classic cars." Great. He'd just given the group's Lothario and Josie common ground.

"I spotted her while she was snapping photos of a '59 Chevy Impala that was parked a few cars down from me. I wasn't the only one who had taken notice of Josie. There were more men watching her than looking at the car. It didn't matter. There was no way she was leaving the event with anyone but me."

Steve shook his head. "We went from talking to the bedroom faster than my car goes from zero to sixty. There was—is," he corrected, remembering her sitting on the edge of the bathtub wrapped in the towel, "a chemistry between us neither of us can explain. But it goes beyond that. I fell in love with her before we left the parking lot that day."

"That's pretty intense," Gib said, all humor gone from his eyes. "So, what happened?"

"I pushed. Hard. I only had a few months before my next deployment. I had no intention of leaving the states without putting a ring on her finger. While she never denied her feelings, she made it clear after she found out I was army, she would not commit to making the relationship permanent. Her dad had been army. She blamed their nomadic lifestyle and his deployments for the break-up of her family."

"But you won her over?"

"Outmaneuvered her might be a better description. I thought I'd convinced her it would be different for us. We were married a few weeks after we met. The time between the wedding and my deployment were the best weeks of my life. I honestly believed she felt the same way."

"But you *were* married?" Gib asked, confused.

Steve walked over to the window and stared at the property next door. "Turned out the minister had let his license expire," he continued with his back to Gib. "The marriage wasn't legal. The County Clerk had to notify a half-dozen couples, including us, that they weren't legally man and wife. Josie attached a copy of the scanned letter to an email. I wrote her that we'd fix it the minute I got stateside. She didn't respond. As soon as it was safe for me to call her, I did. She told me she needed time. Claimed the screw-up was a sign that we'd rushed into the marriage." Steve turned back to Gib and steadied his breath. "She'd already moved to St. Augustine by the time I'd reached her."

"That's a drastic reaction to a case of nerves." Gib's grey eyes narrowed in bafflement.

"I pushed her into marrying me. I thought she loved me." Steve drifted off. What else was there to say?

"Are you still in love with her?"

Steve closed his eyes for a second then opened them as he admitted the truth. "I never stopped. I don't know if I should be proud of that fact or kick myself for being a fool. Either way, it doesn't matter if she doesn't feel the same."

"She came to you when she needed help," Gib pointed out.

"She did." He still wasn't sure what to make of that.

"Is she the reason you're not re-enlisting?" Gib had heard the men talking, expressing their dismay at Steve's decision.

"My *twenty* is up," Steve explained. "Retiring hadn't been in my immediate plans but after watching Colt and Cat together this past summer… I want what they have and I'd like to find it with that woman in there. It's past time we hashed things out. I'd planned on leaving this morning to find her." Steve's gaze drifted toward the hall. "We'll have to see if desperation is the only reason she sought me out. If it is, once she's safe, it's time I walk away."

9

Josie awoke to the sound of a groan. Her own. Exhaustion, or the pain meds Kevin had given her, had allowed her to get some much-needed rest. But now every muscle in her body was screaming to be heard. Her head still ached but it had ratcheted down a few notches since she had awakened in Steve's arms. Pushing up from the mattress, her arms trembled in protest. She hadn't been inactive for this long since she'd dozed off under the potting bench. Then she'd been so terrified upon wakening that her muscles hadn't had a chance to react to the sudden change in position.

Josie willed her long legs over the side of the bed. With support from the nightstand, she got to her feet. Success.

Once on her feet, she gave herself a few minutes, allowing her legs to adjust. The room was covered in shadows but the sun cast strips of light against the honey-colored wood flooring as it peeked through the slits of the plantation blinds. She glanced at the bedside clock. It was a little after noon.

Like in the living room, the bedroom walls were adorned

with stunning photographs of nature. Tropical colors and warm woods filled the room and gave it a calming effect. The place looked, and felt, comfortable. Like a home.

That sentiment was compounded by the bedside photographs, one on each nightstand. The picture on the far side of the bed, showed the beaming bride and groom standing side by side on the sandy beach, the sun setting in the background. The second photo hadn't been staged. The candid shot pictured the tall, handsome man holding a laughing barefoot bride in his arms. The picture caught their absolute joy. Love spilled out from the two-dimensional photo and filled the room.

Steve's former commander was fortunate to have made such a place for himself and luckier still to have found someone special to share it with. Josie had found something similar, for a short time. But as soon as Steve had deployed, her old fears filled her isolation.

When she'd received the letter from the County Clerk, she'd packed a few boxes of personal items and just left. Like a coward. There wasn't a better word to describe her actions. She hadn't been able to face Steve. If she'd tried to explain her reasoning to him, he'd have talked her down off that ledge. She'd done what had to be done.

Picking up the picture of the happy couple, Josie laid it face down on the bedside table.

She achingly made her way slowly down the long hallway toward the main room. Each step sent a jolt of pain through her body, reminding her of the beating and her desperate run for help.

～

AT THE SOFT sound of Josie's faltering steps, Steve turned

away from the window. He'd been staring out at the garden next door where Gib had found her. Thoughts of the dangers she'd faced and the chances she took, still tied his stomach in knots. Hearing her moving about was a welcomed distraction from the nightmare of scenarios he'd imagined her going through.

The woman facing him from the other side of the room looked miserable, not just physically but emotionally. Taking a risk, he opened his arms. She shuffled toward him without hesitation and the break in his heart closed a little. Josie hadn't wavered at his offer of comfort and affection. On some level, she still trusted him.

After Josie's breathing settled to a steady pace, he led her to the couch and watched as she painfully lowered herself to the cushion. How long had she been losing weight? He'd swear she was a good fifteen pounds lighter than when he'd left for Afghanistan.

"Are you okay, Josie? You've lost weight." On top of everything else, had she been sick?

"I'm fine, Steve. I haven't had an appetite lately. What happened while I was sleeping?" she asked, deflecting the question. How many times had he asked about her home or family and she'd used the same tactic?

Why hadn't he realized before that this was what she did? With his training, he should have recognized the ploy. How much of this fucked up relationship fell on his shoulders? Why hadn't he pushed when she refused to talk about her past?

Steve didn't give voice to his revelation. Instead, he told Josie about the man on the bicycle.

"Do you think he was looking for me?" Her color had paled as she'd asked the question.

"He doesn't fit the description of your attacker and with

58

the precautions you took to get here, it's not likely," he told her, giving her hand a squeeze.

"But not impossible," she said, as she pulled back from him.

"Nothing's impossible," he agreed, missing the warmth of her touch. "Don't worry about him right now. It could be nothing. We need to concentrate on the key."

Josie massaged her temples as if kneading them would conjure up the answer.

"Don says the key is a book," Steve prompted. "He recognized it as a book cypher code. It would have to be a specific book you both shared. Did you and Erica have a favorite book? A story?"

"Oh my God, yes. How could I have forgotten?"

"What, Josie? What did you forget?"

"We gobbled up detective stories and mysteries. We read everything from Nancy Drew to Agatha Christie. As kids, we used to send emails to each other in code."

"What did you use to decode the messages? What was the book?"

"I need to get to St. Augustine," Josie said.

"What you are going to do," Steve said, holding her closely, "is tell me what it is."

10

" **A** *Pocket Full of Rye.*"
"A what?"

"*A Pocket Full of Rye.* It's a Miss Marple mystery by Agatha Christie. I should have remembered!" She thumped her forehead with the palm of her hand. *Ouch.*

Shaking off the discomfort, she continued, "We purchased duplicate copies of the book and used it to decipher the codes. Silly, I know, but when we were that age it was exciting to think we could communicate in ways others couldn't understand. I hadn't thought about that in years."

"We need to find a copy of that book. I've seen several bookstores on the island." Steve started Googling them on his phone.

"It would be a miracle if you found the edition we used. We bought them while we were still in middle school. Unless you're lucky enough to find a copy in a thrift store somewhere, we need my book."

"You still have it?" Steve's eyebrows rose in surprise.

"Yes." There were few things she'd hung on to from her childhood because they transferred so often it hurt to toss cherished items with each move. But one box went with her wherever she moved, even now. She kept her most personal, private mementos in it. "It's in a box at my place in St. Augustine. I need to get it."

"You're right, Josie, but you're not going."

"Excuse me?" Josie's eyebrows rose in response to Steve's statement. She hadn't come to him to be given orders.

"It's not safe," Steve stated, bluntly. "Someone could be waiting for you to return."

Steve's argument made sense. Josie slumped back into the cushion.

"Where's the key to your place?" Steve asked.

Josie froze then cocked her head. "I'm not sure," she answered, thoughtfully. She'd stuffed her keys, identification and what little cash she had left in the pockets of her jeans before tossing the purse in a dumpster. She hadn't given them any thought since she'd crawled onto the sandy beach.

Josie bit her lips against the urge to moan as she pushed to her feet. "If my keys aren't in my jeans, I've lost them."

Steve steadied her. "Gib took them. They needed washing."

"No doubt. Hopefully, my ID is still in them, too," she added.

A quick call from Steve to Gib confirmed that Gib had found her meager personal possessions. Steve left to retrieve the items and to give the keys to Troy, who'd been tapped to retrieve the book. She gave Steve the location of the box and prayed it hadn't been destroyed or hadn't disappeared along with her attacker.

After Steve left, she made her way from the living room to the small home office at the front of the unit. Gib had insisted that she make herself at home. He assured her that neither Cat nor Colt would object and she was free to use any computer in the house.

An office doubling as a guest room, Josie figured, when she recognized the Murphy bed attached to the opposite wall. Josie settled herself at the desk and booted up the computer.

Working was better than waiting. She would be climbing the walls if she didn't have a project to keep her busy while the book was being retrieved. She brought up Erica's email and then spent the next hour staring at numbers as if by sheer will they would magically transform into words.

STEVE MET Troy at the base of the stairs. While Don and Kevin had been checking the security system at the house and garden center next door, Troy had been patrolling the property. Steve would get Kevin to relieve Troy while Don finished whatever needed to be done to the property next door.

But what should have been a short hand-off turned into a heated discussion.

"I'm doing this for you," Troy snapped, taking the keys along with Josie's address.

"What's your problem?" Steve outranked Troy but while off base and off duty, they treated each other as equals.

"My problem is that woman upstairs. Popping back into your life when she conveniently needs you. I don't like seeing my friends being used." Troy shoved the items he'd been given into the pocket of his jacket. He started to say more but then turned in military precision toward his truck. His silence said more than any words.

"She needs help," Steve shouted after him. Troy just waved him off and got behind the wheel. The argument had been intended as a wake-up call. Every member of the team knew that Steve wanted Josie back but he didn't have to be told that you don't always get what you want.

Steve watched the dust of the crushed shell lot settle, wishing his heart could do the same. Troy had a point but it didn't matter if Josie had come to him or he had found her. Just as the dust settled, they would settle things between them once he was sure Josie was safe.

He texted Kevin then waited at the foot of the stairs. The shrubs next to the driveway parted a minute later and both Don and Kevin jumped the short fence.

"What's up?" Don asked, looking toward the spot where Troy had parked. "Where's Troy?"

"He's left to get the book. It'll take between ten and twelve hours round trip. Can you two split the watch?"

Before they answered, Rick, who had been at the station, arrived bearing pizzas. From the look on Rick's face, Steve knew he was delivering more than just a late lunch.

"You've found something." Steve said to him, flatly.

"Yeah. Let's go upstairs," Rick suggested. Kevin snatched a couple of slices before he slipped around the side of the building. He'd be on sentry until Don relieved him.

"I've been in touch with Detective Corello," Rick told him when they reached the kitchen. "He's the Tallahassee detective who helped out with the Montgomery issue this past summer."

"I remember the name," Steve said.

"It doesn't look good for Josie's friend, I'm afraid," he told Steve in a voice that wouldn't carry. "Do you want her involved in this conversation or do you want to keep her out of it?"

Steve didn't have to think. Josie trusted him with this.

That was one thing he couldn't afford to lose—her trust. "I'll get her," he said.

The minute Steve stepped into the small office, Josie was on her feet. It wasn't easy to watch. She grimaced at the sudden movement but didn't complain. The tough Josie was back.

"What's wrong?" Josie asked.

"Rick's here," he told her. "He has some information on Erica." She didn't wait to hear if Steve had anything else to say. He sidestepped to let her through the door. She was a woman on a mission.

Rick and Don had grabbed some paper plates and set out the pizza boxes on the living room coffee table. Rick was holding a slice of pizza in his hand, Fold Hold style, when Josie flew into the room. He'd just taken a bite, not anticipating her speedy arrival. Steve gave Josie points for remaining silent while Rick chewed. She'd surprised him by not peppering Rick with questions before he was capable of answering.

"Well?' she asked as soon as Rick swallowed.

"We have a good contact with the Tallahassee PD," he said, wiping his mouth with a napkin. "After I contacted him, he checked on your friend. Normally, he'd dispatch a black and white to do a welfare check but, as a favor, he made the drive himself. He didn't get an answer at the door so he looked through one of the windows. The place had been tossed. That gave him probable cause to enter."

"Did he find her?" Josie asked, while Rick took another bite. This one small enough he could still talk and chew.

Steve put his hand on her shoulder and gave it a squeeze, letting her know she wasn't alone.

"No," Rick reported. "The place was empty. Corello said

there were no signs of a struggle but the place was a wreck. He's waiting for forensics to get back to him."

"There's another thing. Possibly more significant," Rick continued, setting his plate on the table.

"More significant than a missing person's place being torn apart?" Steve asked, his hand tightening on Josie's shoulder. He immediately lightened the grip when Josie dropped her shoulder in obvious discomfort.

"Unfortunately, yes. Corello found the record of the call Josie made to the Tallahassee PD. However, there was no outgoing call to the St. Johns County Sheriff's office for a follow up inquiry with Josie. Someone knew about the call. Josie's name was flagged. We don't know by whom."

"Then Josie's right," Steve confirmed. He removed his hand from her shoulder tightening it into a fist. Anger and fear electrified him from head to toe. "Somebody does have access to information funneling through law enforcement channels."

"That's what it looks like. Corello and I will be communicating via our private cells for the time being. Nothing between the two of us will be going through regular channels," Rick assured them. "Due to the break-in and search of Ms. Stratocas's apartment, however, he requested a check of her recent credit card activity and telephone calls."

"Who the hell can he trust?" Don asked.

"Not requesting that information would be even more suspicious once the break-in was reported and there was no way to avoid that. Corello has a guy in his IT unit he's confident can help and will supply him with information under the table."

"I still don't like it. All this activity is bound to sound alarms. Call Troy," Steve said turning to Don. "Let him know we've confirmed a leak. Tell him to be careful."

"Why does Troy need to be careful? Do I even want to know?" Rick asked.

"Nothing illegal. He went to retrieve the book from Josie's place. She remembered the key."

"Well?" Rick prompted him.

"An Agatha Christie mystery," Josie told him. "We used it to send coded messages to each other when we were kids."

"Troy has Josie's key and permission to enter," Steve explained to Rick.

"While you have him on the line," Rick told Don, "tell him not to disturb anything. No one has reported the attack on Josie yet. Technically, her place is still a crime scene."

11

After Steve goaded her into eating a slice of pizza—proving her point that he could talk her into—or out of —just about anything, Josie excused herself. She wasn't comfortable with Steve's friends. They knew what had happened between her and Steve and the story wasn't a pretty one. While the men had been polite, and charming if you threw Gib into the mix, she didn't feel at ease with them. Wearing only an oversized t-shirt, didn't do much to raise her level of self-esteem. She hoped that once she had clean clothing, her confidence would improve. They'd be ragged and torn but clean. Maybe Troy could grab some of her clothes while he was getting the book. She'd talk to Steve.

The headache she'd acquired from her run-in with the tree had receded and her ability to think had returned. Whatever Erica was working on was hot and, most likely, related to politics. Weak as it might be, there was a chance Josie could find a link between Erica and one of the PACs or lobbying groups based out of Tallahassee. Fingers itching to get to the keyboard, she began with a general search then started to follow the threads.

STEVE DISCARDED the remnants of the impromptu meal and set the kitchen to rights. Kevin remained on guard duty while Don was working on the code downstairs using one of the studio's computers. Rick had returned to the station. Gib had taken off. He had a business to run. He was alone in the unit except for Josie.

Steve mind kept returning to the woman working at the other end of the hall. He found himself pacing. The patience he'd learned in the army had deserted him. Eventually, his pacing brought him to the closed door of the office. He'd planned to leave Josie alone and give her space—that phrase again—but concern for her injuries and, damn it, his desire just to lay eyes on her, had him reaching for the doorknob.

Quietly, so he didn't startle her, he let himself into the room. The woman at the keyboard didn't move, didn't react to the intrusion. Josie was so focused on what she was researching that she didn't sense his presence. He'd seen her in that mode when she had her teeth into a story. Her dedication and thoroughness had gotten her noticed in her field. If she was making progress with this mystery, then it would be best to leave her to it. He shut the door behind him as quietly as he'd opened it.

STIFF FROM SITTING TOO long and, no doubt, from her recent beating, Josie stood up and stretched her aching muscles. Her concentration broken, she noticed the house was no longer silent. The music of Bob Seger pulsated from the other end of the hall. *Oh, God*, did that bring back memories. How many nights had they made love to the sound of "Night Moves"?

Josie's skin warmed as she smiled at the flashbacks. Steve was a passionate lover. On a different level, he had a passion for all things classic. Rock 'n' roll. Muscle cars. Motorcycles. Josie often thought he'd been born in the wrong decade.

Josie followed the music to the kitchen where Steve sat in the breakfast nook as he scribbled notes on a yellow pad. A steaming mug of coffee sat on the table within his reach. The sight had her yearning for the mornings he'd been home. She'd awaken to find him in their small kitchen. Coffee made, a cup ready for her. Each morning had settled that place inside her that quivered with fear at the thought that they wouldn't last.

But the day he'd shipped out, those feelings of security quickly vanished and her phobias had flooded in. She'd been selfish, but knowing that didn't make her fears any less real. Would she ever move past them? She'd already tried and failed. Love and attraction alone didn't make for the perfect match. They were proof of that. Accepting his proposal hadn't been fair to Steve and had brought them both heartache.

Josie didn't know how long she stood there before Steve looked up from whatever he was working on. Once he did, however, he didn't have any trouble reading her thoughts.

"Don't, Josie. Don't go there now," he cautioned her. "Let's sort out one problem at a time."

Shamefully, relief flooded through her. He was right. One thing at a time.

STEVE LIFTED a shopping bag from the bench seat beside him and held it out for Josie. "Gib dropped off some stuff for you."

Gib had stopped by with a bag of toiletries and a variety of clothing, including several pair of delicate underwear still bearing price tags. Steve had scrutinized his new friend closely. Gib just smirked at the unspoken question. Colt's business partner enjoyed nothing more than getting under someone's skin. Steve had watched him bait Colt often enough while Colt and Cat danced around one another this past summer so Steve knew better than to give in to the urge to question Gib's motives. He suspected Gib was disappointed that Steve hadn't risen to the bait.

"That was sweet of him," Josie said. She'd managed to hit the nerve Gib had missed. *Sweet.* She thought Gib was sweet.

"I'll deal with Gib." Steve simmered. "Why don't you put some clothes on before the guys return?" Gib was bringing sandwiches for everyone on his way back from his shoot. Rick planned to stop by when he got off duty and bring them up to date on any intel he dug up. As they handed off sentry duty, Don and Kevin would be by to grab a bite. The men had seen enough of Josie's long, shapely legs as far as Steve was concerned.

JOSIE DIDN'T NEED any additional prompting. Having clean clothes to wear was sufficient motivation but Steve's sudden mood change was the clincher. Taking the bag from Steve, she left the kitchen, then paused. She'd forgotten to ask him to contact Troy about bringing some clothes from the condo. Josie weighed the bag in her hand against Steve's mood and decided not to ask. Whatever Gib had gotten her would have to do.

She hadn't made it through the living room, though, when she recognized the sound of Steve's phone. The tone of his voice had her stopping in her tracks. What she heard next had her retracing her steps.

"Don't," Steve said after a short pause. "We'll let Rick handle it. Did you get it?"

Josie didn't have to ask what "it" was. She held her breath and waited while Steve listened to the other end of the conversation. He disconnected without saying another word.

"Well?" she asked.

"I'm sorry, Josie, but your place was ransacked. Your computer is gone. As far as any other items that might have been taken, Troy doesn't know."

The news about her rental and the destruction was expected. The man had already begun tearing the place apart as she'd run out the kitchen door. She had very few things she cherished enough to miss.

"What about the book? Did they find the book?" she asked. If Troy had it, then her box stuffed with memories would not have attracted the man's scrutiny. Most everything else she'd left behind could be replaced.

"It would seem whoever searched the place didn't care very much for Miss Marple. Troy is on his way back with it now."

STEVE CALLED Rick to fill him in on what Troy had reported. He watched Josie as he repeated details of the information he'd been given. Her expression remained neutral as he described the damage that was done.

"I didn't want Troy being held up with questions by the authorities," he explained to Rick. He'd wanted the book in their hands. Not being held for evidence. "The only item he touched was the book."

Rick made a half-hearted argument about removing property from the scene of a crime but he wanted the key as badly as Steve did. Finally, he said, "I'll take care of it."

"Don't say a word about Josie being here," Steve reminded Rick.

"I'm not going to make that kind of mistake, Steve, but sooner or later it's going to leak out."

"Just do the best you can," Steve asked his friend.

"I'll see you in an hour or so," Rick said. "I should have additional information to share by then."

Steve faced Josie as he ended the call. "Are you all right?" Was it a bad sign she was taking the news of the destruction so evenly?

"I'm fine. It's just stuff."

Steve studied her reaction closely. She didn't appear the least bit fazed by the news. From his limited experience, most women would be horrified at the idea of someone digging through their personal items. Then again, he didn't remember her putting much stock in anything material. She'd moved into his place with her clothes, computer, a few pieces of cookware and a box that she'd shoved to the back of the closet and never opened. He'd expected his small apartment to be crammed from floor to the ceiling when she moved in but a few drawers and some closet space were all she'd requested. He'd been grateful at the time that she traveled so light but now he questioned the reasons behind it. Hell, she hadn't even said a word about the lack of an engagement ring.

"I'm fine, Steve," she repeated now. "What are you working on?"

He accepted her deflection but tucked the revelation away. It was another clue he'd missed.

"I'm setting up a rotation schedule for the security," he

indicated the pad on the table. In reality, he'd completed the schedule shortly after he'd checked on her a couple of hours ago. Unlike last summer when Colt had the entire team to back him up, Steve had a handful of men to work with. He considered calling some of those who'd left the island early but put that thought aside until they knew what they were up against.

Instead, using his phone, he'd spent the last couple of hours searching for information on Josie's friend, Erica and learning about PACs and opposition research. He hadn't liked what he'd found but it had kept his mind occupied and his fears for Josie manageable.

"We should have enough men so no one has to pull watch for too long," Steve told her. "Troy will be back in a few hours. Once he's rested, he'll be good to go. Rick can help if it gets tight but I'm not putting him on the schedule for now."

"What about Gib? He said he was an honorary member of the team."

Gib, again. Steve recognized the twinge of jealousy.

"Gib doesn't have the training," Steve explained. "He can handle a gun and he'll help where he's needed but mostly he's our scrounger. You need something? Ask Gib. He has a way of making it happen. As for being part of the team, he may not be army but he is definitely one of us. He sealed his status when he took a bullet for Cat."

"Cat seems pretty important to all of you."

The statement was made without inflection but if he wasn't mistaken, Steve wasn't the only one dealing with a bit of jealousy.

"Cat, and Gib for that matter, are special to us. Do you remember me telling you Colt had some issues after his last mission?"

"I remember. You were worried about him."

Steve never shared what happened on his tours. The team rarely spoke of their missions themselves. That particular tour had been worse than all of the others combined. Everyone had been affected by it and that one horrific day. Steve had no intention of telling Josie about the depravity they'd witnessed. He'd like nothing more than to forget the sounds of the screaming children and the sight of blood-soaked dirt as their parents tried unsuccessfully to protect their young.

The team had been lured into an ambush. Colt had recognized the danger before any of his men were injured or killed. Collectively, they had managed to take out the enemy but not before many of the villagers, who were being used as bait, had been slaughtered by the Taliban.

Every man carried a heavy burden due to the events of that day but Colt had been in charge and he had laid the blame squarely on his shoulders. No one had been able to dissuade him. None of the team had been able to lift him up because they were all, frankly, fighting their own demons upon their return. Colt had resigned and remained sullen and withdrawn—until he'd set foot on Sanibel. His sanctuary, he'd called it.

"Shortly after Colt arrived here," Steve told Josie, "he met Gib, who happened to share Colt's passion for photography. Then he, literally, ran into Cat. Those two share another kind of passion."

"Between them, they managed to pull Colt from the edge. Gib and Cat reached out and found the man who we'd thought we'd lost. They're family now."

Steve didn't miss the shadow that crept over Josie's features as he'd related the story. "What's wrong? You okay?"

"I'm just dandy," she remarked then spun on her heels and marched down the hall toward the small office.

Steve watched her retreat. And that's what it had been—a retreat. He had no idea what had come over her or what had triggered the sadness in her eyes. There was so much he didn't understand about her, so much he hadn't taken the time to understand. Hopefully, it wasn't too late to find answers to the questions he was only just now asking.

~

"KEVIN'S TURN ON SECURITY DETAIL?" Rick asked, scanning those gathered in Colt's living room.

"He just relieved Don," Steve said, indicating the soldier who was sitting at the dining room table that shared the living space. Don was inhaling one of the sandwiches Gib had picked up.

Steve leaned forward, resting his elbows on his knees, hands clasped, anxious to hear Rick's report. "We'll fill both him and Troy in later. What do you have?"

"Detective Corello reported the break-in at Josie's to the St. Augustine police, citing an anonymous source," Rick began, before taking a pull on the beer he'd just opened. "Prior to making the call," he continued, "Corello had given his IT guy a heads up. As we suspected, someone accessed the record of Corello's call. Since this last report never mentioned Erica, it confirms whoever is behind this is looking for Josie, as well."

"His IT guy wasn't able to trace the ping?" Don asked from across the room, annoyance lacing his question.

"Not yet, but he's still tracking. If they find anything, Corello will call," Rick assured him. Narrowing his eyes directly at Don, he added, "And I don't want to hear the results from you first. Got it?"

Don stared at him for a beat then nodded in unspoken

agreement. Without the direct warning, Steve was sure Don would have made an attempt to hack his way into the Tallahassee PD's system. Steve wished Don hadn't agreed so readily.

"Have you come up with a plan regarding the bicyclist?" Rick asked Steve. "I can't station one of our officers to watch the place. Especially since we can't be sure he's got anything to do with this mess."

"Got it covered," Gib answered for Steve. As Steve looked over at Gib, he noted Josie was visibly wilting. She slumped forward on the cushion next to him. Her skin was pale beneath the bruises. She'd gotten little rest today so it was no wonder the circles under her eyes had darkened. Steve didn't point out that her lips quivered ever so slightly. She was doing her best to hide her fear and exhaustion. He wouldn't call her on it. Today had been another day from hell. She was entitled to both.

"We have two bikes hidden along the north side of the Copeland building." Steve finished what Gib started. "If anyone spots the guy, grab one the bikes and follow." The bicycles belonged to Gib and Colt. Both men used them routinely on Sanibel to run errands or enjoy a ride on the island's endless bike trails. After Gib had returned that evening, he'd pulled both bikes from the shed at the back of the property.

"Just tail him at this point. We need to know where he is staying," Rick added. "If he's an innocent tourist, we don't want to scare him but if he's not, then we'll know where to find him."

"We all set next door?" Steve asked Don.

"Yep. I checked out the security. It's a good system. Alarms on the house and cameras cover front and back of the property. We can access the cameras from my laptop and our phones. Rick pulled strings and we now have Internet service over there." Don paused. "The place didn't need any house-keeping just some sheets for the bed which Gib got for me. So, we're good to go."

"You ready to move?" Rick asked Steve but he was eyeing Josie.

Steve had been keeping one eye on Josie, as well. Her eyelids kept drifting shut then snapping open again. She'd been fighting sleep as they waited for the key to be delivered. But exhaustion leaped hurdles over anticipation when the body had had enough. Steve decided to give her a little help, casually swinging Josie's feet into his lap. He continued to talk security issues with the men. He didn't dare glance in her direction because he didn't trust himself not to smile. One lesson he had learned during his short stretch as her husband was that Josie loved to have her feet massaged. He continued the foot rub while he talked to the guys. As he predicted, she was sound asleep within minutes.

"Neat trick," Gib grinned.

Steve openly smiled before quietly asking the guys to gather their stuff. He then lifted Josie into his arms and headed out the door.

12

J osie awakened disoriented, confused, and terrified. She'd dozed off on the couch at Colt's. Where the hell was she? She struggled to catch her breath as panic crawled up her spine. Her heart beat against her breastbone so hard and fast it hurt. Every beat pounded in her eardrums. Breathe. She needed to breathe. After a few gulps of air, releasing each slowly, her heart began to steady.

As the sound of her thumping pulse dissipated, her hearing returned. Steve's baritone voice drifted into the room. Her nerves settled the rest of the way and she allowed herself to study her surroundings. The limited daylight allowed in through the closed blinds told her she was no longer in the unit above the studio. This bedroom was smaller and sparsely furnished. There were no family photos or decorations. The room was plain and simple and didn't possess the feeling of home she'd experienced yesterday. At least, she assumed it was yesterday.

The men had been talking about the house next door before she'd drifted off. They must have made the move and she didn't remember a single step. She did remember the foot rub, though. Damn, Steve still had the hands of a magician. She was a little annoyed that she hadn't been allowed the opportunity of making the move on her own two feet.

All the toiletry items Gib had acquired for her were in the adjoining bath. After she washed her face and brushed her hair, she stared at the reflection in the mirror. She looked like she'd been at the losing end of a catfight and no amount of makeup would hide that blatant fact.

Based on the animated voices that were growing louder, the timing of the phone call to Steve last night and the daylight that streamed through the opaque glass of the bathroom window, Josie assumed Troy had returned with the book.

As much as Josie wanted answers to the riddle Erica had dumped in her lap, she still hesitated before joining the group. *Family*. That's what Steve had called them yesterday. A family. The term had hit her dead center and had hurt just as much as any of the blows she'd recently received. She'd had a chance to be part of that family but she'd run not understanding all that she was leaving behind. It wasn't until yesterday that she'd understood the depth of her loss. Because she'd left the man she loved—as if that wasn't bad enough—she'd also missed the opportunity to be part of something more. To be part of a group of people who truly cared for one another. But it was too late for wishes and dreams that couldn't come true.

The bedroom and bath may have been smaller, but this place appeared much larger than the shotgun style unit above the photography studio. The bedroom she was in connected to the foyer. Across the entry space, Josie could see a longer hallway that led to additional rooms.

She followed the voices to a separate dining area and found the men huddled over Don's shoulder as he quickly flipped through pages of her old Agatha Christie novel then transferred the information to a pad of paper. Gib and Troy were arguing while Rick and Steve threw questions at Don. The men seemed to be having some trouble with the code.

"What's the problem?" Josie asked. All heads turned in response to her question. Steve's assessing look made her skin warm. He wasn't seeing the battered woman who had greeted her in the mirror. Instead, his look was sensual and wanting.

"Are you certain this is the right book?" Steve asked, clearing his throat as he held up the dog-eared copy of *A Pocket Full of Rye*.

"How many copies do you think a person would own?"

"We're getting letters but they don't make any more sense than the numbers did," Don said, scratching his head.

In that instant, Josie remembered the simple twist that she and Erica had added to the book code. She was a bit stunned, though, that a Special Forces team hadn't figured it out. *Jeez*. "Reverse the letters."

"What?" Steve asked.

"Since you already have the letters, reverse them. We decoded the last number first and so on. Zeros are spaces, if you haven't already figured that out."

Don shook his head at the childish ploy, but smiled.

"It worked," she responded, smugly.

As Don did what she suggested, Josie noticed Rick was now riveted on the pad Don was using to jot down the decoded letters. The color drained from his face as Don's hand moved back to the next set of numbers. She leaned over the laptop but she couldn't make out the first name from where she stood. Josie knew people who could easily read upside down but, unfortunately, she wasn't one of them.

"Don't bother," Rick told Gib when he pulled out his

phone and began tapping keys. Googling the name, no doubt. "Shit," Rick added, under his breath.

"WHAT IS IT?" Steve asked. Rick's cop face was in place—he rarely wore it when he was with his friends.

"Finish the list," Rick instructed, ignoring Steve's question. Gib, as usual, didn't listen. A low whistle crossed his lips as he read the results of his search.

"What's going on, Rick?" Steve asked, insistent this time.

"I'll tell you in a minute. Let him finish," Rick said, this time with a bit more snap.

Despite Rick's directive, Gib had continued to search each name as the document was decoded. Steve moved so he was looking over Gib's shoulder as he simultaneously Googled the names on his phone as they appeared on the pad. The quick search showed that all the men appeared to be prominent in their respective, but diverse, fields. Four of the six were businessmen. Two were public officials.

When the last name was decoded, Steve addressed to Rick. "You know those men?"

"I know McClaren," Gib volunteered, before Rick could answer.

"How?" Steve asked.

"We did some photography work for his business. Very cordial. I wound up doing the shoot for his daughter's wedding. He has a good reputation in this area," Gib shrugged.

"Rick?" Steve prompted his friend for more information.

"I agree with Gib on McClaren," Rick started. "He owns a chain of luxury car dealerships. He's based out of Bonita

Springs at the southern end of the county. I've never heard anything negative about him."

"And the others?"

"I know Deets by name only. He's a State Attorney in Morgan County," Rick said, then hesitated, impressing upon Steve the importance of the man at the top of the list.

"It was the first name that freaked you out. Why?" Steve pressed.

"I didn't freak out," he stated, defensively. "Luis Esteban was a Representative in the Florida State House. He died a few weeks ago." Rick's expression had turned grim.

"How did he die?" Steve asked, his radar going up. It could have been due to natural causes but based on Rick's reaction, that was unlikely.

"He was killed by a hit and run driver while jogging near his home in Central Florida. The Florida Highway Patrol hasn't made any progress. The car that hit Esteban was found abandoned. It was reported stolen shortly before the accident. The owner has been cleared. The Florida Department of Law Enforcement was called in after forensics found that most of the vehicle had been wiped clean."

"They think his death was a homicide?" Troy asked.

"I'd be thinking along those lines if I were on the case. There's always the possibility a car thief ditched his ride after the accident. But FDLE sent out a bulletin asking for any leads regarding Esteban. They'd have dropped the case after an initial review if they didn't think there was more to it. There has got to be a reason they are hanging onto it."

"We need to check those names thoroughly," Steve told Don. "Make sure nothing has happened to any of the others."

Steve ignored Don's flying fingers while his mind digested the ramifications. Had a car thief accidentally killed a jogger or was the death of Esteban intentional? With his name on Erica's list, Steve was inclined to believe the worst. He rubbed his thumb and forefinger together, expelling nervous energy.

"Could Jason or that Senator help?" Steve asked Rick. Jason Waters was Cat's former boss and a close friend of hers and Colt's. He'd also recently retired from the Office of the State Attorney General. He'd had the team's back when Cat was in trouble. They'd also received assistance from a State Senator who had been in the sniper's crosshairs along with Cat.

"I'm not comfortable calling Senator Lucas without more information." Still, Rick pulled out his phone. "But Jason might be able to shed some light on the names."

13

While Rick looked for Jason Waters on his contact list, Steve pulled out a chair from the dining room table and offered the seat to Josie. Once she was seated the other men followed suit. Rick put his phone on speaker then hit the call button.

"We have a situation here," Rick told Jason as soon as he answered.

"Is Cat okay?" Jason asked immediately, the tone of his voice was strained and anxious. He was like a father to Cat.

"Colt and Cat are still in the Keys. I'm assuming they're doing just fine." Rick assured him.

"I should hope so. They're on their honeymoon," Jason replied. "What is it then?"

"A friend of Steve's is involved in something." Rick proceeded to lay out the details they had thus far. "Two of the names on our decoded list are involved in politics. We wondered if you had any information on them."

"What are the names?"

"Representative Luis Esteban and State Attorney Aaron Deets."

After a few thoughtful moments, Waters responded, "I can't tell you much about either man. I was sad to learn about Esteban. I never met him personally but he was respected, although I wouldn't call him a political powerhouse. Why don't you give Lucas a call about him?"

"And Deets?" Rick asked.

"I met him once at a fundraiser. He was an ass."

"Mr. Waters? This is Steve. So, you're saying you don't like the guy. Can you be more specific?"

"Call me Jason," he said, then continued. "I only met him that one time. Had a swagger. He came across as arrogant. He's had a strong conviction rate, though. Tough on crime candidate. He also has a reputation as a power seeker. And that's about as much conjecture as you're going to get from me. I don't know the man but he didn't go out of his way to make me feel comfortable with him, I can tell you that much."

While Steve stood behind Josie, hands kneading her shoulders, Rick ran down the list of remaining names in the event any of them struck a chord with Jason but none of them were familiar.

"I can make some calls," Jason offered. "See what I can find out."

"Don't," Rick quickly warned him off. "Someone is already casting a net. We don't want you getting caught in it."

"If you say so. That would have to be one hell of a net, though. Let me know if I can help," Jason added before disconnecting the call.

"Unfortunately, that wasn't much help," Don said, rocking back on the rear legs of the dining room chair.

Steve scanned the others at the table. "Anyone pick up anything I didn't?" Steve asked them.

"Other than the fact that Deets won't be getting a Christmas card from Ellie and Jason?" Gib joked.

"Yeah. Other than that." Steve turned back to Rick. "What about Esteban?"

Rick thumbed a few buttons on his phone in answer to Steve's question. "Rick Wilcowski for Senator Lucas." Rick waited silently on the line for a few minutes. "Thank you. I'd appreciate that."

"He's unavailable," Rick told the group. "They'll have him call me."

Steve wasn't surprised. A State Senator would hardly be waiting around for a phone to ring. "I'm not sure we're headed in the right direction anyway," Steve said. "It doesn't feel right. You have two on the list that are connected to state government, true. But on the surface, the others don't appear to have anything to do with politics or each other."

Steve couldn't say why but the politics link didn't click for him. Something, though, had to tie those names together. Something that Erica had failed to share in her email to Josie. Each time he thought of the danger that woman had put Josie in, his anger bubbled to the surface. Steve turned toward the window to hide his flaring temper. She'd been a friend of Josie's so he did his best to hide his caustic feelings. If he started slinging insults at a person she'd once been close to it might break the tenuous bond between them. Getting angry at someone who may very well be dead didn't solve anything. They needed a break.

The timing of his anger couldn't have been better. If he hadn't turned away at that moment to compose himself, he wouldn't have seen a bicyclist across the street from the studio next door. The man was partially hidden by the shrubbery that grew along the path between the two properties so comparing him to Troy's mystery man wasn't possible. But this man wasn't moving. What were the chances that a male biker would be planted in the same spot two days in a row?

"Looks like our guy might be out front again," Steve said, turning back toward the group. Troy didn't need any prodding. He double-timed it to the door. Troy would know if it was the same man he'd spotted yesterday. If he was, Rick would determine who owned the property and then plan accordingly.

Don brought up the feed on his laptop from the camera located closest to the biker. The video equipment was directed at this property not the studio next door. What view they had of the man was obscured. *Damn it.*

"Gib, would the studio's surveillance cameras have picked him up?" Steve asked.

"Our cameras are directed to the front of our property. None of them would pick up anything across the street."

Steve let out a frustrated huff. He'd expected as much. That would have been one break too many.

"He doesn't resemble the man from St. Augustine," Josie told them, studying what she could see of the man on the screen.

"Troy will get a picture, if he can, but I agree. He doesn't fit the general description of your Detective Watson," Steve responded.

The object of their scrutiny pedaled out of the camera's range. Shortly after the man disappeared, Troy was seen crossing the street on one of the bicycles and falling in behind him.

While Troy chased after their visitor, Steve and the others went back to reviewing the list of names again. The obvious commonality their initial search uncovered was that all the men lived in Florida. Aaron Deets was the State Attorney out of Jacksonville. James Scagliotti owned a large, elite marina in Sarasota. Peter DiSantis was a real estate broker in West Palm Beach. Martin Roemer was the chairman and owner of an independent bank in Miami. Anthony McClaren, as Gib had said, owned several high-end automobile dealerships located in different cities in South Florida but was headquartered in Bonita Springs. Finally, Luis Esteban had been a State Representative from the Orlando area until his death. Without more than just their names to go on, finding out what these men had in common was going to take serious research.

"Any input on where to start?" Steve said, opening the floor to discussion.

"What about McClaren? We shouldn't have a problem getting in to talk to him. I can give him a call," Gib offered.

"It's an idea," Steve said, reaching for his ringing phone.

"I can confirm he's the same man I saw out in front of the studio," Troy told Steve when he answered. "He let himself into a condo. I've got the address, if you're ready."

Steve scribbled down the information and handed it to Rick. If it was a rental, then they needed the name of the tenant. If the bicyclist was neither the owner nor a tenant, it would confirm his worst fear.

A few minutes after placing the call, Troy rejoined the group. Steve hadn't recognized the address but the speed with which Troy returned told him the bicyclist's condo was nearby. Another reason to be on alert. Most vacation rentals were located closer to the water. Those dotted throughout the interior of the island, tended to be owned by snowbirds that only used the location during the winter months. They typically weren't used for short-term rentals. Rick would confirm it one way or the other.

"Josie," Steve said. "Think carefully. Did you talk with anyone, call anyone, do anything that could lead someone to you? Calls placed from someone else's phone? Use a credit or debit card?"

"Nothing! I used cash to buy stuff for my cuts and a little food for the road. And that was in Daytona after I ditched my car. My phone barely made it out of the driveway before I tossed it in the river. A lot of kind souls offered me the use of their phones but I didn't take them up on it. I had a growing fear that Big Brother was watching. By the time I got here, I was paranoid. God, I even stole a boat rather than hitch a ride to the island!"

Stunned, Steve watched Josie as she hesitantly turned her head toward Rick. Her eyes were wide. She'd just realized she'd let it slip that she'd committed a felony in front of an officer of the law.

"If you're talking about the boat that drifted loose from the marina on the other side of the causeway," Rick said, pocketing his phone, "it was recovered and returned to its owner. I've not heard of any reports of a stolen boat."

"Thank God," Josie whispered, dropping into a nearby chair.

Josie wasn't aware that Steve was staring at her. Her hands covered her face. Her long fingers kneaded her forehead. She'd stolen a boat? *Christ*. He wouldn't have thought her capable of committing such a daring act. Desperate was more like it. It telegraphed the depth of her fear as she struggled to get to him. Steve would have continued to gape at her if Gib hadn't nudged him.

"She's had enough, Steve," he said, moving to Josie's side.

"Come on, Josie," Gib said, taking her elbow in his hand. "You need rest and I'm thinking you've had your fill of testosterone for one day."

Gib putting his hand on Josie brought Steve back to the moment. "I'll take her," he snapped at Gib.

"I don't need help." Josie bit back at both of them. Her chair almost toppled over as she bolted from it. "I'm going to find some aspirin and lay down. I have a headache."

As Josie headed toward the bedroom, Gib looked sharply at Steve. "I'll get her some aspirin unless you know where to find it."

Steve didn't answer. Gib would know where Cat kept her first aid supplies, and knowing Colt she had one at the nursery, but Steve could certainly locate it. "You need to drop the macho crap with her," Gib continued. "You'll push her farther away—unless that's your plan."

"Don't tell me how to act around my wife," Steve growled.

"She's not your wife, Steve. Even if she was, ordering her about and hovering is not helpful. You need her talking to you. Not shutting down."

"What makes you such an expert?"

"I know women."

"You'd better not know *that* woman." A brief silence descended on the room. Everyone present understood Steve's thinly veiled threat.

"I don't poach," Gib snapped, showing one of his rare flares of temper.

Gib was a man of honor. Steve's warning had been insulting. "Sorry," Steve offered.

Gib nodded his acceptance of the apology then headed to get the needed pain reliever for Josie.

"I've got to get back to the station," Rick told Steve. "I'll let you know what we find out once I talk to the owners of the condo."

Don got to his feet, as well. "And I'm due to relieve Kevin."

"I don't get it," Troy said to Steve. The four men had walked as far as the kitchen together. As soon as Don and Rick were out the door, Troy had turned toward his friend.

"What don't you get?" Steve baited him. It was time to clear the air and find out just where Troy stood.

"Why would you want her after what she did to you? She breaks you in half then shows up here expecting you to be at her beck and call. What sort of a person does that?"

"Keep your voice down," Steve hissed.

"Why are you still protecting her?" Troy argued in a softer but stronger tone.

"What would you have me do?" Steve asked. "Throw her to the sharks? I asked her to become my wife because I loved her. I still do. I'll be damned if I'll let anything happen to her."

"She screwed you six ways from Sunday. She wanted nothing to do with you until she needed help. She's using you." Troy slammed his fist on the breakfast bar he stood next to for emphasis.

The truth of the statement hit Steve more squarely in the chest than Troy could have imagined. He had to give his friend credit for putting his thoughts out there in the open.

"That very well may be," Steve reluctantly agreed, "but it's my heart that's engaged—not yours. If you want out, then leave. I'd rather have you out of the picture than worry about whether or not you care enough to give this one hundred percent."

"I'll always have your back, Steve. You know that," Troy was adamant. "I'm just not sure that *she* deserves it."

"Since when do we decide whether to help someone based on our likes and dislikes? Haven't our tours taught us that much?" Steve asked. "I'm not going to argue with you about this, Troy. You're entitled to your feelings. If you want out, then go. There'll be no hard feelings on my part."

"It's you I'm concerned about. What happens after this is over and she takes another hike? We all know how her leaving affected you the last time."

Steve put his hand on his friend's shoulder and gave it a squeeze. "Troy, I appreciate your concern but you don't need to worry about me. One way or the other, I need to know if she and I can make a marriage work. If we can't, I'll move on but we can't broach the subject while this shit is hanging over us."

Steve gave Troy a stern look. "So? Are you in or out?"

Troy stared at Steve as the minutes ticked away. The man's jaw was set. His green eyes studied Steve's. Steve returned the stare, not giving an inch. He respected his friend and teammate—appreciated that he had his back both physically and emotionally but Steve couldn't afford to have someone on this team who didn't have Josie's, as well. Troy would be a liability if he wasn't willing to risk his life for Josie's. It was what they did as a team. They risked their lives every day protecting complete strangers.

Of course, in Troy's mind, Josie wasn't a stranger. She'd hurt one of their friends, which made her just shy of an enemy. Steve appreciated the loyalty but, what he needed now was total commitment for Josie's sake.

Troy blinked first. "I'm in," he said, answering Steve. "And I'll stay as long as you need me. I won't promise to like that woman but I'll do my damndest to keep her alive. Good enough?"

"It is," Steve answered, with a nod. "If I'm willing to give her a chance, I'd hope you'd be big enough to do the same. But the most I'll ask of you is that you keep her safe."

"Let me grab a couple of hours sleep and then I'll be back. You can let me know where you want me then."

Troy had hit some sensitive targets with his argument. Regardless, Steve couldn't see himself walking away from this situation.

"What was all that about?" Gib asked joining Steve in the kitchen just as the rear door clicked shut.

"Could she hear us?" Steve asked, shooting a concerned look over Gib's shoulder.

"Voices. Not words. What happened?"

"Troy has an issue with Josie. Hopefully, we resolved it."

"What's his problem? She's nice. Scared but nice. Troy hasn't spent enough time around her to dislike her. Hell, I've never met a woman he *didn't* like," Gib said, a hint of amusement in his voice. The two men routinely competed for women's attention when Troy visited the island.

"His issue has to do with my history with Josie," Steve said.

"I know you, Steve," Gib said, putting his levity aside. "You wouldn't be putting this much effort into winning her back if you didn't think she was worth it."

"Thanks, Gib."

"I hope things work out the way you want," Gib slapped Steve on the back. "You need anything before I take off?"

"There is one thing. Can you make a run to the store sometime today? We're going to need provisions over here." While they'd checked out the Copeland property for security purposes, no one, including Steve, had thought to stock the kitchen with essentials. If they were going to use the Copeland house as a base, they would need to be fully stocked. Steve pulled out his wallet. He wadded up what cash he had and held it out for Gib.

"No problem and put that away," Gib told him, tucking

his hands in his pockets. "We'll square up later. If you need something before then, you're welcome to what Colt or I have on hand."

After Gib took off, Steve went to check on Josie. This time he didn't try to talk himself out of it. He needed to see her.

Steve quietly opened the door to the bedroom. Josie was sleeping soundly. He propped his shoulder against the door frame and inhaled the scent in the room that was uniquely Josie. Her chest rose and fell softly as she rested. Bruises, now turning a sickly yellowish purple, still dotted her face but she looked relaxed in sleep. Troy's warning that she would leave him had brought that possibility front and center once again. If that was her plan, this time, he'd have the reasons spelled out to him before he would let her go. If he'd asked questions prior to their marriage there may have been a different outcome. Instead, he'd ignored the signals. But as much as she'd hurt him—as much as he still ached from the wounds she'd inflicted—he still couldn't imagine a life without her in it.

It was her beauty that had caught his eye but it had been her strength, independence, and fiery compassion that had reeled him in. He would have never pegged her as someone who would run from a problem. She'd made her fear of marrying into the military clear. He'd dismissed it and thought he'd convinced her that their love was permanent. That nothing would stop him from returning to her after each tour. But he'd shipped out so soon after the ceremony it, more than likely, reinforced that fear.

Fear was a powerful motivator. Fear had him pushing her into the marriage. Fearful that if he didn't tie her to him legally, she'd have too much time to reconsider. It looked like they both had trust issues.

He'd found the woman he wanted to spend the rest of his life with and he'd helped chase her away in his rush to tie her to him. He should have waited. Proved that he'd be back without a piece of paper tying them together. A piece of paper that was now worthless.

14

J osie cleared the sleep from her eyes as her stomach growled. How long had she slept? She did a double take of the bedside clock then looked toward the closed blinds where light filtered in. She glanced at the clock again to confirm her assumption. *Holy crap.* She'd not only slept through the afternoon, but all night. Her body had hit the wall and it had taken the time to recoup. Now, what she needed was coffee then food.

Thankfully, her muscles protested less today than they had the day before as she got out of bed. Progress. After a quick stop in the bathroom, Josie barefooted it toward the kitchen. She smelled fresh coffee. Thank God, somebody had started a pot.

"Good morning. Feeling better?" Josie took a second to catch her breath. She'd been intent on her mission for caffeine. She hadn't noticed Gib sitting in the overstuffed chair. The living room, like the bedroom she'd slept in, was sparse. That single chair along with a couch and a coffee table was all that remained. Josie understood from Gib that the furniture were remnants left by the former owners.

"Much better," she finally responded. "Where is everyone?" The place was quiet.

"Steve's taking a turn on watch. Don's next door researching the backgrounds of those men." Gib had put the word *researching* in finger quotes. "The less we know about his work, the better."

"No Rick?"

"He's got a day job. He's at the station. He'll come if we whistle." Gib said with a wink and a smile.

Josie returned the smile. Gib wouldn't have lasted long in the military, assuming he'd wanted to join. His attitude was a little too flippant for the ranks of the army.

"And that would leave two, right?"

"I suspect Kevin will be showing up soon. Troy had the late shift. He's catching some shuteye."

"He doesn't care for me," Josie stated quietly. It had been obvious by the looks Troy shot her way that he wasn't keen on the idea of helping her. And while they hadn't been able to make out what was said last night, Josie had recognized the voices and the tone. She didn't need a transcript to know what the debate Troy and Steve were having centered on.

"It doesn't matter if he does or doesn't like you. He's given Steve his word that he will help. He won't break it."

"I don't get any of this."

"Give it time. We just got the names deciphered."

"Not that. I don't understand why you're all so willing to help me." Josie explained, a cup of coffee now in her hand. She'd settled on one of the two bar stools at the breakfast counter. Gib topped off his cup and joined her.

"Friends help friends, Josie. Why is that hard for you to understand?"

"I don't have any friends with the kind of bond you guys have. And after the way I treated Steve…" Josie let the rest of

97

the sentence drop. They all knew and yet here she sat with one of Steve's friends sharing a very good cup of coffee. Coffee Steve hadn't made from the taste of it.

"I don't understand what happened between the two of you," Gib said, reaching for a bag of bagels. "But if you need to talk it out or just need someone to listen, I'm told I'm pretty good at that."

Josie smiled at the handsome man. "I imagine you charm a lot of secrets out of women."

"Never any more than they want to tell," Gib assured her, with a sexy grin as he dropped the sliced bagel in the toaster.

Josie slid off the stool. "I'd half expected Steve to kick me to the curb, assuming I found him," she said, pulling butter, cream cheese and jelly out of the refrigerator. Had the place come fully stocked or had the shopping been done while she was out cold in the bedroom?

"Wouldn't blame Steve if he had," Josie continued. "I shouldn't have come here. It's not fair to him."

"Why isn't it fair to him? It's obvious he's still in love with you. It's written on his face every time he looks at you." Gib ripped a couple of sheets off a roll of paper towels, folded then in half and set them beside the paper plates and plastic knives on the breakfast bar.

"That's why it's not fair," Josie found herself fighting back tears. She hated this. Her mind continued to battle with her heart. It was exhausting.

"You're not planning to stay with him. Is that it?"

Gib's expression was a combination of pity and anger. She preferred the anger. It's what she deserved.

"It's difficult to explain," she said, taking her seat again.

"Have you explained it to Steve?"

"No." She stared at the bagel Gib had dropped on the paper plate in front of her.

"You don't strike me as timid so why are you afraid of Steve?" Gib asked, slicing another bagel in half.

"I didn't say I was afraid of him," Josie responded, a chill in her voice.

"Well, you sure as hell are doing a good job of acting like it. You're afraid to talk to him. Maybe you ought to ask yourself why."

Josie gave the back of Gib's head an icy stare as she tore off a piece of her bagel and rolled it between her fingertips. "This is none of your business."

"I beg to differ with you," Gib said, turning to face her. "Steve is a friend and by extension, so are you. I wouldn't want either of you hurt."

The caffeine or the conversation had left a bitter taste in her mouth. Her gaze dropped to the cup of coffee that had grown cold. Her appetite was suddenly missing. "You don't always get what you want," Josie muttered.

Gib either didn't hear or chose to ignore the comment. He took the cup from between her fingers. Josie gaze didn't turn away from her hands that had been holding the cup of coffee.

"I'm headed out to the garden," Gib said, changing the conversation as he rinsed their cups. "I'm the keeper of the plants while Cat's away. Why don't you join me?" Once again Gib sported a dazzling smile. He'd transformed back into the handsome charmer.

"Why not?" she agreed, slipping off the stool without much enthusiasm.

"I know the basics," Gib explained once they were out the back door. He reached for a pair of gardening shears that were hanging on a hook on the side of a garden shed. "Cat made sure I knew enough not to kill any plants while she was away. I can deadhead and spot most malevolent insects. That's the extent of my gardening skills. Forced upon me by the hellcat Colt married. God help me if something disastrous befalls one of these plants while she's gone." But Gib was smiling as he reached into the shed and pulled out a spray bottle and handed it to Josie.

"What am I supposed to do with this?" Josie asked, turning the bottle so she could read the label: *Insecticidal Soap*.

"Cat's a big believer in organic gardening. If we discover any of those bad boys, we zap them with the soap. It smothers them." Gib reached into the shed and this time pulled out a small pail. "Follow me," he said and disappeared along a path through the thick foliage.

"You do this every day?" Josie asked when she caught up with him. The garden was a jungle—an organized, colorful, fragrant jungle. Open space consisted of the maze-like walkway and a small gazebo. The path curved and twisted, exposing a new view, a new species at every turn.

"It doesn't need more than a walk through most days but this place is so damn peaceful, I've been here every day since Cat got the lease on the place." His lips curled ever so slightly as he once again glanced over his shoulder at Josie. "Don't tell Cat," he chuckled. "She'll have me doing this daily and call it therapy."

"I may be gone by the time she gets home," Josie said as she felt her chest tightened.

"Does Steve have any say in that?"

"Legally? No. But I won't run off again without a word if that's what you're worried about."

"Concerned, Josie, not worried. It's sad to see two people who care for one another unable to figure out how to make it work."

She should have turned back to the house at that point. She didn't need lectures. She'd given herself enough to last a lifetime. Thankfully, Gib grew silent as he inched his way down the wandering stone path stopping every so often to give a plant a closer inspection. They reached a large, glossy leafed hibiscus covered in bright sunshine yellow flowers the size of her hand.

"Stunning, isn't it?" Gib commented.

"Yeah," Josie agreed. "We don't have flowers blooming this time of year in North Carolina."

"This is Florida. Some variety of flower is always in bloom." He snipped off one of the wilted blossoms. "But then you have flowers and trees in the Spring that put some of our best to shame. Do you miss North Carolina? Is that home for you?"

"I don't have a home," Josie answered.

"Everybody comes from somewhere," Gib countered.

"We transferred too often for me to have what I would call a hometown," Josie said, watching Gib as he continued to cut off dead blooms and toss them in a pail.

"What about family? Anybody going to be concerned if they don't hear from you?"

"No siblings. My dad is God knows where. He filed for divorce from my mother the day I turned eighteen." Her voice reflected her disgust for the man. Josie didn't miss Gib's tiny hesitation as he reached for another spent flower. She'd said too much.

"And your mom? Won't she be worried about you?" Gib didn't glance her way as he'd asked the question. His tone was nonchalant. Part of her wanted to walk away another part welcomed the release of the history she'd kept to herself. She didn't talk about her parents or miserable childhood to anyone.

Josie sighed. "No. She's remarried. New husband. New life. It's worked out well for both of us."

Gib refrained from any further interrogation while he finished deadheading the large hibiscus then inspected the underside of a few leaves. "We're almost done. You up to finishing?"

Josie wasn't anywhere near one hundred percent but the sunshine warmed her skin. "I'm good as long as it's my turn to ask questions," Josie responded.

Gib continued his trek through the garden. "Shoot," he said as he rounded another curve in the pathway.

She never got the chance.

15

A beefy, hairy arm lashed out from the dense foliage and caught Josie by the waist. Air whooshed out of her lungs. There wasn't time to cry out before a large hand clamped tightly over her nose and mouth. She couldn't breathe. She thrashed her head from side to side, trying to dislodge his grip. She twisted, turned, and scratched. She couldn't open her mouth to bite him as he had effectively sealed it shut.

"Get out of my way," the gruff, baritone voice vibrated in her ear, "or I'll break her neck."

Josie froze. Gib was standing an arm's length in front of them. What had felt like minutes must have been seconds. Gib had only been a few steps in front of her. Josie had been so focused on her fight for freedom that she'd forgotten she wasn't alone. Her eyes widened as her attacker tightened his grip. Her vision started to blur.

Panic should have dimmed her senses. Instead, it sharpened them. She still had a grip on the spray bottle of insecticidal soap. God only knew why she hadn't dropped it but it didn't matter. She had a weapon. Praying the man remained focused on Gib, she raised her arm, closed her eyes, and blasted him.

"Bitch!" the man cried out.

Josie dropped to the ground gasping for air. Her eyes were burning from the residual spray that had seeped in through her closed lids.

Blind but breathing, she crawled away from the scuffle behind her, ignoring the sting from her already damaged knees. She heard a cry of pain then a thud as something heavy hit the ground.

STEVE VAULTED OVER THE FENCE. He spotted Josie on her hands and knees on the stone path that wove through the garden. A stranger lay motionless a few feet behind her. Gib stood over the man.

"Josie," Steve said with a tremor in his voice he didn't attempt to hide. "Are you hurt?" he demanded.

"My eyes," she explained, plopping onto the ground then began to rub them furiously.

"What's wrong with your eyes?" Steve moved her hands out of the way so he could check her. She blinked repeatedly then clamped her eyelids shut.

"What happened to her eyes?" he demanded as Gib approached.

"Soap," Gib said, joining them a little short of breath. "She sprayed him with insecticidal soap. She must have gotten some in her eyes. We need to flush them."

Steve looked over his shoulder. Troy and Don had followed him over the fence. Troy now had the man on his feet and in an arm lock. Don was on his phone, probably calling Rick.

"I'll take care of it," Gib said, reading Steve's thoughts. He sprinted toward the house.

"Are you hurt anywhere else, Josie?" He helped her to her feet then led her to a nearby small garden bench.

"I couldn't breathe," she told him. "Scared me."

"I'm sorry, baby," he said, squeezing her close. How had this guy gotten past him?

"Where is he?" Josie asked, cocking her head, eyes still closed. Her muscles were trembling beneath Steve's grasp.

"Troy's got him," Steve assured her as Gib returned. "You're safe." *For the moment, anyway.* This wasn't the end. He could sense it.

"Lean your head back a little, Josie," Steve said as Gib uncapped a bottle of water. "We need to flush the soap out of your eyes." Steve used his forefingers and thumbs to spread her eyelids open and hold them there while Gib emptied the contents of the bottle over both her eyes.

"Here you go," Gib said as he grabbed her hand and placed a wad of paper towels in it. Josie used them to wipe her face. "Better?" Gib asked.

"Uh huh." Josie blinked a few times then nodded. "Thank you."

"You hurt anywhere else?" Steve asked again.

"My knees took a hit. I think I reopened a few cuts."

Small specks of blood dotted the light denim of her jeans. They weren't bleeding heavily but Kevin would have to take another look at them. "Where's Kevin?" Steve shouted, knowing one of the men would have contacted him.

"On his way," Don answered.

The slamming door from across the drive confirmed Don's statement. The sound was quickly followed by the wail of sirens.

"Will that be Rick?" he asked Don.

"And company. This guy needs a medic," Don said, indicating their captive.

Steve scrutinized the man Troy still had in an arm lock. Blood was darkening one sleeve of his shirt. He glanced at Gib who responded with a shrug. A pair of pruning shears lay on the ground near their unwanted guest. Blood glistened from the sharp, curved tip.

Steve didn't bother to ask for any details. Rick would be grilling Gib soon enough. Besides, he could care less how the man had been injured.

"You okay?" Steve asked Gib who was rubbing the knuckles of one hand.

"I tend to use my hands for more gentle sports than pugilism, but I'll be fine," Gib quipped. "Smart lady. If she hadn't sprayed him with that soap, I wouldn't have had a shot at him. He had her plastered against his body like glue. I couldn't touch him without hurting her."

Steve turned to Josie. "Do you recognize him?"

"No," she answered, still rubbing her irritated eyes.

"He is our biker," Troy informed them.

The sound of sirens drew closer. Their time for questioning the intruder was growing short.

"What did you want with Josie? Who sent you here?" Steve demanded.

"I don't know what you're talking about. I saw this garden and decided to check it out," the guy grunted. "I need a hospital. That son-of-a-bitch tried to kill..."

Steve took a step toward the intruder, leaving Josie in Kevin's care. His fists were clenched, his jaw as firm as steel girders.

"I'm pressing charges against those two," the man said, ignoring Steve.

"You're not real bright, are you?" Troy snorted.

"The bitch tried to blind me," the guy insisted, squinting his eyes.

"It was soap, you idiot." If Steve hadn't been so angry, he'd have laughed. "What did you want with her?"

The intruder didn't answer.

"Who sent you? Why were you after Josie?"

This time, the man smirked. "What would any man want with a nice piece of ass?"

What little control Steve had left evaporated. His knuckles tightened as his arm reared back then plowed with lightning-quick speed into the man's jaw. *God, that felt good.*

TROY WAS HAULING the man to his feet as Rick appeared on the path that threaded through the garden. Steve was prepared to take the heat for hitting the guy, but Rick didn't ask.

The instant their prisoner realized the police had arrived he started screaming for medical help. Rick spoke quietly to one of the men in uniform then turned to the guy Troy once again had in an arm lock.

"You'll get help but first, why don't you tell us what you're doing here?" Rick asked, matter-of-factly. His calm demeanor was nothing new. During the time they'd served together, Rick would often take the lead during interrogations of prisoners. Good cop to Steve's bad cop routine.

"I was trespassing. No big deal. It's a misdemeanor. That crazy woman attacked me. I want to press charges. She—" The man swallowed his words as Steve took another step toward him, crowding his space.

"Let's cut the crap," Rick said to him, turning a blind eye toward Steve's menacing posture. "You and I both know you have a record and we're going to know all about you as soon

C. F. FRANCIS

as we run your prints. How many convictions have you had? Remember this is a three-strikes-you're-out state. You could go to jail for a very long time. Especially if this woman presses charges."

"I know people—" the man started.

"And I guarantee you we know even more people. Now, if you don't want to spend time in prison getting that pretty face and other body parts messed up, you'd better start talking."

Rick was bluffing. Steve knew that Rick couldn't legally withhold medical attention. He was in full agreement with Rick's ploy—the man's desire for help could be used to their advantage.

"I'm bleeding here," their captive begged, clenching his wounded arm. He surveyed the group looking for an ally. His expression fell as he circled back to Steve.

"Okay. Okay." His shoulders dropped in defeat. "I was told to watch the place next door for a tall, thin woman with long, dark hair."

"Who told you to watch for her?" Steve demanded. The guy recoiled at his tone. "I don't know. I got an envelope in the mail with a cell phone, address and instructions."

"And you don't know who sent them to you?" Rick questioned. "You go where you're told for no reason?"

"There was cash in the envelope with a promise of a lot more if I found the woman and sent a picture."

"That's it? All they wanted was a picture?" Steve didn't believe it. "Then why did you try to grab her?"

"If I was going to be paid a couple grand for pictures, I figured she was worth a hell of a lot more in person."

The bastard was lucky that Rick was present because Steve would have likely killed the asshole and buried his body in the garden.

"Have you reported in? Did you tell anyone you found her?" Rick asked.

The man didn't respond.

"The sooner you answer, the sooner you'll get help," Rick explained.

"I haven't contacted anyone since I spotted her this morning," he told Rick, indicating Josie with the tilt of his head. "Now call the paramedics, damn it."

Rick signaled one of the officers and an EMS unit pulled into the driveway.

"Son of a bitch," the intruder raged. He'd figured out he'd been had.

Steve could care less. "Where's his phone?" he asked quickly. The paramedics were off-loading their gear. He wanted to check out the phone. Once the police seized it, they'd never see it again.

"Go to hell," the man spat at Steve.

"That wasn't a request."

Don patted down their captive while Troy held the struggling man. Once the phone was retrieved from the man's front pocket, Don tossed it to Steve.

"You know I need that," Rick warned him.

"Let Don take a look at it. It's a burner but he may be able to get data off of it faster than your guys can."

"It's evidence, Steve."

"At least let me get the contact numbers," Steve argued but he was already inputting them into his phone.

"I want to be the first to know if you find anything," Rick warned him. "Now, I need statements from all of you."

Josie's assailant was loaded into the rear of the EMS unit

accompanied by one of the officers that arrived with Rick. While the remaining members of the Sanibel PD did their respective jobs, Rick directed her and the others into the house to get statements.

"Okay, Josie," Rick said, "start at the beginning. When did you become aware of the man?"

"Not until he grabbed me. I had absolutely no inkling anyone was in the garden with the exception of Gib and myself. The guy immediately covered my mouth and nose. I couldn't shout. Hell, I couldn't breathe let alone scream," she told Rick. She could still feel the panic bubble up inside her as she'd tried to inhale and couldn't.

"I'm sorry, Josie," Gib said.

"Don't be." The sincerity in those gray eyes touched her. "It's not your fault. You got the bastard," she praised him, smiling for the first time since the attack.

"After you blasted him with the soap. Smart."

"Yeah, that was fun." Josie's eyes still burned.

"I'd like to know how he received that puncture wound in his arm." Rick directed the question at both Josie and Gib.

"You know what caused it," Gib answered. "You bagged the pruning shears. Cat's going to kill me if she doesn't get those back."

"Cat's not your problem right now, Gib. I am," Rick snapped. "You need to explain why you stabbed him."

"It was more of a case of him stabbing himself. Seriously," Gib added as Rick gave him a look of disbelief.

"He was flailing his arms all over the place after Josie hit him with the spray," Gib explained. "I had every intention of trying to subdue him but he stumbled into me. I was still holding the shears. That was it. I'd wasted enough time trying to dance around him. I hit him hard enough to make certain he wasn't going anywhere." Gib started to rub his knuckles again. "Steve arrived about that time."

"What did you see?" Rick asked Steve.

"The asshole was already on the ground when I got there. Gib was headed toward Josie. I got to her first." Steve pulled her a little closer. "I can't believe I didn't see him," Steve berated himself. "Did we get anything on video?"

Don had already retrieved the laptop from the kitchen counter. Everyone remained quiet while he tapped several keys on the device. "Nothing," he said after looking at several screens.

"He's either a mastermind or just plain lucky he wasn't spotted," Troy jumped in. "My vote is for the latter. Did anyone notice he didn't have a means to get Josie out of here once he'd grabbed her? I spotted his bicycle about a block away."

"Maybe he was going to call Uber for a ride." Josie smirked.

"This isn't funny, Josie," Steve chastised her.

"It kinda is," she replied. "I have this picture in my head of being stuffed into the basket of a bicycle while he peddles like crazy. You know? Remember that scene from the *Wizard of Oz* when Margaret Hamilton grabbed Toto and took off?"

"You're a bit bigger than a terrier," Gib smiled.

"Why the hell did you let her out in the garden to begin with?" Steve snapped at Gib.

"I'd already done a walk through…"

"Wait just a damn minute," Josie said, interrupting the two. "I'm right here. Don't talk about me like I'm the family pet. You don't make decisions for me. You make them *with* me."

"You're the one who came looking for help." Troy turned

toward her. "You shouldn't argue with your personal bodyguards."

"Troy…" Steve started to warn his friend off.

"It's okay, Steve," she said turning to face Troy directly. The man was starkly handsome but he had fire in those emerald-colored eyes. He also had a point. She could ignore Troy's comment but that would only allow the pot to continue simmering until it boiled over.

"You don't like me," Josie said. "I get that. You have every right and believe it or not, I agree with you.

Troy's eyes narrowed. If he was waiting for a counterpunch, he was going to be disappointed.

"I've made of lot bad decisions," she continued. "One of them was coming here— bringing Steve, and by extension, the rest of you into this mess. I'm sorry about that. All I ask is that I'm not treated like a pawn. That I'm included in decisions as long as I'm here."

"And then you'll be gone," Troy added, his distaste for her ringing in his tone.

"Steve's fortunate to have a friend like you. I envy him," Josie responded without addressing the pointed comment.

She never went toe-to-toe with anyone—not on a personal level. This was new territory. Give her a good story with the promise of a meaty center and she'd get to that center one way or another. But personal stuff? She was happy to bury it under the nearest rock she could find. She'd proven that point with Steve. Why had it taken her so long to grow a spine?

As far as Troy was concerned, hopefully now that their cards were on the table he would, at least, tolerate her. Steve didn't need to play referee in addition to everything else she had put on his plate.

She looked over at the man with whom she'd once exchanged vows. Troy's statement had hit him hard. The light in his eyes had dimmed, proving that Troy had every reason to hate her.

If she could go back in time how far back would she go? If they'd never met, Steve would never have been hurt. But, as she'd proven over and over again, she was selfish. If she was granted that wish, she would have still wanted the time she'd had with Steve before he'd been deployed. Those months had been magical. They would never be repeated but she had the memories. She didn't have a fairy godmother or a genie in a bottle. She couldn't undo the hurt any more than she would be able to stop the pain that was yet to come when all of this was over.

16

Steve shook off the sting of Troy's words, the reminder that Josie's plan was to leave him once the danger had passed. He had his own plans. She'd had enough time and space. He'd get his answers this time. Right now, however, he had to think and think like a soldier.

How the hell did anyone know where to look for her?

"Josie, there's no way they could have tracked you here unless you used a credit card or made a phone call."

"I didn't call, text, or email a soul. Not even you. I don't know how they found me!"

"Where's your ID?" Rick turned to ask Josie.

The question had Steve snapping his head up. "What the hell has that got to do with this?" he barked, still trying to get a grip on his anger.

"Could have a lot to do with it."

"It's on the counter in the kitchen," Josie answered.

Gib left the room and returned with Josie's card case.

"You didn't change it," Rick stated as he looked at her driver's license and then flipped through her credit cards. "None of them."

"Changed what?" Gib asked.

"Her name," Rick explained.

Steve snatched the license from Rick. Josette Boussard Brody was printed boldly across the top. A little bit of his heart melted.

"But I haven't used them since I left St. Augustine," she argued, confused. "How could they use them to trace me?"

Rick had figured it out first but now the answer was clear to Steve. "They didn't, Josie. They used mine," Steve told her.

Steve's stomach churned knowing that someone had found Josie by following his credit card trail. To do so the party would first have to be aware of the marriage. That would be the easy part as long as they'd had Josie's full name. Tracing the credit card usage of a member of a Special Ops team, however, would take some doing. Due to the covert nature of their work, Special Forces members had added layers of security on all their transactions and communications. The fact that whoever was behind this was able to break through those layers added another degree of severity to their problem. Who the hell were these guys?

Steve led Rick away from the others so Josie wouldn't know how much this development had shaken him. "It might be a good idea if Josie and I take off." he said to Rick once they'd reached the kitchen.

"I disagree," Rick countered, his jaw set.

"They know where she is." *Wasn't that obvious?*

"You're not thinking, Steve. We don't know that for a fact. This guy could be one of any number of drones sent out in search of information. He says he hasn't reported in. We'll know soon enough after we get a good look at his phone. Whoever these people are, they're good. Sure, you could drop out of sight for a while but eventually you'd have to surface.

Then where would you be? Alone with no one having your six. Hiding isn't going to solve this. It will just postpone it. We all know you're worried about her but you can't protect her twenty-four seven. And if we're going to sort this out, we're going to need her help."

Josie must have overheard part of the conversation because she shouted to Steve from the living room. "I'm done running, Steve. As long as I'm welcome here, I'm staying."

"I don't like it," Steve grumbled, returning with Rick to the main room.

"As if we couldn't tell," Josie muttered.

"I hate to be redundant but could this be the work of Gravestone?" Gib asked. "Finding Josie wouldn't be difficult for them."

"After that fuck-up this past summer, I'm still convinced their days of subcontracting are over. And there is no way either of the men who came after Josie are professionals," Rick said.

"They still make me nervous," Gib admitted.

"They make us all nervous," Rick agreed.

"Rick, can you keep our friend off the radar for a while?" Steve asked. Once the name of their visitor was keyed into the law enforcement network they might as well have Josie 'check-in' to Sanibel on Facebook. The arrest would send red flags to anyone who had eyes on the system. "I have an idea."

17

"I'm listening," Rick said, but hesitation laced his response.

Steve's former comrade-in-arms trusted him. A very thin line divided law and justice, however. Rick had walked it often enough for Cat. He'd probably thought he was done with that balancing act.

"We don't know how but whoever is behind this shit will know the minute that our intruder is entered into the system," Steve explained. "Once that's done you'll be confirming Josie's location, assuming the guy is telling the truth about not reporting in that he's found her."

"And what am I supposed to do? Let him go?"

"Of course not. But can you keep him under wraps? Put him in a safe house, book him under a John Doe or any name that would keep his real name out of the system? Then we use his phone to continue with the updates. Updates that say there is nothing new to report. It could buy us time."

"It is a solid idea," Rick agreed. "But let me talk to my captain and run a few scenarios through him. I need to bring him up to speed on this anyway."

After Rick left for the station, Kevin re-examined and cleaned Josie's knees. Then Steve told Kevin and Don to get some sleep. Troy would take the next turn on guard duty. The small contingent of men would make for some long nights and little rest. It would've helped if a few more team members had stayed on the island after the wedding but you worked with what you had—and what he had now were good men. Even Troy, who made his dislike for Josie clear, would give his life to protect her.

At Steve's suggestion, Josie was now working on Don's laptop in the bedroom searching for what she could find on the names from Erica's list. She'd started her research at the dining room table but several times he'd caught her giving him longing looks, followed by a cloud of sadness that would shadow her face.

He tried to ignore it. She'd made her intentions clear. She planned to leave him—again. He couldn't force her to stay nor did he want a forced relationship. He did want to know why she believed so firmly they weren't meant for each other. Why did she believe they were better off apart? He'd asked her before in text messages, emails, and voice mails. She'd simply said it was for the best.

Why did he continue to punish himself? He was starting a new life. It might be best to start it with a clean slate.

But she was here now. And if she felt that fate had intervened in their marriage he had every right to believe that fate had delivered her back to him. He'd never believed their marriage was a mistake. Their months together had been more than just heat—a heat that had yet to fade. There was a connection that was deep, emotional, and fulfilling. He couldn't believe that connection was one-sided. If he did, then how could he ever trust his judgment again?

THANKS TO THE WELL-STOCKED KITCHEN, Josie and Gib were able to throw together a late lunch of sandwiches. Rick either had an uncanny timing for food or he had news. Based on his sullen expression, it was the latter.

Rick said nothing as he took a sandwich off a platter, placed a handful of chips on his plate and grabbed a drink. Josie followed him to the dining area where Steve, Gib and Kevin were chowing down but didn't enter. She leaned against the doorframe that separated the kitchen from the eating area. She'd nibbled on a sandwich while she'd prepared the food. Right now, the roast beef she'd consumed was threatening to make a reappearance. She had a feeling she wasn't going to like what he had to say.

"There are no records of Erica using her cell phone since that last text to Josie," Rick said after he swallowed his first bite. "There hasn't been any recent credit card use by her, either. The Tallahassee PD will continue to check her call history and her credit card trail."

"That's not good, is it?" Josie sensed Rick's pessimism.

"She might be hiding like you did," Rick answered, quickly. Too quickly.

"But you don't think so."

"I can't say, Josie. I wish I could tell you but I don't know that answer. She's not been in contact with any of her clients and her family hasn't heard from her."

"What else do you have?" Steve asked.

"The body of a man was pulled from the Matanzas River. He fits the description of Josie's detective. Drowning is a possibility but his death is currently being ruled as suspicious since they found a contusion on the back of his head. The body was stripped of all identification but it didn't take long for him to be identified. His real name was Ron Sykes. He has a long rap sheet. Mostly for assault. He was out on parole." Rick pulled out his phone, clicked on a few apps then turned the phone toward Josie. She left her perch at the doorway and crossed the room to look at the screen.

"Is this the man who attacked you?" he asked.

Josie studied the mug shot of a man in need of a shave. His hair was dark as were his eyes. The cocky grin on his face made her blood turn to ice crystals. "That's him. That's the man who called himself Detective Watson."

"What do we know about him?" Steve asked.

"Right now? Not very much. Remember, we're trying to keep a low profile by working through Corello so information is a bit slower in coming. They are looking into his history. Known associates, etcetera. I told Corello about our bicyclist." He held up his hand to stop Steve when he started to object. "We need to know if the two are connected. He can't work blind any more than I can."

"They're cleaning house," Steve said.

"I agree." Rick nodded. "Which worked to our advantage. Once we suspected the body belonged to Josie's attacker, the captain had no problem going along with your idea to keep Samuels out of sight and off the books. That's the name of our bicyclist. Sam Samuels, if you can believe it. He goes by Sammy."

"Where is he?" Steve jumped on the name.

"I was told he's been taken care of. In other words, don't ask. I have Sammy's phone and enough text history to be able to replicate his text pattern. We'll continue the 'nothing to report' texts for as long as it works."

"So, what now?" Josie asked.

"Now we start looking hard at those names on that list," Steve answered.

When Josie wasn't searching the internet for information about the men, she'd been feeding data given to her by the others into a spreadsheet that Don had created. The more information they found, the more columns were completed. Sex, age, date of birth, birthplace, and current residence, were all listed on the sheet along with family information. Still, with all the searches, the only two common denominators they'd discovered were gender and the state in which they resided—Florida.

"There's got to be at least another link that ties them together," Steve mused. "Gib, why don't you and I take a ride in the morning and visit McClaren." The headquarters of McClaren Luxury Imports was in Bonita Springs, which was about thirty minutes away. It was time to start asking questions of the men on Erica's list.

"If I can drive the Mustang," Gib grinned.

"In your dreams," Steve responded. "While we're gone, someone needs to start making calls," Steve said to the others. "However you want to do it. Split them up or one of you be the main contact. Whatever works best for you. Find out if they are willing to talk or see if you can get a reaction to the other names on the list.

"We're going to have to invent a reason for the call. We can't tell them we're working with law enforcement." Steve looked to Rick for confirmation.

"We have no official reason to question them like we did when we had a sniper loose on the island," Rick agreed. "Use your cells if they're secure. Better yet, get burners. The fewer people who know your location, the less likely they'll be able to trace Josie here."

"You don't think they're going to give out information to a stranger on the other end of the line, do you?" Gib was obviously skeptical.

"May I make a suggestion?" Josie offered.

"What have you got in mind?" Steve asked.

"Well, Esteban wasn't a household name but he was a State Representative. Whoever calls could claim to be a research assistant for a journalist. Tell them that you understand they knew him and ask for their thoughts on his passing. It's not very far from the truth."

"They're going to ask questions about the journalist," Steve countered.

"You don't have to know the name of the journalist requesting the information. Tell them you are part of a pool of researchers who do work for different journalists or news organizations. It's a stretch but most people don't know how the media operates. They may fall for it."

"It might work. Most people like seeing their name in print," Rick agreed.

"Alright, then. We've got a plan," Steve confirmed, as he ushered the group out the door. "Gib, call when you're ready to go in the morning."

18

The bedroom was only a few steps away. Was she supposed to lock herself in along with her fears or invite the man she'd longed for to join her? It had taken this personal act of terror for her to realize how much she'd missed his strength and his touch. She wanted to be wrapped in his arms again. The same arms that had held her tightly to his chest when she'd awaken in panic from the terror that had chased her here. How long had it been since she'd felt safe, loved, and protected?

"If you need me, I'll be out here on the couch," Steve said.

The fluttering in her chest was replaced by an ache. Why had she assumed he'd want the same thing? Steve was a good man. A man that deserved better. But it didn't change the fact that she still wanted him. Wanted the safety and security she felt when they were so close they became one. It made no sense that she felt the need to push him away and still want him at the same time, but she did.

She dropped her gaze and studied the woodgrain pattern of the flooring. "You don't have to sleep on the couch."

"I'm not leaving you here alone, Josie." Steve's tone was defiant.

"I don't want to be alone," she said, her eyes still averted. He hadn't understood. God, how much more could she muck this up?

The toes of his shoes crept into her field of vision. "What are you saying, Josie?" He touched her chin then tilted her head until their eyes met. Her nerves danced in the most sensitive place as she grew damp. He'd touched her many times over the last few days but tonight the sensual pull was too great to ignore. Was it her close call today or had her will to keep her distance worn down? She didn't care about the reason. She wanted Steve.

"I'm saying there's a king-sized bed I'm willing to share."

Confusion then sadness flashed across his face. With his understanding came realization. She was asking for tonight—not a future. Flushed from embarrassment, she wrenched herself free of his touch.

"Sorry. Bad idea," she mumbled and turned toward the bedroom. Her body still tingled from his touch. She had to escape. She'd do something stupid if she stayed in the same room with him.

"Josie. Wait."

Why did that have to sound like a plea? Because it had, she was unable to walk away. But she didn't turn. Couldn't face him. The heat that radiated from him chased away the chill as he drew close. Reflex had her squeezing her thighs together in need. Did he have to stand so close?

"Are you sure this is what you want, Josie?"

She turned and nodded. God, yes, she wanted him. "I'm being selfish. I don't want to hurt you, Steve. I've never wanted to hurt you. That's why I left."

"You couldn't have hurt me more, Josie. I still don't understand why."

Josie quieted as she once again studied the patterns in the wood grain floor. This idea had been another monumental and impulsive action that had turned out badly. She was becoming a gold medalist in major mistakes.

"Why won't you tell me? What is it that is so horrible you won't share it with me?" Steve asked.

The question hit a nerve. "Like you shared with me?" she snapped.

"I don't understand."

Josie didn't sense any anger in his response. Simply puzzlement.

"No, I don't suppose you do," Josie said, her shoulders slumped in defeat. He had never let her in. His silence during their time together was another confirmation that she'd made the right decision in leaving.

THE DARK, wavy locks streaming from the crown of Josie's head were all he could see as he looked down at the woman in front of him. She was now staring at the floor as if something on it held her interest, making it impossible for him to read her expression. Was this the time to press the issue of their marriage? He couldn't fix what he didn't know was broken. The subject had been broached. He could press her for answers. He had every right. But as he watched, her shoulders sagged and her breathing hitched. She was hurting.

Sex wasn't the answer but it was a damn good distraction. What difference did it make why they slept together? He'd been celibate since he'd left for Afghanistan. Legally, he'd been free to sleep with anyone he wanted. He'd only wanted Josie. She was offering him the chance to be with her again. Even if she walked out of his life tomorrow, he'd have another night with her. Another night to remember.

Steve cupped the sides of Josie's face, and nudged it upward until their eyes met.

"We never had issues in the bedroom. There's no reason why we can't enjoy each other again if that's what you want," Steve admitted.

Minutes ticked past. She'd said nothing further as her blue eyes bore into his. Had she changed her mind? Then she wrapped her arms around his neck, pulling his head down until her lips crushed against his. She opened her mouth, inviting him in. Instinct took over as he pressed her closer and deepened the kiss. His tongue met hers, stroke for delicious stroke. The kiss was carnal and long overdue. *God*, this was his Josie. A night hadn't gone by that he hadn't yearned for the taste, the feel, the scent of her.

He tightened his grip on her silky hair while his free hand traced the length of her spine. Cupping her ass, he forced her hips into his. She arched her back, ever so slightly, the movement pressing her core against his erection. Steve almost embarrassed himself. He pulled away from the kiss and her gyrating hips.

Once the erotic contact was broken, that damn sanity began to creep in.

"Are you sure?" he asked again, idiot that he was.

"Look at me, Steve," she begged, holding his gaze, her palm brushing his beard-roughened cheek. "Look at me."

Steve did as she requested. The desire remained but tears now pooled in those deep blue eyes.

"I want you, Steve. That hasn't changed."

Her declaration would be enough for tonight. He kissed

her again hard and quick, then lifted her into his arms. When she nipped at his ear, he stumbled. Only sheer determination had him making his goal of the bedroom.

In deference to her injuries, Steve laid Josie gently on the bed. As he yanked his shirt over his head, Josie reached for the button on his jeans. She'd forced the zipper down before he could toss the shirt aside. Once she had access to the object of her desire, she didn't wait for Steve to shed the remainder of this clothing. Her fingers found his erection and began to stroke.

Carefully, he removed her hand and stepped out of his jeans. Josie shimmied out of the shorts she'd changed into after her fall in the garden. Her panties were tossed into the corner of the bedroom along with Steve's clothes. Once again, she reached for his cock.

"Come here," she implored. A salacious grin crossed her face in the shadows as he joined her on the bed, straddling her. He grabbed the hem of her shirt so he could have access to her breasts. She batted his hands away then lifted her hips, reaching to guide him in. He got the message. They'd both been so long without each other.

He was already damp with precum before she began to stroke her tender flesh with the tip of his erection. Sweat beaded at his temples as he continued to rub against the heat of her wet, hot core. No longer able to hold back, he lifted her hips further into the air and dove deep.

Her breath escaped her lungs as he entered her then buried himself deep inside. A moan signaled her pleasure when he reached between them, finding her sweet spot with his thumb and bringing her over the edge. As soon as she tightened around him, he began to move. She repeated his name with each stroke as he quickened his pace. Within seconds, he was over the edge as well. Every muscle of his body went taut as she wrung him dry.

Steve dropped to the mattress beside her and pulled her close, lightly kissing her hair. Josie rested her head on his chest. Within a few minutes, her breathing steadied and her body relaxed. She'd fallen asleep in his arms.

19

J osie slept soundly as Steve dressed for his meeting with McClaren. His t-shirt was bunched up around her hips giving him a view of her well-rounded backside. He'd never gotten the opportunity to remove her shirt. Josie had quickly fallen into a deep sleep. He, on the other hand, hadn't slept at all.

The minute they'd finished, he'd wanted her again. That hadn't changed. Making love with Josie had always been off the charts but something stronger drew him to her. Something special that made him fall hard.

They had both needed the release last night. But he wanted more. He wanted his wife back—not just in his bed but in his life. What would it take to make that happen? He pulled the rumpled sheet from the foot of the bed and covered her body then left the room before he was tempted to wake her.

≈

"YOU MIGHT WANT to let up a little on the gas," Gib suggested as they barreled south on U.S. 41. "McClaren isn't going anywhere. He's expecting us."

Steve eased his Mustang back to an acceptable speed for the busy, commercial six-lane highway. His thoughts had been racing, but that didn't mean his car had to keep pace with them.

"You wanna tell me about it?" Gib asked.

"It's none of your damn business," Steve snapped, taking his eyes off the road long enough to sneer at Gib.

"I wasn't talking about last night," Gib laughed. "Why don't you tell me about her?"

"Josie?" Steve's eyes flashed from the road to his passenger.

"Who else would we be talking about?"

"I told you what happened between us. What else do you want to know?"

"Could the split between the two of you be connected to what's going on now?"

The question had surprised Steve but Gib was his usual unfazed self. "I can't imagine how. Why?"

"Just a thought. She's in Florida. You're in Florida and so is everyone else who seems to be connected to this shit." Gib drummed his fingers on the arm rest of the passenger door.

"I'm relatively certain that Josie and I are both in Florida at the same time this 'shit' is going down is just a coincidence."

"Why is she in Florida? Didn't Josie live in North Carolina?"

"She moved right after she got the letter from the clerk's office." Steve shifted the gears with a little more force than was necessary.

"I still don't understand that move," Gib said.

"That makes two of us. Josie was always skittish about

marrying me. Marrying anyone in the service, for that matter." Steve kept his eyes on the road as he wove through the traffic.

"I can understand her hesitation to marry you." Gib smiled when Steve gave him a cross look. "What's her problem with the military?" he asked, more seriously.

"I'm not sure. Her dad was army. She didn't talk about her parents much but what I do know isn't pretty. They separated while she was still in school."

"Why separate? Why not divorce?"

"An interesting question." Steve said half under his breath. "She would never discuss it. I did ask if she wanted to wait to get married until her family could attend the wedding. She said they wouldn't come so it didn't matter."

"She told me her mother remarried. They don't communicate at all," Gib told him.

Steve gave his friend a sideways glance. How had he managed to get that out of her? She never talked about her family.

Gib didn't comment further so Steve asked pointedly, "What's on your mind?"

"I spent time with her the other day before and after the attack. She's no wuss. I wouldn't tag her as a runner."

Neither had Steve until he'd received her email telling him she'd relocated to St. Augustine.

"Turn here," Gib told him. "Why don't you drive a vehicle with GPS? You know they make them now, Steve" he chided lightheartedly, closing the directions app on his phone.

"You're riding in a classic," Steve reminded him with a knowing grin as they pulled into the lot of the luxury dealership. They'd driven the Mustang at Gib's insistence.

Walking into the showroom, a young man sprinted past the other salesmen to greet them. "Are you trading that in?"

he asked, his eyes locked on the Highland Green '68 Mustang GT.

Steve smirked at Gib. "Told you. A classic." The kid was all but drooling over the car. He was going to be disappointed. "We have an appointment with Mr. McClaren," he told the salesman. "He's expecting us."

"Sure. Sure. I'll take you to his office." He gave the car a longing look. You'd have thought someone had taken away his puppy.

Steve and Gib were led up a short flight of stairs to Anthony McClaren's mezzanine office. A glass wall gave the occupant a panoramic view of the shiny, expensive luxury automobiles displayed on the showroom floor below.

McClaren stood as they entered the office. Steve estimated him to be in his mid-fifties. His salt-and-pepper hair was meticulously groomed and he wore a crisp, white button-down shirt as a backdrop for a striking hand painted tie. A navy-blue suit jacket hung over the back of his chair.

"Mr. McKay." McClaren reached for Gib's hand. "Good to see you again. How have you been?"

"Fine. And it's Gib, remember?"

"Yes, of course."

"This is my friend, Lieutenant Steve Brody." Gib introduced the two men.

Steve took the man's hand. He had a good grip.

"Happy to meet you, Lieutenant, and thank you for your service," McClaren addressed Steve.

Steve simply tipped his head in acknowledgement.

"I gather from your call that this visit isn't about photography or vehicles. What can I help you with?" McClaren asked, getting right to the point.

"As I mentioned, we're looking into a problem on behalf of a friend," Gib said. Steve had asked Gib to start things off since he was acquainted with the man. "Would you mind telling us if you knew State Representative Luis Esteban?"

"Why do you want to know?"

Steve responded to the question. "Your name had appeared on a list along with his and four others. We're trying to find the connection. Esteban is dead," Steve added.

At the blunt statement McClaren's eyes widened and his head snapped back as if he'd been slapped. The information was news to him.

"What sort of list are you talking about? Where'd it come from and how did Mr. Esteban die?" McClaren fired off the questions in rapid order.

"The Representative was killed by a hit-and-run driver near his home in Central Florida. The state is investigating. At the moment, I can't share information about the origin of the list as it's part of an investigation. But the list is just that —a list. Regardless of its origin, we have no other information other than the names that are on it. We're trying to connect them. Did you know Representative Esteban?" Steve asked again.

"The name is vaguely familiar. Of course, it could be because he was a public figure or I heard about his death on the news."

Both were reasonable possibilities. Steve gave McClaren the list of names. The room was deathly silent as the man studied the paper Steve had placed in front of him.

"You know, there is something familiar about them but damned if I can tell you what it is."

"What about college, organizations or a board you might have served on together?" Gib tossed out.

McClaren's tanned brow wrinkled further as he fought a battle with his memory. "I'm sorry," he said. "I wish I could help you but I can't tell you whether I know any of them or not. Now, I have a few questions for you," McClaren added.

"Shoot," Steve leaned back in his chair. Sometimes questions were as good as answers.

"Why is this important to you? I'm as curious as you are as to why my name turned up on that list with these men but I'd like to know your connection."

That wasn't what Steve had expected but he answered it freely. "The list was sent to my wife." The statement was simpler than explaining the convoluted relationship between him and Josie. "She was attacked by someone wanting it. I want to know why and by whom."

"I'm sorry to hear that. I hope she's okay. Do you believe the people on the list are in danger?"

"To be honest, I have no idea." Steve admitted. "To be safe, I'd watch my back."

"I'll do a little digging and if I find a connection," McClaren said, "I'll call you."

Steve gave McClaren his number and he and Gib headed back to the car.

"You disappointed?" Gib asked.

"Disappointed? Yes. Surprised? No," Steve said. "It was a long shot. The names could be connected for any number of reasons—or no reason at all. But there's got to be a connection somewhere."

The young salesman who'd taken them to McClaren's office was hovering by Steve's Mustang when they returned to the lot. Respectfully, his hands had remained in his pockets as he eyed the interior.

"She's a beauty," he told Steve.

"Appreciate you keeping an eye on her," Steve said to the young man.

Gib slid into the passenger seat. "Do you believe McClaren?"

"I don't think he was lying. His reaction to the news of Esteban's death was sincere. We'll be hearing from him if he remembers anything. He's worried now."

20

Muscles that hadn't had a workout in months objected as Josie stretched. She still ached from the beating as well as the tumble to the garden floor. But muscles that had nothing to do with the attacks were making themselves known this morning. Those aches were a pleasant reminder of the frantic lovemaking with Steve. It hadn't solved their problems but it had been a hell of a nice diversion. And she'd slept in Steve's arms again.

A sliver of ice-cold guilt cut its way through the warm memories. Last night was a stolen moment in time and she was the thief. She had been upfront with him but had her physical need given him false hope?

The outline of where Steve's head had laid was still visible on the pillow but his side of the bed had grown cold. It was after nine. Steve had always been an early riser. Plus, he and Gib had planned to visit McClaren. Hopefully, they'd learn something new during the visit.

Josie dragged herself out of bed and into the bathroom. A shower was very much in order. As she pulled her t-shirt over her head her eyes caught a shiny reflection in the mirror. Her gaze dropped to the gold chain that hung around her neck. If she'd fully undressed last night, Steve would have seen the wedding band hanging on that chain. How would she have explained that? When news came from the county, she'd removed the ring. She'd had no right to wear it. But removing the ring had felt like an amputation. The pain hadn't eased until she'd placed the ring on a chain and it settled close to her heart.

Breathing grew difficult as the game of tug and war resumed between her heart and her mind. She would not repeat her parents' mistakes. Neither she nor Steve deserved that hell. Fate had stepped in to save them both. Why was she tempting it now?

Tears filled her eyes as she unhooked the chain. She dropped it, along with the simple band, into the small cosmetic bag Gib had brought her filled with toiletries. If Josie was giving Steve false hope by sleeping with him, knowing she wore the ring would make things even worse.

AFTER HER SHOWER, Josie went in search of coffee. "Good morning," she said as she passed Don who was seated at the breakfast bar plugging away on this laptop. "Is there any coffee left?" she asked, indicating the cup next to the computer.

"Help yourself," Don told her. "It's fresh. I dumped that shit Steve made."

Steve liked his coffee strong. When he'd been home, she'd gotten into the habit of adding a cube of ice to thin down his sludge so she could drink it. She'd never said a word because what newlywed would complain when their husband went to the trouble of making her coffee every morning?

She turned toward the coffee pot before she had another fit of tears. What the hell was wrong with her?

"Steve's back," Don said, making her jump.

"Is he?" Josie asked, trying to play it casual, while she attempted to pour coffee into a cup with unsteady hands.

"Yep. He's relieving Kevin," Don said. "We're stretched a little thin until Colt gets back."

"I hope this is over before then. When are they due to return?"

"Don't have an exact date. A few more days, at least. Gib is handling the business so there's no rush." She noticed Don was focused on her hands as they tried to hold her cup steady. She was not having a good morning.

"Did Steve say whether they had any success?" she asked, hoping to distract him.

"They got nothing out of McClaren. Troy is next door attempting to get through to the remaining men on the list."

"What are you doing?" Josie asked, looking at the computer.

"Hacking."

Her eyebrows rose at the blunt statement.

"You didn't hear that," he warned her quickly. "*Research.* I'm doing research."

"Okay," Josie smiled. "What sort of *research* are you doing?"

"Finding out everything I can on those men."

"Anything I can do to help? I feel pretty useless."

"As a matter of fact," Don started, "I was developing a spreadsheet, trying to discover what they may have in common. You think you could take that over while I continue my, umm, research?"

"I think so." Josie grinned again. "I've used similar methods to put stories together. What have you got?"

Josie and Don worked hand in hand for the remainder of the day. He'd pass her information as he dug it up. Her hands steadied as she started picking apart the information to enter on the spreadsheet.

Josie had descended into her comfortable world of gathering facts and data when Don suddenly stood and reached toward the back of his jeans. She'd been with him all afternoon and hadn't noticed a weapon tucked in his waistband under a loose-fitting shirt. The weapon was at his side when someone tapped on the rear door. When Gib entered the kitchen, Don slipped the weapon back into his jeans. Gib was followed by Troy and Rick. Each carried a bag. The contents smelled suspiciously like Italian food. Josie's stomach grumbled.

"I guess it's my turn," Don said. He closed the program he'd been working on. He stuck his hand in one of the bags and grabbed a container of food then headed for the door. He stopped and turned to Josie, "We'll pick up where we left off after I catch some shut-eye. You have a nice evening."

Have a nice evening? The air quickly left Josie's lungs as she stared after him. Did he know what happened last night between her and Steve? Did she care?

STEVE WATCHED Rick pull into the crushed shell lot behind the studio. He'd been expecting Rick. Steve received a text minutes before to advise him of Rick's eminent arrival. If someone was on guard, you warned that guard of incoming to avoid being in their crosshairs. While the plan had been to meet later that evening, Troy had called to request a sooner, rather than later, face to face with Rick and Steve. The request wouldn't have been made lightly.

Since none of them had eaten, Rick had offered to swing by Momma's Italian Restaurant for take-out. As his truck pulled in behind the studio, Gib and Troy appeared from the building to help him unload. Steve didn't make a move toward the vehicle. He had a job to do until relieved.

The trio disappeared into the Copeland's place. Steve inhaled the cooling night air while his foot quietly tapped the sandy soil beneath it. As he waited for Don to relieve him, Steve's eyes darted from one corner of the garden to another looking and listening, for anything out of the ordinary. No buzzing of mosquitos this time of year—killed by the first major drop in temperature or seeking protection from the cooler air until spring. One of the tiny lizards that were abundant in the area scurried through the mulch. In the twilight, the mockingbirds had yet to stop serenading each other. An owl hooted off in the distance calling to its mate. The only sounds not provided by nature were the ticking of Rick's truck engine as it cooled and the occasional car passing by out front on Periwinkle Way.

Don exited the building. He stood under the outside light for a nanosecond before moving into the darkness. The slight pause had been a signal to let Steve know he was ready to go.

It took Steve less than a minute to reach the door. Other than a couple of quick glances through the window, he hadn't seen Josie since he'd left her that morning. The picture of her rounded ass had stayed with him most of the day. She'd offered him her body last night. Nothing more. But he'd take it again if she offered.

As Steve entered the house, his eyes immediately locked on Josie. She was staring at him or, it appeared, through him. Her color was off. Her skin was flushed. Then Josie quickly excused herself.

Steve followed in her wake but she made it to the bathroom and shut the door in his face. Was she sick?

"Josie? What's wrong?" She didn't respond.

"Josie!" The voices and sounds from the kitchen had ceased. Steve ignored the silence as he reached for the doorknob.

"I'll be out in five minutes." The lock on the door clicked.

The voices at the other end of the hall resumed as did the rustle of plastic bags and aluminum containers but not a sound emanated from the other side of the door. Five minutes. He'd give her five minutes then he was going through that door.

"Can't a woman use the facilities in peace?" Josie asked when she swung open the door and faced the wall of his chest.

"What's up with you?" he asked. "A few minutes ago, you looked ill." His gaze swept the length of her frame. He saw no hint of illness or new injury to her physically or emotionally. She looked good. No, she looked fantastic. He tamped down his sexual response to her closeness. No time to go there now.

"Just hungry," Josie answered. "Is that dinner I smell?"

Steve stepped out of Josie's way as she swept by him, ignoring his question. What was with the chameleon act? She'd escaped from the kitchen agitated or upset but had reappeared from the bathroom calm and in control. He'd talked to her later about the sudden change when they were alone. He grinned at the thought of another night with her.

Josie and Steve were the last to help themselves to the food. He sat next to Josie on the couch, his friends' strategy obvious to him. He appreciated their matchmaking but that wasn't his main concern at the moment.

He turned to Troy who was shoveling in a forkful of pasta. "What's going on?"

"Martin Roemer," Troy responded as he munched. "The second name on the list? He's dead."

"What?" Steve managed not to spit out his food. "When?"

"How?" Rick added.

"Why didn't that show up on our search today?" Josie sat her plate on the coffee table

"Start at the beginning," Steve said, taking control of the conversation.

"I kept calling different departments at the bank until I reached one of the vice presidents. 'Off the record' he told me that Mr. Roemer had passed away several days ago."

"Why wouldn't Don have come across that today?" Steve asked, repeating Josie's question.

"Because he died on Saint Martin while on vacation," Troy said. "His death hasn't been officially reported here. They've got to be worried about business repercussion when it's announced. They're prepping for that possibility."

"And the cause of death?" Steve asked.

"Don't have it. The person I talked to either didn't know or didn't want to share." Troy told them.

"Well, crap," Josie sighed as she slumped against the sofa cushions. "Two dead from the same list? You know this can't be good."

The information lodged in Steve's throat threatening to choke him. No, this couldn't be good.

"Where was he from again?" Rick asked, pulling out his phone.

"He lived in Miami Beach," Troy answered.

"I'll get hold of the Miami-Dade County Sheriff's Office off the loop," Rick said, as he scrolled through a screen. "They need to be informed that his death could be connected to another investigation. Their coroner needs to do an autopsy."

"Does anyone else have another bombshell to drop?" Steve asked.

"That's my big news. I've hounded the offices of Scagliotti, Deets, and DiSantis," Troy added. "No return calls."

"You take over for Don in the morning," Steve said to Troy. "Let Kevin have a swat at them tomorrow. If we don't get a response, we'll start calling their homes. I hate to get families involved if it's not necessary."

"You know we're shooting in the dark here, don't you?" Rick asked. "These guys might not know anything."

"They're the only lead we have," Steve answered defensively. "Unless our bicyclist has been more forthcoming."

"He's in the dark as much as we are."

"Nothing from his phone?" Gib asked.

"No messages have come in. I've continued the texts," Rick told the group. "I don't know if it's working or not, though. There is always the possibility they had code words that he hasn't shared but he's obviously scared. I don't think he'd keep that to himself."

"What about my contacts?" Josie asked.

"What contacts?" Steve said, eyeing her cautiously.

"I could try to reach some journalists in their respective cities. It's better than doing nothing."

"No, it's not and no, you won't." The words were out of his mouth before he'd thought to soften them.

"Excuse me?" Josie responded. Her eyebrows raised, her voice shrill.

Bam. Not a good start to what he'd had planned for the remainder of the evening. "We're trying to keep your location a secret, remember?"

Josie's eyes narrowed. "That guy found me," she countered. "What difference does it make now?"

"He might have just gotten lucky," Steve argued. "We have no idea how many other locations may be on their radar. How many others may have been sent out to check places you could have gone. If you contact one of your sources or colleagues, you could inadvertently be pinpointing your location. If they knew you were here, we'd know it by now." His skin prickled. For her to reach outside their protective circle they currently had her enclosed in could be suicide. He wasn't letting her take that chance. "We can discuss it again if nothing develops tomorrow," Steve told her, offering her an olive branch.

Josie studied his face. He hoped his expression conveyed concern not fear. In truth, she was more than likely right. They had found her.

Her knee bounced rhythmically as she contemplated his argument. "Agreed," she finally said. "But, Steve, I'm not letting it drop indefinitely."

21

Josie grabbed their empty plates and headed for the kitchen after everyone had left. Over her shoulder she said to Steve, "I want a gun."

"What?" Steve was fully on alert.

"I want a gun."

"Why do you need a gun?" He would take care of her—unless her plan was to shoot him for last night. They still hadn't broached that subject.

"You know that I can use one. I need to take some responsibility for protecting myself." She paused. "I need to know that I can."

Sure, she could shoot. They'd spent plenty of time at the base's gun range. He'd made certain she could handle a gun before he'd been deployed. But he was here. It was his job to keep her safe, damn it. "You don't have a permit for the State of Florida, do you?" he countered.

He recognized her "No-Shit-Sherlock" look. "Pardon me for not having time to apply for one on my run through the state."

"Don't get upset, Josie. You don't need to be armed."

"I wasn't upset but I'm definitely heading in that direction. I want a gun so I can protect myself, if necessary. I'm not doubting the ability of you or your friends to keep me safe. But give me some credit for being able to take care of myself. I'll keep it in the bedside table so no one knows I have it, if that's what you want."

"Is there a reason to believe I might not share that bed with you again? That I won't be here if you need me?"

"No." Josie answered but her gaze was now riveted on the kitchen's tile floor.

"No? No, what?"

"No," she said again. "I know you won't leave me, Steve."

"Like you did me?" Steve grabbed onto her words and flung them back at her. He saw her eyes close and her lips quiver. He didn't care. Couldn't contain it himself. "Would you have wanted me in your bed if you hadn't needed my help?"

JOSIE'S HEAD WHIPPED UP. Steve loomed over her waiting for an answer.

"You're wanting this to be more than just sex," she said. Did they have to discuss it? Couldn't they simply crawl between the sheets together and forget everything else?

"Hell, yes, I want more. The question is, why don't you?"

"I didn't come here for this argument." Josie snapped back.

"No, you didn't. You came here for my help and my body." The words lashed out at her. Josie lost her ability to speak. Instinctively, she wanted to argue but she couldn't

Lovers Key

deny he was right. Her teeth bit into her bottom lip, not caring that the previous injury to it stung as she did so.

"What about it, Josie?" Steve continued to hammer the point home. "Was it good for you? Do you want to go another round? I suppose I could get it up but it better be worth the effort this time. You were asleep before I had you fully undressed."

Anger rippled off him in waves, crashing into her so hard she was in danger of being sucked away by the rip current. The ferocity of his temper blindsided her.

Still, she held her ground.

"Why are you so angry? I didn't lie to you."

"No, you didn't," he agreed. "You wanted sex. Just sex. You got it. Are we done now?"

"We were done before we started," Josie muttered under her breath.

"What the hell is that supposed to mean?"

Josie rocked backward as Steve crowded her space. "You don't understand…"

"No, Josie, I don't. I don't understand any of this shit. You've never offered a friggin' explanation other than 'we rushed things.' That's bullshit and you know it."

"It isn't bullshit. We did rush things."

"It's bullshit as far as you and I are concerned. One month. One year. One decade. It wouldn't have made a damn bit of difference. We've had a connection since the moment we met. No amount of time or distance will change that and you know it."

"You don't understand," she repeated.

"How am I supposed to understand if you won't explain it? Why won't you open up to me?"

"Oh, like you opened up to me?" Now she had something solid to sink her teeth into.

"What the hell are you talking about? We talked all the time when I was home. I didn't keep anything from you."

"Of course, how could I forget all the times we reminisced about your missions," she said, sarcasm dripping from her voice. "Not once did you bring up the subject. Not once in the months we were together did you tell me if it was hell, or brutal, or even if it was just fucking hot. Seven goddamn months out of your life every year and I know nothing about them. How you felt. What you did." *Shit*. Her dam had cracked. She bit her bottom lip again hoping to stem the breach. If she started down this road he'd have the scent. He would counter all her points and win. That wouldn't help either of them.

"You thought I should tell you about the hell we went through?"

"You openly worried about your former commander but you never once offered me a glimpse into your feelings."

"Because I wanted to forget!" Steve shouted as he stalked to the other side of the room. "Colt wasn't the only one affected by those missions. Do you think we come home and want to relive them again by telling stories?" His lungs expanded, sucking in a breath. After a few deep pulls of oxygen, he turned on her again.

"You want to know about our missions? You want me to tell you about our friends whose limbs we couldn't find or recognize? The young men misled by fanatics to blow themselves up along with anyone they could take with them? You want to know about the children—the babies—we saw slaughtered?"

"Colt resigned because one of our missions went south." Steve continued, raking his hands through his hair. "He wasn't at fault but it didn't matter. He was going over the edge. We were all worried about him because he was our friend. We were worried about him because each of us saw ourselves in him. If Colt could fall, then so could we all."

"So, if it's all the same to you," he snapped, his face red with fury. "I'd rather not drag out those horrific memories to share."

Josie's lips remained sealed. She'd asked. Now she had the answer. All this time she'd selfishly thought she'd been locked out of the boys' club. She clutched her arms tightly at her waist. It kept her from reaching out for him and pulling him close—to ask for forgiveness and absorb some of his pain. A gesture that would have been rejected by the angry beast now stalking across the room. He used every inch of space in the galley kitchen before he turned back toward her.

"Is that what fucked up our marriage?" His eyes narrowed "You didn't get all the gory details you wanted so you felt left out?"

"No! I didn't understand," she said. "I'm sorry."

"You're sorry about what?" he yelled, throwing his hands out. "Leaving me? Feeling left out? Sorry for keeping secrets? What are you sorry about, Josie?" Each question hit like a blow to her body.

"For being selfish," she admitted.

"Oh, so now we're back to last night." His pacing stopped as he swung on her.

"No, we're not back to last night. I was talking about our marriage. I left to protect you. Thinking you didn't care about me enough to share was only the cherry on top of a list of reasons. All you did just now was knock that cherry to the floor. The reasons still remain. I would have hurt you sooner or later, Steve, so I ripped the bandage off and left."

"You're not making any sense. What reasons?"

"Explaining them to you won't change them. Doesn't my leaving prove to you that you're better off without me?"

"So, I get to splay open a vein for you but you can't give me the reasons why I lost you? You're right, Josie," he snapped. "You are selfish. Maybe I *am* better off without you."

THE BEDROOM DOOR slammed shut but it did little to muffle the sobs coming from the other side. Steve's blood sizzled, which was a step down from boiling. There had been times during his tours that he raged against the inhumanity—the insanity—of war. Tonight, his rage had been directed at Josie. It had been their first outright argument. His stomach sank knowing it might have been their last.

As his blood dropped from sizzling to simmering he began to dissect her words. *You're better off without me.* How could she believe that?

And a few minutes ago, he'd agreed with her.

Steve found himself circling the living room but then vacated that space as sobbing from the bedroom overflowed, filling it. He flung open the refrigerator door and snatched a beer off the shelf, pissed they hadn't stocked something stronger. Damn it, he could still hear her gut-wrenching tears —or was he imagining that? Was the sound stuck in his head, running on a loop? Beer in hand, he stepped outside craving the cooler air. Hoping for a cooler head.

"Wondered how long it would take you to get your ass out here," Gib said, startling Steve.

Man, he was in bad shape. He hadn't checked the vicinity before he exited. What if Josie had been with him?

"What are you doing here?" Steve asked, noting the bottle of beer dangling between Gib's middle and index finger. He was leaning against the outdoor shed.

"Waiting on you. Thought you could use another target after you got done with Josie."

"You heard us?"

"Colt and Cat probably heard you in Key West."

"Christ." Steve leaned against the building then sunk to the ground next to the storage shed. The earth was cool. He could feel the dampness through the seat of his jeans. The blackness created by the dense foliage stared back at him. A perfect reflection of his mood.

"Not quite that bad," Gib said, joining Steve on the ground, resting his forearms on his knees. "Did you guys get your laundry aired out?"

"Nope. I'm afraid it just got dirtier. We've never argued like that."

"Might be past time you did," Gib suggested.

Steve huffed then took a long pull on his beer. "This coming from the island Lothario."

"My parents were happily married but they still had their clashes. As their son, I don't like to think about it, but I'm pretty sure the make-up sex was worth it," Gib said. He proceeded to drain what was left of his bottle.

"Well, Josie and I aren't married and I don't foresee any make-up sex in my future. Hell, I might as well relieve Don. I'm not getting any sleep tonight. You want to take the couch? I'd hate for her to wake up and be alone."

"I have a perfectly good bed, thank you. So, no, I won't take the couch."

Steve shook his head from side to side, still thinking about the yelling match. "Something is going on in her head and I don't know how to get it out. She's convinced she made the right decision to leave."

"Is that what had you two raising the rafters?"

"Part of it. She thought I'd shut her out because I didn't discuss my tours. Like any of us do."

"Did you set her straight?"

"It wasn't pretty but, yeah, I think so. Why?"

"Seems to me you may have solved one problem. You know what they say about eating an elephant?"

"I'm not certain I like the metaphor," Steve grimaced. He'd probably eaten elephant in one or two of his more exotic and unusual base camps but he'd rather not picture it, thank you.

"Whatever. It's still one spoonful at a time."

Gib had a point. And Steve's blood had cooled. He still had time to solve this puzzle—to find out if the bridge between him and Josie could be repaired.

"No date tonight?" Steve asked Gib, rising to his feet.

"Well, my initial plans didn't include sitting on the hard, damp ground," he replied brushing off the seat of his jeans, "and discussing your wife."

"She's not my wife," Steve quickly corrected Gib.

"Nuances. She is to you."

Steve looked once again into the darkness. "It was just sex last night."

"Sex is a good place to start."

Steve smirked. "You would know."

22

Standing in front of the closed bedroom door, Steve gathered his nerves. *Nerves*. He'd run head first into battle and they'd been easier to control. But he'd been trained for battle and knew what to do. This was new territory and it had come without a training manual. He'd never had to make-up with his wife. Gib was right; he'd never thought of Josie as anything but his wife since the day he'd slipped the ring on her finger.

He listened through the door while his thoughts danced through the various scenarios, the cause and effect of any action he might take, should he proceed with this mission. Josie could be sleeping or she still needed time to calm down. Then the sound of her blowing her nose reached him and, for some reason, it made him smile.

"Josie? May I come in?" Polite, right? Or had that been a mistake. Asking gave her the opportunity to say no. He should just go in. Check on her, make sure she was okay. He was still staring at the doorknob, weighing his options, when the bedroom door opened.

Josie stood on the other side of the doorway, wearing the

worn t-shirt he'd given her the day she'd arrived. His personal favorite. The one from Charleston. His eyes shifted from the t-shirt to her face. The vision tore him up inside. Josie's nose and eyes were red. Her skin was pale and clammy. One hand was on the door. Her other grasped a wad of tissue as it trembled.

She didn't say a word to him as she turned away. He followed her into the room but waited outside the bathroom door as she blew her nose a second time. Again, he smiled. He couldn't say why.

"Are you okay?" he asked as she walked past him and settled on the edge of the bed. The handful of fresh Kleenex should have been a warning but he was slow to pick up on the cues tonight. As soon as the question had been asked, her eyes filled with tears again.

"Please don't cry anymore, Josie." How could an adult produce that many tears?

"I'm sorry," she said, sniffling. Her voice cracked.

"So, you've said." He wanted to take back the comment the minute it left his lips. It wasn't what he'd said but how he'd said it. Obviously, there was still some anger he needed to ratchet down a notch or two.

"My turn to be sorry. I didn't mean to snap," he explained. "I didn't know I could lose my temper like that, at least not with you."

"I deserved it," she confessed.

"No one deserves that kind of anger or the words I said. I am sorry, Josie."

"When are you going to realize that this is my fault?"

Steve reached for her hand but she pulled away. To keep from trying again, he stuck his hands in the pockets of his jean. "I don't believe that. There are two of us here. It takes two to make a marriage just as it takes two to argue."

She remained silent and stubborn. *One bite at a time*. One wall had been dismantled tonight. He'd keep chipping away at the others for as long as Josie, or time, allowed. "I hear make-up sex is pretty good," he joked.

Josie's head snapped up.

"Want to make-up?" He'd asked the question as lightly as he could manage but a lead weight had settled in his stomach. At least sex was common ground. Neither of them could deny they were good together.

"You still want me?"

In every way possible. But he kept the thought to himself. "The theory is worth testing. You game?"

She cast her eyes downward. The floor had held much of her attention tonight. He lowered himself onto the bed next to her and waited for her answer. It about killed him.

After an eternity, she laid her hand on his. He clasped her fingers. She didn't retreat, returning the squeeze. Steve took that as a *yes*. Tenderly, he kissed her pouting lips. He nipped and suckled before engaging his tongue. She didn't pull away, instead opening for him.

One hand slipped under her t-shirt and found her breast. He cupped it, rubbing his thumb over the nipple. Hard and tempting. He yanked the shirt over her head then dropped to his knees in front of her and feasted on each breast. His hands clasped her waist so she couldn't escape his need. She leaned in, offering him more.

He lapped and tasted until she was writhing in anticipation. His hands moved from her waist to the elastic band of her panties. He gently pushed her against the bed, continuing his feast until she laid flat against the mattress. He broke away and quickly removed her skimpy undergarment.

Blood boiling in lust instead of anger, he rushed to shed his clothing. But instead of joining her on the bed, he once again knelt in front of her. Her knees were still draped over the edge of the mattress. He lifted them over his shoulders and inhaled her scent. He planned to take it slow. No wham-bam-thank-you-ma'am this time. Tonight, he would *make love* to her.

Josie let out a little yelp as his tongue touched her tender flesh. The sensation had her raising her hips to meet him. The moment he began to suckle, her muscles tightened. The reaction heightened his desire to please her. She grasped his hair and moved against his tongue. It wasn't long before a scream tore through the room as her climax overtook her.

Steve didn't stop when her cries began. Instead, he continued the ministrations until she collapsed, gasping for air, against the bed. He was rock hard and hurting but her musky fragrance drew him to the valley between her legs. The allure was stronger than his need. He dipped his head to the source of the scent.

"No, Steve, I can't stand it!"

"You can, Josie. Please…"

His plea must have done her in because her head dropped against the mattress in surrender. Surprising him, she spread her legs wider, giving him more access. Again, he lapped and teased the tender flesh, his desire to bring her to that same peak, urgent.

He lifted her hips further into the air and eased himself inside her. He withdrew with excruciating slowness before burying himself in her to the hilt. He repeated the tortuous act until she began to clench around him. As she did, he took them both over the edge.

23

"Well?" Gib asked Steve the next morning over a cup of coffee. Gib had tapped on the Copelands' door earlier, a bag of bagels from Bailey's Market in one hand, an empty mug in the other.

"Well, what?" Steve ask, taking the cup from Gib's hand.

"Is it as good as they say? The make-up sex?"

"Lower your voice," Steve admonished him. "Josie's still sleeping."

"Wore her out, huh?"

"You sound like a high school girl," Steve said.

"How would you know? And that's a sexist statement, isn't it?"

Gib had a point. "We are not discussing this," Steve told him firmly but he was grinning over his cup.

"Don't have to." Gib smiled back.

"What are they up to next door?" Steve asked, his voice lowered so he wouldn't disturb Josie. She wouldn't wake up for another hour or so. She had never been a morning person.

"Don is getting some sleep before he heads back over

here to work with Josie." Gib grinned again. "I told him to take his time."

"Will you stop?" Still Steve couldn't help but smile again. How did Colt get any work done with this jokester around?

"Kevin is outside."

"Troy on the phones?"

"Will be when the businesses open. Speaking of which, I talked to Rick. We have an idea to light a fire under the reluctant names on the list. We wanted your take on it."

"What is it?" Steve asked.

"Obviously, the researcher story isn't flying. Nobody has returned his calls. What if we add a little bait to it?"

"What sort of bait?"

"Next message Troy leaves states the story may be evolving and it concerns banking regulations. Nothing more. All these guys are in business with the exception of the State Attorney. Every one of them uses a bank unless they stuff it in a mattress. Might be enough to get them to call back and find out what we know."

"Or get their attorneys to call," Steve said.

"I doubt they'll want to pay an attorney their hourly rate if they're honest people. If it were me, I'd make the initial call before talking to an attorney."

"Hmmm. Okay. I see the bait. How do we reel them in?"

"I'm just the guy throwing out chum. You guys have to hook them."

"I'll talk to Rick." Steve called Rick and they spent time on the phone working out the kinks to a plan. Troy would call DiSantis and Scagliotti. Rick was confident that Senator Lucas would agree to a backup story as long as they didn't go too far. No one would contact Roemer's family. Unless some lead developed that led directly to him, they would be left alone to mourn.

"McClaren isn't a problem," Steve said to Rick. "He's cooperating. I'll touch base with him later and let him know about Roemer. The news might jog a memory loose. Our big problem is going to be Deets. He's not going to fall for any smoke screen. I might have to show up on his doorstep."

"That's not a bad idea," Rick agreed. "Give me a little time to reach Lucas. I'll let him know what we're doing. He should be able to arrange a meeting with Deets. I'll call you back."

~

BY MID-AFTERNOON, Steve felt the investigation had started moving forward. Rick had spoken to Senator Lucas who arranged for Steve to meet with Deets the next morning. Jacksonville was a five-hour drive from Sanibel—four, if Steve didn't get stopped for speeding. Fortunately, Gib remembered McClaren had a private jet. He'd offered to make the call and arrangements.

And so, by 8:00 a.m. tomorrow, Steve would be wheels-up on his way to Jacksonville.

Don and Josie were once again at the dining room table working together. Josie had arrived in the kitchen smiling and freshly showered about an hour after Gib had left for a photo assignment. Steve was grateful for that intervention. Gib could be merciless in his teasing. The old Josie he'd known might have gone toe-to-toe with him but the one he was watching now was hanging on by some very thin threads.

Steve sat at the breakfast bar, fine tuning his list of questions for Deets. From where he sat, the dining room and Josie were in full view. He found himself studying her more than the sheet of paper in front of him.

While Don plodded along, punching keys, or clicking the

mouse, Josie sorted through information. She continually twisted her hair around a finger. A nervous habit. He'd seen her do it from time to time when they'd been together but hadn't associated it with nerves until now. How had he missed that signal? He was trained to read tell signs. And what about her inexplicable five-minute bathroom break yesterday? A wreck of a woman had entered but a calm, collected person had emerged. There appeared to be a lot he had missed.

But deciphering Josie would have to wait for another day. If he pushed her now, she might snap. *One bite at a time.* And, currently, they were eating off entirely different menus. The investigation had taken center stage.

His phone vibrated against the granite countertop. He gave Josie another concerned look before he grabbed it.

"I've got something," Troy told him.

"What? Someone else dead?" Steve asked. He saw both Don and Josie turn his way.

"No. But Scagliotti returned my call. We've now got a connection, at least between three of the names," Troy said.

"Scagliotti remembered two of the names, DiSantis and Roemer. They attended the same summer camp in the Florida Keys while he was still in high school—a camp for well-to-do families to send their kids while their parents flew off to Europe or wherever. He didn't know if they were still in operation. That was over thirty years ago."

"Did you get specifics? Year? Name? Location?" Steve asked.

"Just those basics. And that was like pulling teeth."

"Was he nervous?"

"Not at first but when I pushed for additional information on the other names, he got a little jumpy. He was adamant, though, that he had not been in contact with anyone from the camp since that summer."

"Give me what you've got." Steve jotted down the information about the camp. "Bring Kevin up to speed," he said to Troy. "I'll give Rick a call. If you hear from DiSantis, let me know," Steve said as he disconnected the call.

"Middle Keys Aquatic Camp. Roemer, DiSantis and Scagliotti all attended at the same time. See what else you can find out," Steve handed the paper with the camp information off to Don.

Don snatched it out of his hand, "Already on it."

"I have a contact at the *Miami Herald*. I could call him," Josie told Steve.

"No, Josie," Steve said. "Not yet," he added as her eyes darkened. "If we don't get anywhere, then we can bring it up again. Let's see what we can find out first. It's for your own protection."

Josie didn't argue but she didn't answer, either. She turned her back to Steve, dismissing him. Okay. She was pissed. He'd experienced more of her temper this past week than he had in the months they'd been together.

When she remained silent, he took that as an agreement. He wouldn't be able to keep her off the scent for long, though. She was a journalist and possessed a natural instinct to dig for answers. But they currently had other options. Other options that wouldn't require Josie to stick her neck out. Besides Don's hacking skills, Rick had his contacts in law enforcement.

Steve got Rick on the phone and filled him in. Rick would immediately contact the Sheriff's Office in Monroe County where the camp was located to see what he could find out about the place. Steve then placed a call to McClaren.

"Yes. I remember that place," McClaren said when Steve mentioned the name of the camp. "I'll never forget it."

"What makes it so unforgettable?" Steve asked. He noticed Josie's head cock in his direction out of the corner of his eye.

"A girl disappeared during the two weeks I was there."

"What?" Why the hell hadn't Scagliotti mentioned that fact to Troy? Steve's grip tightened on his phone. A warning siren was going off in Steve's head.

"Not something you're likely to forget," McClaren told him.

"Exactly what happened."

"We were awakened one morning just before the end of our two weeks there. We were told by our counselor to stay in our cabin. Word spread anyway, like it does around kids, that a girl had gone missing. After the staff finished their search, the authorities were called in. Once the cops arrived, we were all assembled in the community area to be questioned by the police while others searched the property again." McClaren paused. "I remember Esteban now. He was sitting next to me at that time."

"What was the name of the missing girl?" Steve asked.

"Ruth. Same as my mother's. Her last name escapes me."

"We'll find it," Steve told him.

"Do you know if they ever found her?" Steve asked the question but he already knew the answer. The sort of shit they were wading through didn't center around a runaway who later came home. It seemed they'd just found the cover to their box of jigsaw pieces. They had a picture. They could now start putting the puzzle together.

"Not that I'm aware of. The rumor was that she'd run away but I don't remember any official conclusion. It could still be a cold case, for all I know. The papers carried it for a while but eventually I stopped following the story."

"What about the others on the list? Do any of the names ring a bell now?" Steve waited.

"Yes. I remember DiSantis and Scagliotti. They were seated next to me during the group questioning. I'd participated in a few team sports with them but we weren't close. The two of them shared a cabin with a couple of other guys. I'd totally forgotten about them. I would never have remembered if you hadn't found the connection."

"And the others? Deets and Roemer?" Steve prompted him.

"They could have been their roommates. There were two other boys besides Deets and Roemer in their cabin. I don't remember their names but all four were in front of Esteban and me the day of the questioning."

"Appreciate your help. Oh, and thanks for the use of your plane tomorrow," Steve added just before he disconnected. Steve thought he heard McClaren say something but if McClaren was talking to him, he'd call Steve back.

24

Josie's heel tapped rhythmically against the floor beneath the chair. She was going to crack the tile at this rate. Steve had filled her in on his conversation with McClaren and she was even more anxious to reach out to her contacts. Her inability to talk to people who might be able to supply information about the men on the list, the camp, or the girl made her as anxious as a caged lion—able to see her prey but unable to reach it. Steve had lectured her again on the danger she'd put herself, and possibly others, in if she reached out to her sources. It was "the others" that had stopped her from ignoring Steve's warning. She didn't want anyone else hurt on her account.

Don was in his zone as he researched the camp. They'd put the spreadsheet aside. For now, they were focused solely on the camp angle.

Josie could have grabbed the tablet and started her own research but she'd seen what Don could do. She'd be wasting her time. The man was a Picasso on the keyboard. She wished she had those skills when she researched her stories but with her luck, she'd wind up in jail, doing what he did.

Leaving Don to do his thing, she prowled the house. This place was bigger than Colt's unit next door but after a while it wasn't big enough. She'd headed out to the garden but Steve had stopped her the minute she'd stepped outside. Too dangerous, he'd claimed, and he didn't have the men to spare as her personal bodyguard.

She was itching to do something productive. Anything. After five minutes of quiet meditation away from prying eyes, she emerged from the bedroom on a mission. She found some cleaning supplies under the kitchen sink and started scrubbing. Don gave her a quick, odd look but returned to his project. The work kept her busy and her nerves began to settle.

BEFORE TROY TOOK his turn on guard, he placed a call to DiSantis armed with the additional information. Once triggered, DiSantis' memories of that summer had also miraculously returned although neither Scagliotti nor DiSantis claimed to have a particularly clear recollection of one another. Steve didn't believe it since McClaren seemed sure the two of them had roomed together. Troy had talked to both about the disappearance of the girl. Their comments reflected McClaren's, nothing new was added. But now Rick had a date, time, and incident to investigate through the Monroe County Sheriff's Office.

Gib returned early that evening with the promised groceries. Josie seemed grateful for a change in projects. She'd already cleaned the house from floor to ceiling. The damn place sparkled. Now she attacked the dinner preparation with the same energy. Gib assisted. Steve watched from the doorway as the two zigged and zagged. They got along well. Gib had a way with people. Don, Kevin, and Rick had accepted her, as well. Troy, however, was still out with the jury but he'd kept his opinions to himself and hadn't been offensive toward Josie. That was all Steve could ask.

Steve heard Rick coming up the rear stairs as the group stood in a makeshift buffet line, filling their plates. Rick had called earlier from the station saying he'd be there shortly. Steve had decided to hold off the debriefing for the day until after Rick arrived. One of them would bring Troy up to speed later as he was extending his turn on watch so Don could report what he'd found.

"What were you able to find out about the camp?" Steve asked the hacker once they were all seated.

"It's still in operation. Still catering to wealthy parents who need a place to dump their kids for a few weeks so they can jet off to Greece or some other exotic place. They're open during the summer and for Christmas and Spring breaks."

"Who the hell drops their kids off at a camp for Christmas vacation?" Steve asked.

"Apparently, enough people that the camp can afford to operate that time of the year."

"What about the girl?" Josie asked. Her reporter's instinct would have her blood racing to track down that story since she'd heard about the missing girl. Steve had taken every opportunity to reinforce her fear that "Big Brother" was still watching. While Don had the skills to hide his tracks when looking for information, Josie didn't.

"Ruth Carr is the name of the missing girl," Don continued. "That information came from a newspaper article—not from the camp's records. The problem is they hadn't entered the digital world yet. What I did find is sketchy, at best. I've got the names of a couple of counselors who were employed that summer. Current records don't show them associated with the program any longer. I'll see what I can find on them tomorrow."

"I can reach out to my source at the *Miami Herald*. They would have covered that story," Josie told the group.

"No, you won't," Steve stated quickly and emphatically. "How many times do we have to go over this?"

"Steve, I'm not stupid. I'll be careful when I talk to my contacts but reporters often know more than the police do about a crime," Josie argued. "It might help."

"I said, no."

Josie's response to his order was a lethal glare accompanied by the rat-tat-tat of her foot on the floor. With the exception of the tapping noise, silence engulfed the room. Eyes shifted from him to Josie and back again.

Gib smiled. "Steve, didn't you learn anything watching Cat and Colt last year? I'd stop poking this tiger, if I were you."

Steve looked at Josie. Unlike Cat who went verbally toe-to-toe with Colt, Josie's anger was contained. Still, there was fire in her eyes. Her foot continued to slap the wood on the floor beneath it. She was pissed. He'd lashed out. He was trained to keep his emotions under control in countless situations but this was Josie. This was different.

"Umm. I touched base with the Monroe County Sheriff's office," Rick said, redirecting the conversation. "The investigation fell under their jurisdiction. They've got a records clerk digging for information on the case. Same situation as the camp, they were in the beginning stages of computerizing documents. Not all the information from that time got scanned into the system. They are physically going on a hunt through their cold case files in storage. They've also sent out a request to current and former MCSO staff to inquire if anyone remembers the case."

"What else did you find?" Steve directed the question to Don.

"The article, which was from the *Herald*," Rick's eyes shifted to Josie's for a second before he continued, "speculated that Carr might have been a runaway. Her parents had recently separated which was the reason she'd been sent to the camp. Her parents thought it would be better if she was elsewhere while her dad moved his personal items out of the house."

"That's it? That's all you've got?" Steve was hoping for more.

"I've just scratched the surface at this point. I'll keep digging."

Josie was no longer completely tuned in to the conversation. She was paying more attention to her cuticles than listening to the men. Some things didn't change. She was mentally going through the list of people she could call. It was what she did. Dig and report. He couldn't take the chance right now and turn her loose.

Steve's phone vibrated on the coffee table distracting him from Josie. As soon as he saw the caller's name, he hit the speaker button.

"Someone tried to kill me!" McClaren screamed before Steve could say anything.

"Take a breath and tell me what happened," Steve said, trying to calm him down.

"A car tried to run me off the road."

"Did you call the police?" Rick asked.

"I just finished talking with them," McClaren answered. "The deputies took the information but they're writing it off as another case of aggressive driving. I tried to explain about the list. That two of the names on it were dead. They looked at me like I'd been drinking!"

"And you're positive it wasn't an aggressive driver?" Steve anxiously leaned over the phone.

"Son, I've driven this route home a hundred times over. I've seen aggressive drivers every day. I was a target. I'm sure of it. Fortunately, my Jag isn't just pretty. It has a lot of horsepower under the hood and I know how to handle it."

"Where are you now?" Steve stood up, reaching for the phone on the table.

"Almost home."

"Good. Give me your address. I'll meet you there. You didn't happen to get a license number?"

"I wish I had but everything was happening too fast."

Steve disconnected after he got the address. "You want to ride along?" he asked Rick.

"Might be interesting. I'll get ahold of the Sheriff's office on the way. Find out what they know. And Steve? Don't make me give you a ticket for speeding."

"Funny," Steve said, snatching his keys off the counter on his way out the door.

JOSIE'S TEMPER had settled after everyone had left but her curiosity had not. She couldn't think of any reason she couldn't contact her friend at the *Herald*. He'd have no way of knowing where she was unless she told him. Even the NSA wouldn't think to connect the two of them.

Without her phone, Josie's contact list was gone. Using the burner Don had purchased for her, she called the newsroom at the paper and got Roberto's number from a fellow reporter. She'd done some freelancing for the *Miami Herald* and had met Roberto on one of those occasions. Since then, they had reached out to each other from time to time in search of a lead.

An hour and a half later she had several pages of notes on the missing girl and the investigation that took place after her disappearance. Roberto had to dig through the archives to find the crumbs she was looking for but he'd come through. She'd been careful not to tell him why she was researching Carr's disappearance, and to his credit, he hadn't pushed. He was intrigued by the cold case, though, when she started asking questions. He'd gotten more curious since her number appeared as *unknown caller* at his end. There weren't too many reasons a reporter would go to the trouble of hiding their location or contact information.

Roberto confirmed what she had suspected that Ruth Carr had never been found. Her parents, who were in the middle of a divorce at the time, were both investigated and cleared. Camp counselors were also investigated, and while there had not been an official sex offender registry in the area at the time, all the known offenders were located and questioned. After weeks of following leads that had led nowhere, the case grew cold. The parents, no longer fighting over custody, had come together and hired a private investigator. A reward was also posted. Nothing on the girl was ever found after that night. She'd told friends she was going for a walk on the beach and never returned. Most assumed she'd run away. Hopefully that was the case but considering the deadly activity that surrounded them now, Josie presumed the worst for Carr.

But now they were armed with the names of other attendees, camp counselors and family members. It wasn't an all-inclusive list of those in attendance that fateful night, but it was a good start. Steve, however, was going to be livid when he discovered she'd made the call. Reaching out to Roberto was a risk—albeit a minor one. Going any further would be taking unnecessary chances.

It was a little after nine o'clock when she'd finished. Josie figured she had time for a shower before Steve returned. She still sported bruises along with aches from the beating and her nighttime activities. A hot shower would be just the ticket.

The Copelands' master bath was much smaller than the one next door but what it lacked in size it made up for with its modern amenities. The stand-alone shower sported jets that were strategically positioned in the walls, making it perfect for massaging sore muscles. Josie was sure the former owners enjoyed the pulsating water after a day spent tending their huge garden. She turned on the water to let it warm as she began to undress. As she bent over to tug off her jeans, the opaque window behind her shattered.

25

Steve and Rick had just passed through the toll booth and were on the bridge to Sanibel when the call came in from Kevin. Steve answered the phone and put it on speaker. No blue tooth in this classic.

"Josie is going to be all right," were the first words out of Kevin's mouth.

"What? What do you mean she'll be alright? What happened?" Steve pushed the gas petal to the floor. His Mustang roared past the car in front of him. All talk about speeding was forgotten.

"Someone took a shot at her through the bathroom window."

"She was shot? Are the paramedics there? You still at the house?" There were no hospitals on the island. *Damn.* He could be headed in the wrong direction. He checked the road, preparing to do a one-eighty.

"We're still at the house," Kevin said. "The EMTs are here. The bullet missed her, Steve. She has shrapnel wounds from the glass. Her back took the brunt of it."

She wasn't shot.

She wasn't shot. She wasn't shot.

Shrapnel.

"How bad? How deep?" The car went airborne as it flew over the last span of the bridge.

"There's a lot of blood. I can't tell how bad or how deep. The paramedics are taking over."

"Put her on the phone," Steve demanded.

"Back off, Steve," Rick snapped at him, yanking his own phone away from his ear. "We're almost there and she doesn't need you stressing her out."

"Let me talk to her," Steve said, this time with restraint. "I need to talk to her."

"Steve?"

"Josie? You okay, baby?"

"Yeah but it hurts. Ouch!"

"What? What happened?"

"They're working on my back. Fuck!"

"Steve." Kevin said into the phone. "Concentrate on getting your ass back here in one piece and let them do their job. I won't leave her."

"Turning onto Periwinkle now," Steve told him.

"What did you find out?" Steve asked Rick. His friend had been on his phone since he heard Kevin's announcement. The car fishtailed to the left, its tires smoking as he made the turn then accelerated on the straight road. The smell of burned rubber hung in the car.

"Black-and-white units had already been dispatched when I reached the station. I called Don and told him to make sure all our guys were inside. We don't want anyone becoming a target."

True, but Steve would have preferred their team to be searching for the gunman. They were experienced at hunting snipers.

First responders had the front and rear of the Copeland's place blocked so Steve pulled into the lot behind *Island Images*. He slammed on the brakes and was out of the car before the dust of the shell lot settled. He leaped over the fence that separated the two properties. Fortunately, Rick was right behind him, badge extended, or Steve would have had to plow through a few uniforms to get in the back door.

Steve ignored Don and Troy who were giving statements to officers in the living room. Hell, he was moving so fast he almost slammed into the wall as he turned down the hallway toward the bedroom. Gib was standing guard at the door. He stepped aside as Steve approached.

Steve had to remember to breathe. Panic wouldn't help. Green Berets didn't panic but he couldn't spot Josie through the sea of medics who surrounded the bed. A large plastic bag stuffed with bloody gauze pads sat on the floor. A blood pressure cuff, gauze wrappers and other items he couldn't identify were scattered across the comforter. Sweat beaded across his forehead and temples as he imagined the worst. Then he saw the long, denim-covered legs between those of the uniformed trousers of EMTs. Josie was sitting upright while they attended to her injuries. *That was good. That had to be good.*

Kevin said something to Josie's caregivers because the sea of men in front of her parted, leaving Steve with a clear view of Josie. His pulse settled into a rhythm he recognized as "battle ready" then calmed as the picture in front of him registered.

"Where the hell is your shirt?"

Josie was sitting on the edge of the bed, clasping a bath towel to her bare chest. Her face, which had been resting against her hands, whipped up at the sound of his voice. Her dumbfounded look confirmed he'd spoken the absurd question out loud.

"I decided to take up stripping," Josie answered but with no rancor or snap to her voice.

Fear was no longer doing a drum roll in his chest. Steve's heart and hands steadied as he gently clasped her arms as he squatted on the floor in front of her. He looked at the paramedics. "Are you transporting her to the hospital?"

"We were discussing that," one of the men still attending to her answered.

"What's to discuss?" Steve asked.

"She doesn't want to go and we can't force her. It wouldn't hurt but her wounds are more bluster than serious. She's going to hurt like hell for a couple of days, though."

"Josie, please." He pushed her hair behind her ear, snatching a quick look at her back. Blood continued to seep from the cuts on her pale skin.

"Baby, I'd feel better if they checked you out at the hospital."

Josie didn't respond. Her chin rested on her chest. "They know," she whispered, the sound of defeat resonating across the room.

"Yes," Steve confirmed, dropping a kiss to her hair. "They know you're here."

STEVE LOST the argument regarding the hospital. Josie was already on shaky ground, so after getting Kevin to sign off on the decision, he hadn't pushed. She agreed to let Kevin monitor her injuries. That was the best he was going to get. He'd watch her closely.

As worrisome as Josie's injuries were, a bigger problem had just sailed through that bathroom window. With the EMTs and officers gone, Don was outside kicking himself in the ass. He'd been sweeping the garden for intruders when the shot came from the street side. The fact that they had limited personnel resources had been punctuated by the shattered window. A chill worked its way down Steve's spine.

Rick had called his captain and arrangements were made for tighter patrols near the property.

"Find out what our bicyclist has been up to," Steve told him. "Confirm that he hasn't found a way to report to his handler."

"Already done. The guy is terrified. He has been ever since they found Sykes' body floating in the Matanzas River. He's not contacted anyone. I've been using his pre-paid phone but haven't received a single response. We don't know if the two are related, Steve."

"Well, who do you think took a shot at her if it wasn't the guy at the other end of the phone—or someone he sent?"

"If we learned anything from Cat's trouble this past summer, it's that we can't assume because we're being led in one direction it doesn't mean there isn't something requiring our attention elsewhere."

26

After helping board up the shattered window, Steve went to the bedroom to check on Josie. She was digging through the dresser drawers.

"Josie, what the hell are you doing? You were just shot. You need to be resting." Steve snapped at her. It didn't help the situation.

"I wasn't shot. I was shot at. And I'm not an invalid, Steve." she said, digging through her meager possessions. "I need a shirt."

"You don't need a shirt. You're going to take something for the pain and get some rest." He didn't raise his voice, this time. He was making progress.

"The hell I am." Unfortunately, Josie wasn't on the same page. Her voice continued to rise. "We have a problem to solve and I can't do it sleeping."

"Josie, I don't want to argue with you." Steve told her.

"Well, you're doing a pretty damn good job of it." Josie slammed the drawer shut and dropped down onto the corner of the bed.

"What's gotten into you? Why are you so angry?" She'd

been through hell this past week. She had every right to be angry but Steve didn't think that was the issue.

"Frustrated. Not angry," she clarified.

Steve raised his eyebrows. She was splitting hairs but he didn't point that out. "Okay. Why are you so frustrated?"

"Because I can't figure out why that damned list is so friggin' important. It's got to be tied to that camp and that missing girl. Roberto said there was a lot of speculation regarding her disappearance. He did some digging…"

"Roberto? Roberto who?"

Silence. Josie was once again picking at her cuticles.

"What did you do, Josie?" Steve asked, enunciating each word.

"Nothing that caused this," she finally responded, jutting her jaw out. "That shooter had to be out there waiting before I made the call."

"What call?" The patience Steve had been so proud of a minute ago was waning.

"Can we save what I found out for the group?" she asked.

STEVE REACHED in the closet and pulled out a button-down shirt and helped her into it. He told her he'd brought it for the wedding. Josie didn't care. She was just ecstatic to have something that was soft and loose and covered her well enough to be seen by others. Once dressed, she turned toward the hallway but Steve didn't follow. He still stood at the closet door, the muscles of his arms, tight and bulging. His jaw was, once again, clenched. Josie retraced her steps and stood in front of him. She prepared herself for what was coming next.

"Go ahead," she said. "Just say it."

"Say what?" he snapped.

"Whatever it is that's bubbling up inside you. I'd rather get reamed in private than in front of your friends."

"You could have been killed!" he shouted at her.

Not what she'd expected. A lecture for reaching out to her contact? Yes. Instead, he was furious because someone had taken a shot at her.

"I'm sorry I scared you, Steve. But it's not like I put a bullseye on the bathroom window. The guy got lucky. Or I did. One of us should buy a lottery ticket. Could be my lucky night."

"It's not funny, Josie. And where the hell was I when someone was trying to kill you? Off chasing a lead that went nowhere instead of where I belonged."

"You were where you belonged. Trying to get answers. You didn't know anyone was going to start taking pot shots at me anymore than I did. What could you have done anyway? How would you have known someone was lurking in the dark?"

"I'm supposed to be protecting you!"

Josie had come to him for help and she'd been harmed while under his care. Of course, he'd feel responsible for her injury. She grabbed his hand. "I'm sorry I scared you."

He gripped her hand tightly. "Don't do it again."

"I'll do my best. Do you want to hear about the call?" she asked in way of a peace offering.

"You can tell me when you tell the others. I'll meet you in the living room," Steve said as he pulled his phone from his pocket. "It's time I talked to Colt. I need to break the news about the damage and bring him up to date."

27

When Steve left the bedroom after his lengthy conversation with Colt, Josie was waiting in the hall. "Why didn't you join the guys?" Steve asked.

"I don't know what to say to them." Josie's eyes darted toward the living room. "As soon as I stepped out there, they all looked so concerned. Even Troy. Why do they care what happens to me, Steve? Why should they care? I've been nothing but trouble."

"Why should they care?" Steve's brow wrinkled and his eyes narrowed. "You're a friend, Josie. Of course, they care."

"I'm not a friend. I'm a problem. How can they consider me a friend?"

Through the shadows cast from the light in the bedroom, Steve scrutinized Josie's puzzled expression. Her brows were pinched together. Her blue eyes sparked with the hint of tears. She was confused and scared. Had he missed these signs of insecurity and anxiety before?

The new-found revelations did nothing to change how he felt about her but they went a long distance in helping him understand a few of her issues. One of them was self-esteem.

He'd thought of her as confident. He'd heard her pursue individuals doggedly on the phone when putting a story together. Perhaps the confidence she showed in her job didn't extend to her personal life.

"Josie, they would help even if you weren't a friend. But you are. You're special to me, therefore, you're special to them. They're family. You're family, Josie, if you'd just have us." He kissed her forehead then pulled her toward the main room.

"Rick take off?" Steve asked.

"He was needed at the station," Gib explained, all the while keeping one eye on Josie. "You okay?" he asked.

"I'll be fine. Thank you."

"Any time." Gib leaned over and placed a kiss on her cheek.

"Okay, I know it's late," Steve said, automatically looking at his watch, "but Josie has some news to share with us."

"Not much but it may help. Roberto, a reporter I know at the *Miami Herald*, dug into their archives and found information surrounding the girl's disappearance. Roberto knows the town, the paper, and where a lot of skeletons are buried. In this case, though, my guess is none of them are buried in Miami."

"What did you get?" Steve asked. He couldn't take back what she'd done. If she had information, they needed to hear it.

"He confirmed a lot of what Don has already found. While speculation was that Carr had run away, her parents never believed it. The divorce may have been hard on her but she was very much loved by both. One theory that was floated around at the time was that it was a stunt to get them back together again. If it was, it went seriously wrong—at least as far as her part was concerned. Her parents did reconcile but she never came home.

"I suspect Rick will get a lot of the same information from the Monroe County Sheriff. I did ask Roberto for all the names mentioned in the articles about the disappearance. They're on that pad on the table." She gestured toward the dining room table where she'd been working earlier. "There's one name that's popped up again. Aaron Deets."

"What about him?" Steve asked.

"Nothing much. A reporter who did the story questioned several of the kids at the camp. Deets was one of them. His responses to the questions about Carr were innocuous. 'Seemed like a nice girl. Kept to herself.' It just struck a chord with me, hearing his name from someone else." Josie shrugged.

"There's more," Steve prompted her to continue.

"Yeah. Roberto gave me the names of a couple of the counselors he found in one of the reporter's handwritten notes. Those interviews didn't make it to any final copy. Not relevant to the articles, I suspect. Their names are on the pad as well."

"I want to talk to Roberto," Steve said.

"I figured as much. His number is at the top of the pad. He's expecting your call."

"Okay, babe, you've had enough for tonight."

"No argument here," she said as she made an effort to stand. Adrenaline had pushed her since the shooting. Steve was familiar with the body's response to the fight-or-flight symptoms. Josie was on the downward slide now and was ready to crash.

"Do you want me to call Rick?" Troy asked.

"Wait until I come back," Steve told them as he got to his

feet. "I want to help Josie get settled. Then we can go over the plans for tomorrow and conference Rick in."

When Steve reached the bedroom, Josie was sitting on the bed, her head bowed. Once again, she was topless. His button-down shirt lay on the bed beside her. His old Charleston t-shirt was clutched to her chest.

"What is it, baby?" Steve asked, quickly making it to her side.

"I can't get the damn thing on!" She looked up at him, her bottom lip full and trembling. She wasn't crying but it was a close call.

This was a different woman from the one who had left the living room. She was tired, hurting and, he suspected, scared.

"Here," he said, opening his palm to reveal a pill. He picked up the glass of water from the nightstand and held it out to her.

"Where did this come from?" Josie said, eyeing the medication.

"Cat had a few pain meds left from this summer. Gib brought them over. Kevin says they're okay for you. Take the pill then we'll decide what to do about the shirt. Why do you want to wear anything?" The sideways glance she gave him after had him explaining, "You might be more comfortable without it."

"I know." She sighed. "I just wanted to prove I could do it."

"Josie, you can do whatever you put your mind to. There's no need to put yourself through misery to prove it— to me or to yourself." Steve couldn't stand to see her hurting. "Come on. Take the pill and in a few minutes, you won't care one way or another."

Josie opened her palm then swallowed the pill.

"Everybody gone?" she asked.

"No, Josie. We're going to call Rick. We need to bring him up to speed on what you found out and go over a few things for tomorrow."

Steve helped her into bed and got her situated on her stomach. "I'll be back shortly. Try to get some rest. Troy will have the watch tonight. So, don't fret. You'll be safe."

"Steve?"

"What, Josie?" Steve gently brushed her hair from her face.

"I realized something tonight while I was trying to keep my mind off the glass they were plucking out of my back."

"What did you realize?" he asked as he stroked her arm softly.

Her eyes drifted shut but she continued to fight sleep. "I don't know why it took someone shooting at me but I know why I ran." Groggy, her voice began to slur.

Steve held his breath, waiting for another insight into her thinking. Another peek into her reasoning for leaving him.

"If I left you, then you couldn't leave me."

"I was never going to leave you, Josie," he told her but she'd already fallen asleep.

28

"**G**ood God, I look like hell," Josie mumbled at her reflection the next morning in the bathroom mirror. The bruises from the beating in St. Augustine had mostly faded but the events of last night had set her back a couple of days. She looked pale, unless you counted the dark circles under her eyes. Her weight loss was underscored by her pronounced cheekbones—but not in a sexy way. Yep, she looked like shit.

"You look beautiful." Steve said, surprising her and, apparently, reading her mind. He was leaning against the doorjamb. She scowled at his reflection. Turning to face him would require too much effort.

"Okay, so you're not at your best," Steve agreed with her silent reprimand. "Give yourself a break. You haven't had an easy time of it these last few days." He turned on the tap in the bathtub. "No shower for you today. Don't want to get that back wet. But a hot bath may help you feel better."

Steve prepared the bath while Josie watched in bewildered silence. Had that tenderness been there all along? Had the combination of his digital camouflage and the heat that flowed between them blinded her to this side of him?

"If you have any problems with your back, let Kevin know," Steve said, bringing her back to the here and now. "Do you need any help before I leave?"

"No. I can manage. Where are you going?" Josie asked.

"Jacksonville. I have an appointment with Deets this morning. Remember?" He'd told her about the trip to see the State Attorney and McClaren's offer of his plane but after last night, he wasn't surprised she'd forgotten it. "We need to talk to everyone on that list. He's the last one alive that we haven't reached and his name keeps floating to the surface."

"Be careful. One of us being injured is enough."

"One of us injured is one too many. Get some rest today."

"I plan to work today, Steve. I assume the restrictions on who I can talk to have been lifted?" she asked.

"It looks like your whereabouts are known. Just don't advertise them and promise me you'll stay inside and away from windows."

"Scout's honor." It would be a long time before she nonchalantly walked by an open window.

TROY AND GIB were in the living room when Steve returned. He wasn't surprised to see Gib as he'd volunteered to run Steve to the airport. But Don had been hunched over the computer when Steve left to check on Josie.

"What happened to Don?" Steve asked.

"He left to catch twenty," Troy said. "He has a program running he said would take a while. I'm keeping Josie company until he comes back."

Steve hesitated briefly. Troy had softened a bit toward Josie but there was still some underlying animosity.

"I'll make sure she stays safe, Steve," Troy promised. "You don't have to worry about that."

"If anything happens at all, call me," he said as he followed Gib out the door.

Half an hour later they pulled into Private Sky Aviation. No check in. No security. No plane changes. *Thank God.*

"Thanks, man. I owe you and McClaren." Steve said, getting out of Gib's truck.

"About that?" Gib said before Steve could shut the door. "I wouldn't mention the plane to McClaren. He kinda doesn't know about this."

"What are you saying?" Steve asked, his eyes narrowing. He looked at the sleek jet waiting for him then glanced at Gib again.

"Don't worry," Gib assured him, "you're not stealing a plane. Just go get your answers."

29

During the flight, Steve had spoken to the pilot and was assured that the owner would have no issue with the trip. The short trip didn't allow for much more conversation. They touched down on the tarmac a little over an hour after they'd taken off from Fort Myers. That left Steve ninety minutes to get to Jacksonville's downtown district for his appointment. According to his GPS app, the airport was about thirty minutes away. With the sleek, black Camaro that Gib had arranged, there'd be no problem making it in time.

The heart of Jacksonville was thick with cars by the time Steve turned onto Monroe Street. After twenty frustrating minutes of searching, he eventually found a parking garage that wasn't full. He made it to the municipal center with a few minutes to spare. He grabbed a cup of coffee from the vendor in the lobby then proceeded to the State Attorney's office. Surprisingly, he didn't have to wait.

Deets stood, hand extended, as Steve approached. The man didn't quite reach six feet and his receding hairline and overly tanned skin made him look older than someone in his mid-forties. Steve accepted the hand he was offered. The cold, sweaty skin was in stark contrast to the take-no-pris-oners attitude the man projected. It could have been nerves that made Deets's hands clammy, but the man clearly didn't give a rat's ass what Steve thought of him. It was obvious from the way Steve had been rushed into the State Attorney's office that Deets wanted this meeting to be over as quickly as possible. That would explain why he didn't notice Steve's reaction to the slithery grip. Steve had to force himself not to wipe his hand on his pant leg as he took his seat.

"Whatever you have to ask must be pretty damned impor-tant for a State Senator to demand that I see you. I figured I'd best get this over with or I'd be hearing from Washington next."

Okay. If the man wanted to go head-to-head, Steve was more than willing. "Since you're so curious, I'll get straight to the point. I'd like to know why your name is associated with two men who have recently died under suspicious circumstances and another one who had an attempt made on his life."

"What the hell is this?" Deets slammed his hand flat against his desk. "Some sort of smear campaign?"

"Why would you think that?" Steve watched the man closely. Body language often spoke louder than the words a person was saying.

Deets settled into his chair, his arms crossed over his wide chest. Taking his silence as the go-ahead, Steve gave him the names of the others on the list with him.

"State your damn business and then get out." Deets snapped.

There were red flags flying everywhere. The man was combative, yes, but Deets wasn't just taking a defensive posi-tion; he was taking an aggressive one.

"Okay. Two men, Luis Esteban and Martin Roemer, are

dead. Investigations into their deaths are ongoing. Anthony McClaren had an attempt made on his life last evening. The person who sent the list is missing and the woman who received it has been beaten and an attempt was made on her life."

"You still haven't explained what this has to do with me and why it is important to you," Deets countered.

So much for a show of compassion for the dead and injured. The man was a cold fish. "I would think it would be important to you since your name is grouped with these men. Men who are dead or have been targeted. Do you want to tell me how you're connected to them?"

"Why don't you tell me?" Deets asked.

"Excuse me?" Steve eyes narrowed.

"You didn't force your way in here on the chance I might be able to give you information on these names. You've made a connection already or you would have simply put in a call to me or had your puppet Senator do it for you."

Whoa. What was with this guy? He hadn't given a straight answer yet. Then to assume that Steve controlled a State Senator... Something was definitely off. "First of all, we have called. Those calls weren't returned. Secondly, you are correct. We have made a connection. Would you like to know what it is?"

"By all means."

"Do you remember the time you spent at Middle Keys Aquatic Camp?" Steve again studied the man for tell signs. Deets was careful. He didn't move. That alone was telling. He had prepared for this meeting and had no intention of giving anything away.

"That was over thirty years ago." Deets pointed out the obvious.

"A girl went missing."

"So?"

Had Deets gotten so jaded working as a prosecutor that his response to a girl's disappearance was "so?" "Can you tell me anything about it?" Steve asked.

"Woke up one morning and we were told she was missing. The camp was on lockdown until the authorities arrived and searched it again. She hadn't turned up by the time I left for home."

"Did you know her?" Steve pressed. Deets's answers were too pat. Too rehearsed.

"Just in passing. The girls and boys didn't mix much. Guess they thought it was safer that way," he answered with a smirk.

"Nothing else you can tell me?" Steve asked, ready to write this interview off.

"No. I was dumped at the camp by my parents and was bored to tears for the entire two weeks. That was the only interesting part."

Interesting? The man thought a girl's disappearance was interesting. Would Steve have had the same reaction at fifteen? He certainly hoped not. "What about the names on the list. Do you remember any of them?" The State Attorney had barely glanced at the paper Steve had handed him.

"I suppose they were there at the same time? No. I didn't make friends. I was just biding my time." Deets was on his feet before Steve asked any further questions.

"What is it that you want? Are you working for the girl's parents? Why do you care what happened to someone thirty years ago?"

"Because people are dying. Isn't that reason enough?"

"People die every day. We don't go on crusades to solve

their murders and from what you've told me they're not people you know. Why do you care? What's in it for you?"

Did this guy believe everyone had an angle? "What about Josette Boussard? Do you know that name?" Steve didn't miss the quick flash of recognition, although he gave Deets points for recovering quickly.

"Can't say that I do." The answer was a little too quick. "Now if you'll excuse me," Deets said rising from his chair. "I've got important work to do. I hope I've answered all your questions."

He left his number and asked Deets to call him if he remembered anything. The chances that Steve would hear from him again were slim.

JOSIE PLANNED to touch base with a few journalists who might have been familiar with the case of Ruth Carr but first she needed to call Roberto. She hadn't warned him to keep a low profile if he'd planned to dig any deeper. They still didn't know who was looking to silence Josie or why.

Unfortunately, Roberto had already contacted Carr's parents, although nothing new had been gained from the interview. There had been no word of their daughter. According to Roberto, they'd accepted the worst. They were sincere in their belief that she did not run away but had been taken from them. Roberto regretted that his phone call might have given them false hope of finding her remains. Josie promised that if she found out anything about the missing girl she would pass it along to Roberto so that he could share it with the Carr family. For the time being, she suggested he keep his head down.

After ending the call with Roberto, and hopefully putting

him off the scent of a story for now, she placed a call to Mike Haskins. She and Mike had shared a by-line a couple of years ago about the sugar industry, Big Sugar as it was known, and how it was at odds with environmentalists and the tourist industry in Florida. They made a few enemies when the story ran but nothing that concerned them. Mike had said if they didn't piss off a few people, they weren't doing it right.

Mike was now retired but he'd been a reporter for the *Key West Citizen* at the time of Carr's disappearance. He would have had his finger on the pulse of the story, even if he wasn't actually involved in the writing and researching of it. He still lived in Key West and was doing well as an author of detective thrillers set in the island city.

"Mike? This is Josie. Josette Boussard. Remember me?" she asked after he'd answered with an abrupt "Hello." She hadn't spoken with him in years.

"Josie? How the hell are you?"

"In a bit of trouble. I'm hoping you can help." Josie first apologized for the lack of communication.

Mike brushed it off quickly. "That street goes both ways. What can I do for you now?"

Having learned her lesson with Roberto, she started by telling Mike to keep the information and her call to himself. As she expected it would, the warning brought out the newshound in him. "What the hell is going on that could make this conversation dangerous?"

"Well, it all began with an email…" Josie proceeded to tell Mike her story, starting with the email from Erica and ending with her dodging a bullet.

"Sounds like you have quite a puzzle on your hands. I'm glad you're okay. Now, you're saying that all the men on this list were at the Middle Keys Aquatic Camp at the time Ruth Carr disappeared?"

"Yes. So far, that's the single link we can find between them. Do you remember the incident?"

"Like it was yesterday. I covered it. Hell of a thing, her disappearing like that. I interviewed most of the girls who were there at the time. None of them noticed any sign of her being angry or despondent. Unhappy, yes. Her parents were breaking up. That's hard on any kid. But both her parents swore that she would never cause them that kind of worry, even with the divorce going on."

"What about the boys and the counselors? Do you remember any of them?"

"Damn. I wish I still had my notes. Left them behind when I quit the *Citizen* but I don't recall anything significant from the young men I interviewed, although I didn't interview everyone who attended. The counselors, of course, were worried. One of their charges had gone missing. Whether she ran away or foul play was involved, she was still their responsibility. A few of the staff were concerned about the camp being sued. Most were genuinely worried about the girl's well-being. I can check with the paper. They may still have my notes on the disappearance."

"Please don't. Whoever is behind this knows if inquiries are being made—at least those of an official nature. I'd rather you not take that chance. Call me, though, if you remember anything else."

"Josie, the names on that list… There are two that rise to the surface when you're talking about the ability to obtain that kind of information. And one of them is dead."

"And the other is a State Attorney. I know. I can't picture him running around killing people. Why would he?"

"I may not be part of the journalistic world anymore but I occasionally have a drink with a few people familiar with the political world. There are rumors circulating that Deets is planning to make a major campaign announcement."

"For what? Governor?"

"Congress."

"Even more reason to keep his hands clean."

"Or his skeletons buried."

30

Steve broke a few speed limits getting back to the airport. Fortunately, he wasn't stopped. He'd called ahead so the pilot knew he was on his way and he buckled in as the plane taxied toward the runway ten minutes after he'd boarded. Once the plane leveled off, Steve was out of his seat, pacing through the small seating area of the jet. Now that his business was done with that asshole, he wanted to see Josie. He'd spoken with her briefly prior to his meeting with Deets. She'd told him not to worry and that she'd be busy on the phone talking to her contacts. But he'd still texted Troy to check in. If she knew he'd gone behind her back to check on her, she'd blow a gasket.

After the meeting with Deets, Steve had tried several times to reach Josie again but his calls had gone straight to voice mail. Troy confirmed she was on the phone and was perfectly fine, but the longer Steve went without speaking to her, the more he needed to hear her voice. He wasn't just worried, he realized, he flat out missed her—and he hadn't even been gone a full day.

As soon as the plane landed, he was on the phone again.

This time Josie answered.

"What?" she barked.

"Is that any way to answer a phone?" he responded, smiling because she sounded so strong. Annoyed, but strong.

"How am I supposed to get any work done if you keep calling me?"

"We've only talked once today."

"Yes, but how many times have you called? I need to talk to people to get answers. Besides, hasn't Troy been keeping you updated?"

Steve didn't say anything. He'd been caught but he wasn't ready to admit to it.

"You shouldn't have texted Troy after every attempted call to me. He either has a girlfriend with an uncanny sense of timing or you were checking on me."

"I have a right to be worried. You were injured yesterday."

"I'm fine," she said, then added, "I have some interesting information to share. When will you be back?"

"We just landed. I see Gib pulling in now. If you're feeling up to it, I'd like to have everyone over to discuss what we've learned today."

He also needed to discuss the phone call he'd gotten from McClaren during his ride back to the airport. He was going to need the team's help with that one.

JOSIE WAITED for Steve in the bedroom. She couldn't decide whether to be pissed or touched by his concern. She was the best judge of what she could and could not do.

Troy, on the other hand, thought the whole situation was comical. Getting Steve worked up was some sort of entertainment for him. He'd played along with him all day, letting Steve pretend Josie wasn't wise to the texting. At least he didn't get his jollies by reporting that she'd fallen prone to a disaster while Steve had been gone. Plus, the teasing had melted a layer of ice between Josie and Troy. She wouldn't call them friends but the tension between them had lessened. Odd, because Troy was the only one in the group who had her pegged.

The rear door slammed shut. A few seconds later she heard Steve's voice. "Where is she?"

"She's out in the garden. Didn't you see her?" Troy answered.

"What the hell?"

Troy's laughter was loud and contagious. Josie was still grinning when Steve stormed into the bedroom. "That wasn't funny," he growled.

"Yes, it was."

The laughter had taken the edge off her temper. Steve dropped onto the bed next to her and pulled her to his chest. His heart was racing but slowed as he held her. Bless the man's heart. She didn't mean to be such a burden. She'd debated again today whether leaving would be best—just slipping out if the chance presented itself. She wouldn't get far before one of them caught her, though. If she hadn't come here in the first place Steve wouldn't know about her trouble and wouldn't be worried. But she couldn't undo that and leaving would compound Steve's hurt and worry. Besides, she'd promised she'd not leave without discussing their past.

"I'm fine, Steve."

"It killed me to leave you after last night."

Josie laid a kiss on his cheek. "It's okay. I felt the same way the day you shipped out. Helpless and worried."

"I won't be shipping out again," he said as he pulled

her close.

"Don't make me the reason you're leaving the army. God, Steve, I couldn't stand that guilt."

"You aren't, Josie. I want to be with you, true. But I've put in my time and thanks to Colt, I've realized there is life after the army. I want that life with you. The time is right, if you'll have me."

Josie closed her eyes. The time for the talk had arrived.

"Have you thought this out? What are you going to do?"

"I have a few ideas. Rick said law enforcement is always looking for former military men or I can go into auto racing," he added with a smile.

Josie didn't return it. "And if I'm not in the picture? What would you do then?"

Steve left her side to shut the bedroom door then took a seat in the single chair that occupied the corner of the room. He leaned forward, elbows on his knees, his fingertips formed a steeple. "I'd be miserable but I'd manage. I need to know, Josie. I need to know why you're so convinced this won't work between us. I deserve to know that much."

He deserved to know. He also deserved more than the person she was—more than the person she was destined to become. So much more. "You've never met my parents," she started.

"No. You didn't like talking about them. That was easy enough to figure out when you refused to invite them to our wedding."

"I don't like them. That's a terrible thing to say but I have no desire to see either of them again. I don't like talking about them either but since telling you about my idyllic childhood might explain why you'd be better off without me, I'll open up that vein you wanted. You're right. You do deserve to know and you do deserve better than me."

"I'll be the judge of what I deserve, Josie." His voice was as strong as steel. "What is it that you believe that makes us wrong for one another. What is it you're scared of?"

"I didn't say I was afraid."

"I've seen fear, Josie and you're afraid. You're afraid of a future with me. I want to know why," he pushed.

"You want to know why I didn't want to marry into the military? Because my dad, career army man and officer, was a womanizer and adulterer."

Steve's eyes widened but she gave him credit for keeping silent. Whether he was reacting to her tone or the statement, she couldn't say. She'd go with the statement.

"He was a man-whore, male slut, womanizer…whatever you want to call a man who sleeps with every woman willing to spread her legs for him. He never wore a wedding band. Saved him the trouble of slipping it off if the opportunity presented itself."

She glanced toward Steve's hands and his bare fingers.

"My dad saw every deployment as a playing field. Not that he was faithful when he was home but deployments made it easier to hide his cheating. My mother didn't report his adultery fearing he'd reciprocate by cutting off her finances. After all, she had a daughter to raise." She spit out the words like a nail-gun. She didn't care.

"He should have been court-martialed. It was a wonder he never contracted some form of STD. Maybe he did. I wouldn't know. I haven't talked to him since I turned eighteen," she admitted to Steve.

Blood rose in his face. "You thought I'd do that? You thought I'd cheat on you?"

"I don't know. Yes. A little... And then there's my mother. Among other things, she's mean, belittling and selfish. What happens if I become a mirror image of her? I already have the last trait down pat. You said so yourself. Do you want to stick around to see what other attractive traits I develop?"

"I'm not your dad and you're not your mother," Steve argued, red-faced.

Josie let out a slow breath. "I thought I'd convinced myself you were different. Then you left. Just like my dad. You left."

"I was deployed, Josie. I didn't leave *you*."

"It was all I knew, Steve. I'd lay in bed alone at night wondering if someone shared yours. Knowing you were in a freaking war zone still didn't stop my mind from wandering there.

"We'd only been 'married' for three months." *Three months, two weeks, and three days, if you were counting the day the certified letter had arrived.* "We were apart longer than we'd been together. My dad didn't hide his indiscretions. I would overhear him and his buddies brag about them on the rare occasions his friends stopped by."

"Like minds attract, Josie. He picked friends with the same lack of morals. The army is made up of good men. Your dad was an ugly exception." Steve argued.

"I know that. Deep down, I know that. But I didn't trust you. What does that make me?"

"Human."

Josie harrumphed. "Doesn't rate real high on the loving wife scale, though. And I wouldn't subject you to living with the person that my mother became. Bitter, vindictive, cold…"

"You're none of those things."

"Yet," Josie countered.

"Why are you convinced that's your fate? Our fate?"

"Because I ran. When I received the news about our vows, I ran like a mouse with its tail on fire. All those fears came slamming back into me. I ran, Steve. Don't you get it?

My family history is nothing compared to that fact. I willingly walked away from you. Shouldn't that be reason enough to end this relationship?"

"Josie…"

She raised her hand to stop him. "You asked. I answered. You have the whole ugly truth now. The stock I came from. My inability to trust. Think about it, Steve. Even if I don't turn into the shrew I had for a mother, why would you want to trust me again?"

"Our 'stock' doesn't make us who we are, Josie. Bad people come from good homes and good people come from bad ones. It's what's inside us that makes us who we are." Steve rose out of his chair and stood in front of her. "The fact that you doubted me hurts. I admit that but I don't believe you'd walk away given a second chance."

"I committed to you once and failed that test."

"True, but that commitment was ripped away by something out of our control. You're a decent, honorable person, Josie. I know that."

"How can you say that?" *How could he say that?* Her eyes burned from holding her tears in check.

"Why are you a freelance journalist?"

"What?"

"Why do you freelance? You're good. You could get a job with any news organization. Why do you freelance?"

"What are you asking?"

"Answer the question, Josie. Why do you freelance?"

"Because I don't like the crap that's published for the sole purpose of selling advertising."

"Exactly. Because you set your standards high. Because you want your stories to be unbiased. You tell stories that need to be heard. What's that if not honorable?"

Josie stared back at him. "Running isn't honorable," she

argued. "You deserve better."

"Where do you get off telling me what I deserve. You made yourself judge and jury of this relationship. You played this break-up game without ever showing me the cards." Steve grasped her shoulders, giving them a gentle shake. "I had no idea what you were thinking—how you felt. Now you act like you care about my feelings but you haven't even asked what they are. You've decided what's best for us. For me." Steve's grip tightened around her shoulders and brought her to her feet so they were face-to-face.

"You're not exactly the sharing type either, Steve."

"Oh, I haven't forgotten our last discussion," Steve spit out.

"I'm talking about now. Not your tours. Since I've arrived here, you've done nothing but tell me what to do. When I've tried to help, I'm shut down."

"For your safety." Steve told her.

"And I was trying to keep you safe—from me."

Steve closed his eyes then pulled her close, pressing her head to his shoulder. "How could two intelligent people be so stupid?"

Josie pushed back enough to look at him, her eyes narrowed. "I mustn't be one of those intelligent people. I don't understand. What do you mean?"

"We didn't talk. You're right about that. You should have told me what you were thinking. We might have argued but I'd rather be arguing with you than have a life without you. You never asked questions. I assumed I knew what was best. Neither of us was very smart."

"I guess not," Josie said. "I'm sorry I doubted you."

"We can get past that, Josie. We can get past anything but the big question is whether you want to. Do you want this relationship to be permanent?"

THE LIVING ROOM was silent when Steve returned. Some of the men were flipping through Cat's gardening catalogues as if that held their interest. No doubt the men had a good idea of what had just gone down behind the bedroom door. Most of them would argue that the talk had been long overdue but none would broach the subject unless Steve did.

He didn't. Instead, he grabbed one of the dining room chairs, straddled it, and filled them in on his meeting with Deets then told them about the call from McClaren.

"McClaren is nervous. His security staff isn't in the protection business and he knows it. He offered me a job as his bodyguard. I told him I couldn't do that but I did tell him I'd put the request for protection out there for us to discuss.

"He's tied to this somehow," Steve continued. "It wouldn't hurt to have one of us nearby. What do you guys think?"

"We're stretched pretty thin but, I agree, it's not a bad idea," Rick said. "It wouldn't hurt our investigation if we got our hands on the guy who tried to run him off the road. He could make another attempt on McClaren. Unfortunately, I can't help you on that end," Rick added. "That's way out of my jurisdiction. But I can help fill in here when I'm not on duty to free up one of you."

They'd be working on a lot less sleep but they'd done it before. Plus, Colt told Steve he'd be back in a couple of days. Regardless of his new marital status, there would be no keeping Colt out of it. He'd wouldn't sit on the sidelines while his friends put themselves in the line of fire. The best option would be to have the problem resolved prior to Colt's return.

With the McClaren issue dealt with, Steve turned to Don.

He'd spent the day hacking into the background of each man on the list, including the two who were dead. "What did you find during your research today?" Steve emphasized the word *research* for Rick's sake.

"No red flags showed up, at least not on the surface," Don said, looking at his notes. "After your meeting with Deets, though, I spent most of my time digging into his history. There's a lot there and it's quite colorful. He's from a wealthy family who made their money in the smelly, but lucrative, paper mill business. Over the years, they've branched out, no pun intended, into other areas including the hospitality industry. That's now the family's major source of income. Most of their hotels are considered resorts and are located here in Florida, though they're slowly expanding outside the state. Not surprisingly, the family and its businesses contributed heavily to his campaign."

"Interesting, but not exactly eye raising," Steve said.

"Well, this might raise an eyebrow or two. Deets has a sealed juvenile record. I don't know what's in it," Don added quickly for Rick's benefit. "But that discovery had me looking closely at his school records. He transferred schools frequently once he hit middle school. Unfortunately, social media didn't exist so I've no public domains to search. I did find the names of a few of the guidance counselors and principals that were at those schools when he attended. They might shed some light on him."

"Interesting but still not a lot of help," Steve said raking his hands through his hair. He'd been involved in missions that took a lot of time and research to pull off. By comparison, this investigation had barely started but it couldn't move fast enough to suit him. Because of Josie.

As if that thought had conjured her up, the door to the bedroom opened. He turned his head. Pride filled his chest as he saw Josie walking toward him. Her eyes and nose were red but her spine was straight. She wasn't hiding. He wasn't wrong about her. She had guts, backbone, and a deep sense of right and wrong. The question was could he make her believe it?

She'd thought he might cheat on her. That stung. The admission would have been a deal breaker if not for the bastard she'd had for a father. The whirlwind romance, the news from the County Clerk and her family history—it all added up to a level of insecurity he hadn't even begun to suspect. Adultery was a court-martial offense, as it should be, but this man had retired comfortably. He could still be brought up on charges and the idea was tempting but it would just open old wounds for Josie. It would serve the son-of-a-bitch right if he was suffering from a host of STDs.

Steve reached behind him and grabbed another dining room chair and pulled it next to him as Josie neared. She gave him a timid smile before accepting the invitation.

After she'd taken the offered seat, Steve turned back to the others present to continue the discussion but they were all watching Josie. Each had a welcoming smile mixed with a bit of concern in their assessing eyes. Steve reached for her hand, telegraphing the message that they were okay. "Go on," he prompted the group.

"Deets was kicked out of his fraternity in college," Don announced.

"That takes some doing," Rick commented. "How does a bad boy get to be a State Attorney?"

"Money," Josie jumped in. When all heads pivoted in her direction, she hesitated.

"Go ahead, Josie," Steve encouraged.

"It's all about money, unfortunately. Candidates with large financial backers or lots of family money have more to spend on the race—advertising mostly. The more advertising —written, spoken or visual—the more ingrained the name becomes in the voter's mind. It's similar to brainwashing. Political beliefs are secondary. Most people believe what they hear. They don't dig deeper. Cynical but true. Unless he had an ambitious or connected opponent, no one would have bothered, or would have reason, to look this deep. Being an asshole is easily overlooked when money is waved around."

"Okay. What else do we know about him?" Steve searched the faces of the men in the room but it was Josie who spoke out.

"He may be planning to run for a higher office," she added.

"How high?" Rick asked, leaning forward, resting his arms on his thigh.

"Congress."

Steve's eyebrows rose a notch in surprise. "He wants to jump from local State Attorney straight to Washington? That's quite a leap. Where did you get that info?"

Josie related the conversation she'd had earlier in the day with Haskins. "Mike's not a journalist anymore but he's always had connections in the political world. If he says it's likely, I'd bet money it was going to happen."

"Could be that's why Deets was so closed-mouthed today," Gib suggested. "He doesn't want his name connected to our investigation."

"Or have the investigation into Ruth Carr reopened. It could be the names on the list can connect him to the missing girl." Steve mused.

"I'll be damned," Gib said.

31

Steve called McClaren to discuss the protection detail and ended by telling him to stay put until Troy knocked on his door the next morning. Troy would be pulling full time duty on McClaren. Staying at his place, driving him to work, and providing security at his dealership. Troy would set the ground rules tomorrow. If McClaren didn't like them then he'd have to pay to hire a private security firm to watch over him. Troy was providing protection but he would continue to seek answers from McClaren while he was there.

Pulling Troy from the rotation at the house meant Steve would be spending additional time taking his turn as sentry. Rick had offered to stay and take a few hours on watch so Don could catch some sleep. That would leave Steve free to spend the night with Josie, assuming she was willing.

Other than the discussion regarding Deets, Josie had said little. He'd thought about sleeping on the couch then verbally kicked himself. Not talking had been a mistake. It was past time to stop that shit. Steve entered the bedroom. Josie was already in bed laying on her side. The covers had been turned down on both sides of the bed. The invitation was clear. This was one instance talking wasn't necessary.

As soon as Steve was under the covers, Josie turned and snuggled against him, resting her head on his shoulder. He'd tried to talk her into taking a pain pill earlier. She'd refused even after begrudgingly admitting that her injuries still bothered her. So, they reached another compromise. Josie promised to take one if she couldn't sleep but for now, she said she wanted to feel him—to touch him.

"I don't deserve this, but I spent too many nights wishing you would mysteriously appear. The ache in my back is a small price to pay to have a dream come true," she'd said, pleading her case.

Steve lay quietly, while Josie stroked his chest. The maddeningly erotic movements had him picturing all the ways he could make love to her. If she didn't stop soon, he would be tempted to try one. She was still battered and given the way she'd squirmed all evening, the cuts on her back were still irritating her.

He'd crawled into bed still wearing his jeans. When Josie had questioned the action, he'd given her the lame excuse that he might need to relieve Rick or Don on short notice. Truth was, the denim kept his erection from pointing due north and, thankfully, acted as a barrier from her wandering fingertips.

Eventually, Josie's hand ceased to roam and her breathing steadied. He crooked his head to confirm that her eyes had drifted shut.

A STABBING PAIN in her back awakened Josie.

"What is it?" Steve asked, suddenly looming over her.

"I'm okay. I just rolled over on my back."

"Let me take a look," Steve said.

She wouldn't win this battle so she turned onto her stomach. She flinched when he turned on the bedside light, quickly covering her eyes against the glare. He carefully removed the bandage that Kevin had applied that morning.

"Well?"

Instead of answering her, Steve grabbed his cell. "Kevin, get over here and bring your kit."

"You didn't wake him, did you? It could have waited until morning."

Steve remained silent. Josie had no idea what he was thinking. She turned her head to look at him. He was staring at the bedroom door, awaiting Kevin's arrival.

"It can't be that bad," she told him but nerves had her tapping the toes of one foot against the mattress.

Steve placed a hand on her leg. "There's some inflammation. Can you stay still until Kevin takes a look, please?"

Kevin walked in and Josie attempted to rise. Steve gently held her in place.

"Sorry, Kevin. I told him I'd be fine until tomorrow," she mumbled into the pillow.

"I think he's the one that's hurting right now," Kevin whispered into her ear. "Let's see what we've got."

"It looks worse than this morning," Steve said as he raised her t-shirt further up her back.

Kevin slipped on a pair of latex gloves and after a few minutes of poking and probing that had hurt like hell, Kevin said, "This would be the reason why." A pair of tweezers entered her limited line of sight, a sliver of bloody glass in its pinchers.

"I thought the paramedics got all that out," Steve snapped.

"It's not surprising they missed this piece," Kevin explained. "It's tiny and was a little deeper. It worked its way to the surface where it irritated the skin. Good thing. Once we get it cleaned out, she'll heal just fine." Kevin pulled out a few additional items from his kit and placed them on the bed.

"Josie, this is going to hurt a little more than the removal of the glass. I'm going to clean the wound and make sure there's nothing left behind. Okay?"

"Knock yourself out," she told him. Steve held her hand as Kevin pressed and squeezed the tender skin surrounding the wound then administered antibiotic ointment. After the bandaging was done, Steve pulled down her shirt and helped her into a sitting position.

"You might as well have left me on my stomach," Josie grumbled. "No way I'm sleeping on my back."

"You can't swallow a pill while you're lying on your stomach," he said, holding out a glass of water and a tablet. "Come on, Josie. I can't get any rest if you don't."

No point in them both going without sleep. She chased the pill down with the water.

32

The next time Josie awakened it was to the smell of coffee. She opened her eyes and saw Steve sitting in the corner chair, a cup of the steaming liquid in his hand.

"Good morning," he said, studying her as he said it. "How are you feeling?" he asked.

She moved her shoulders, stretching her back. "Better. A bit sore but better. Is that coffee?" she asked, her eyes focused on the cup.

"Do you want a sip?" he asked.

"Did you make it?"

Steve grinned. "No, Don did."

"Gimme," Josie smiled as she reached out for his coffee.

Steve sat with Josie, discussing her plans for the day until she'd finished his cup of coffee. He retrieved his cup then left to take his turn on watch. Josie's fingers were tingling to get started. She was free to reach out to her sources today. She caught herself in the silly act of rubbing her hands together in anticipation. It's what she did. Research. Find the truth.

While Don "researched" the additional names connected to Deets, Josie planned to reach out to business associates and community leaders to learn what she could about Deets's personal life. Her cover story would be that she was doing a series of articles on Florida State Attorneys and was currently looking into Deets as a potential subject for that series.

Her phone was at the bottom of the Matanzas River. She was still using the burner phone Gib had picked up for her so she had to dig through her emails to find the phone number she needed. Since the focus was on Deets, all she needed was a phone number for one particular journalist to start this snowball rolling. Hopefully, she'd kept at least one of Peter's emails.

Her fingers flew over the tablet's keyboard and, hallelujah, she'd saved it. The journalist she'd known at the *Florida Times-Union* in Jacksonville still worked for the paper and in another sign of good fortune, still covered the political beat. If he was suspicious of her probing questions, he didn't ask. Journalists were always looking for a scoop but they were also extremely helpful to one another. She promised to let him know if she discovered anything interesting and he was good with that. He shared what information he had on the State Attorney. He didn't mention Deets's rumored bid for Congress so Josie didn't say anything as that wasn't information she could share at this point. There would be no way to keep the reporter off the story if that tidbit was dropped.

Most of what Josie learned from calling Deets's acquaintances was mundane. He was a member of local country clubs, and community and charitable organizations. He was widowed at a young age. No children from the marriage. He was known to date and recently was in a relationship which a number of the people she'd talked to had thought might be serious. For some reason, though, the couple had parted ways. None of those who mentioned it knew why or cared enough to remember the woman's name. Josie was told repeatedly that the woman was much younger and stunning but now out of the picture. Josie had been able to find plenty of photos of Deets but none with his mysterious beauty.

Josie then targeted those a little closer to the SA. Her contact at the *Florida Times-Union*, had also shared the names of several employees who worked at the State Attorney's Office in Jacksonville. She'd need to be a lot more circumspect when she reached out to this group. She didn't want to spook Deets. Josie used the rumor about his run for Congress to ask for feedback on the man, off the record or otherwise. She was casting a wide net with the hope that she'd catch something.

And her fishing technique worked.

After getting through to several of the names on her list, Josie could say without a qualm that "warm and fuzzy" would never be used to describe Deets, at least not by his underlings. One female employee inadvertently dropped the word "creepy" but quickly retracted the description. It was too late. *Creepy*. The word had Josie's antennae rising further. This woman was uncomfortable around her boss. There were certain men who, by simply looking at a woman, could make their skin crawl. Josie'd met a few of them and they weren't easily forgotten. The tone and delivery of the employee's remark reminded Josie of those men.

After talking to the staff members, Josie was itching to speak to the two school counselors Don had located yesterday. The first one was aware of Deets's current position and expressed astonishment at that fact. Josie had asked why but the woman disconnected the call.

The second was a bit more forthcoming but Josie still had to pry the information out of him even after promising that his comments would be off the record. He, too, was aware that Deets was now a State Attorney and admitted to being perplexed by the career choice. He'd expected the former student to eventually end up on the other side of the courtroom. The man didn't hang up when Josie asked why, but he refused to go into detail. He limited his statement to the fact that Deets had been asked to leave the school because of infractions that he, personally, believed should have been a matter for the authorities. The counselor wouldn't elaborate, but the man was bitter that Deets's family money had been able to bury a multitude of sins. He ended the conversation saying he'd been relieved after Deets had transferred out.

At one point during the day, Don slipped Josie the name of a Middle Keys Aquatic Camp employee from the time Carr went missing. Just her luck, the name was Robert—no middle initial—Brown. Besides the common name, Don had made a notation that Brown had taught scuba diving to camp attendees with little to no experience in the sport. Playing a hunch, Josie started in Key West and worked her way up the island chain talking to one dive shop owner after another until she reached one who remembered a Robert Brown who owned a place in Key Largo. Key Largo, however, was the home of John Pennekamp Coral Reef State Park—the first undersea park in the United States. As a result, it had a massive number of dive shops. Thanks to the Google gods, though, Josie found one owned by a Robert Brown.

Then, in another stroke of luck, not only was Mr. Brown in the shop that day, but he answered the phone. Introducing herself as a reporter who was researching the young Aaron Deets, Josie asked Brown if he remembered the teenager.

"Do you remember Aaron Deets? He was at the camp the summer Ruth Carr disappeared. Do you remember that summer?"

"Hell yes, I remember that summer session! You never

forget being so close to an event like that. They never found her, did they?"

"No. No, they didn't. Was Aaron Deets a friend of hers?"

"I doubt it. The boys and girls didn't socialize together. The camp made a point of keeping them apart except during supervised activities. Hormones run rampant at that age, you know what I mean?"

Josie avoided commenting. She had a talker, she wasn't going to sidetrack him. "Do you remember Aaron Deets?"

"I was a dive instructor not a babysitter. That was the counselors' job, thank God. They're the ones who had to spend time with those spoiled brats most of the day. You should be talking to one of them."

"I would if I had a name," Josie prompted.

"Hang on a minute." Paper rustled at the other end of the line then Brown was back on the phone. "Try this number. Butch was a camp counselor then. He stayed with the company for a while after I left to open this place. Lives in Key Largo now and still likes to dive. He comes in here to get his tanks filled." He rattled off a phone number.

Josie thanked him for his time then immediately placed the call to Butch.

He was skeptical from the onset.

"Is this about the girl or about Deets?" he asked.

"Deets, unless the two are connected. Are they?"

"Never saw the two together."

"But you remember them?"

"Didn't know Carr except to see her. I don't think I'd remember her if it hadn't been for her disappearing act. Deets was one of the boys I supervised that summer."

"What was your opinion of him?"

"Arrogant. Spoiled. Privileged. But that wasn't particularly unusual. A lot of the kids at that camp felt entitled. They

"Which one?" Josie asked, shutting the refrigerator door, putting her hunger aside. Her stomach was now rolling.

"DiSantis. Our calls are going straight to voice mail and none of the messages we've left have been returned. It would be one thing if he was just avoiding us but he didn't show up for work and his office can't reach him either. He has quite a few demanding, high-end clients so according to his staff, it's unusual for him to be this inaccessible."

"What about family?"

"He's single. No immediate family." Steve explained.

The rolling in Josie's stomach had turned into a tsunami. She pressed her hand to her abdomen in a ridiculous attempt to contain it. "So, how many of us are left?"

33

"Don't you dare include yourself in that shooting gallery." Steve was instantly furious. "You are not a target!" he glared at her.

"The hell I'm not. I was shot at!" Josie glared right back.

"You weren't shot at because you were on the list."

"No. I was shot at because I *have* the list. I'm connected to it."

"So is everyone here," Steve countered.

"Now you're being ridiculous. Using that logic, everyone we've talked to would be a target. This isn't Ebola, Steve. It's not spreading like a virus. The targets are those with a direct link to the list. You know that. Why are you so angry?"

Why was he angry? The honest answer was that he was frightened. She'd summed up his fears and presented them to him in one tight little package. She was a target. Possibly even the bull's-eye. But he'd rather be angry than scared. He'd been in countless situations that would scare any man. He was trained to handle that kind of fear.

"We're going to keep you safe, Josie. I'm going to keep you safe," he promised.

"I know that, Steve. I don't doubt that for a minute but it still doesn't change the fact that I'm a target."

Steve tugged her toward him and held her tight, fighting against the urge to argue. If he admitted she was a target then he was vulnerable, too.

THE WARMTH of Steve's body seeped through her thin barrier of clothing. She needed that warmth, the heat. Fear trickled down her spine like ice water, chilling her from deep inside. She wanted it gone. If she was a target, Steve was as well. He'd made it his mission to keep her safe and if that meant getting between her and a bullet he'd do it without hesitation. The knowledge made her stomach turn. She'd come for help but not at the cost of his life.

Still, what else had she expected? He could do no less.

How the hell had they gotten into this mess? It didn't matter now. She couldn't undo what had been done. She couldn't stuff Erica's email back into the void of the World Wide Web and pretend she'd never received it any more than she could take back her actions—or reactions—following the news that their wedding vows weren't legal. Hiding in Steve's arms wasn't going to change the past, although it felt damned good.

The house around them was quiet. "Where is everyone?"

"Doing what they need to do. We're alone." Steve told her, giving her a devilishly, crooked smile. "Want to make use of the time?"

Josie immediately returned the smile. The reaction came easily and without thought. Before she'd opened up, she'd unconsciously weighed each movement, each word. Would her words or actions inadvertently give Steve hope for their future? Would she hurt him with a gesture or remark? But they'd talked. A conversation had begun. One that she hadn't believed was necessary. She'd been wrong.

Her fears were no longer buried. Once shared, the weight of them had slid from her shoulders. She'd had no idea of the amount of baggage she'd been carrying until it was gone.

Steve's invitation was clear. She melted like butter under his heated look. Placing her hands on the sides of his face, she kissed him deeply and tenderly before stepping back. It took every ounce of willpower to pull away. She wanted him as much, if not more, than he wanted her but her damn reporter's instincts wriggled to the front of her mind. She had a story to tell first.

"Hold that thought," she told him, placing a finger to his lips before he objected. "First, I need to tell you what I've put together."

She went over everything she'd learned about Deets. Given his sealed record and based on her interviews, she had a good idea of what kind of charges were being kept under wraps. "No one outright accused him of a salacious misconduct, but I'm not liking Deets much as a boy," she concluded.

"I didn't think much of him as a man."

"There's nothing concrete in what we've found. If I was doing an actual story, no editor would publish it. There's not enough evidence or corroboration to accuse him of any wrongdoing. But he stinks, Steve. Deets stinks to high heaven."

"I agree. Throw in the fact that he's the only one who could have accessed the information about you and Erica. None of the others on the list, that are still alive at least, would have those connections."

"What are we going to do?"

"We keep digging."

"I've run out of places to look."

"Then we look elsewhere. The men on that list were all at the camp at the same time Carr went missing. None of those we reached today were willing to talk about Deets. They acted like they barely remembered him, but according to the counselor you spoke with, they bunked together. They're nervous. The question is why."

"They're afraid of something," Josie concluded.

"That would be my guess."

"And DiSantis? You think he's okay or there's another one down?"

"I have no idea. He could be running scared. Don's going to look at his background a little harder. If he's running, we'll try to figure out where he's headed. We'll review all the data we've accumulated with the team tonight."

Josie stared into his anxious, deep brown eyes. He was worried. Again, she wished she could travel back in time to stop her burden from becoming his. But time machines didn't exist and now their future was in doubt. All they had was today, the most precious of moments.

"You sure we have this place to ourselves?" she asked, as she pressed her palm to the nape of his neck to pull his lips within a breath of hers.

"For a couple of hours, at least. Don is on watch. Kevin's catching some sleep and Rick and Gib are working."

Josie's eyes sparkled. "We can do a lot in a couple of hours," she whispered.

STEVE TOUCHED his brow to Josie's forehead and closed his eyes, inhaling her scent. So unique that not even the stench of war had been able to erase it. He'd longed for it—imagined it

—every night he'd been away from her. The scent was unique to Josie and when she was near, his nostrils flared seeking more of the intoxicating pheromones. As he absorbed her essence, she pressed her lips to his.

"Hold on tight," Steve warned her. His hands dusted her sides before clasping the firmness of her bottom to lift her off the floor. Her legs instinctively wrapped around his waist. Her core brushed against his now straining erection, the sensation was too much for him.

A bed. They needed a bed. But as Josie began to nibble at his ear, the bedroom might as well have been in the next county. She took the lobe between her teeth and nipped. Steve squeezed her closer. Josie's sudden, sharp intake of breath reminded him of her injuries.

"I'm sorry," he said, grabbing her legs in an attempt to lower her to the floor.

"I'm not," she responded, locking her legs into place.

"But your back…"

"I can be on top," she said, wickedly. "I want you, Steve. Don't deny me this. Don't deny yourself," she added, putting all humor aside.

Her eyes implored him, her dark lashes standing out against her pale skin. Her mouth firm and begging him to kiss the scowl from her face. She didn't blink. Didn't waver.

"You're sure." It wasn't a question. Still, he watched for any signs of hesitation.

"About everything, Steve. Yes, I'm sure."

The back of his legs made contact with the mattress. He fell onto the bed as gently as he could manage so as not to jar her. He reached for the buttons of her blouse, smiling again. "On top, huh?"

34

The door to the kitchen clicked open and Steve bolted from the bed. He grabbed his discarded Glock and jeans in one fluid motion and was out in the hall before the back door had closed. A quick look over his shoulder confirmed that Josie had not been awakened by his sudden movement. He closed the bedroom door behind him.

Sounds coming from the kitchen confirmed what he'd suspected but would have been stupid to assume. His heart rate dropped along with the arm holding his weapon. Unless their visitor was fishing for a beer in the refrigerator, Gib had arrived with dinner.

"Keep it down," Steve hushed as he finished zipping his jeans. "Josie's asleep."

Gib popped his head over the top of the refrigerator door. "I'm guessing that's not all she's been doing."

"What is it with you and my sex life?"

"I want nothing to do with your sex life."

"You damn sure seem interested in it."

"Sex is always interesting. Although, talking about it isn't half as much fun as doing it. Tell me again why I'm spending my nights with you?"

Steve bit his tongue. Gib would love nothing more than for Steve to rise to that twisted bait. He'd seen this act before, though Rick was Gib's favorite target.

"What's for dinner?" Steve asked, pointedly changing the subject.

"Because you've already had dessert?"

"Gib, enough!"

"Okay. Okay. If you don't plan on shooting me with that thing," he said, indicating the gun in Steve's hand, "you can put it away and help me unload the groceries."

STEVE WATCHED Rick as he dropped into the single side chair left behind by the Copelands. He'd grabbed a Cuban sandwich and a beer on his way through the kitchen. His friend had phoned to tell them he was hung up at the station and to get started without him. It was now going on eight o'clock. Kevin was absent, having taken over Don's watch after he'd finished his meal. Don and Gib flanked both ends of the couch, sitting in chairs that had been pulled from the dining area due to the shortage of seating in the main room. Sitting next to him on the couch, Steve could feel the tension return to Josie's body as soon as Rick entered the room. She'd yet to completely relax around him. That wasn't surprising. She'd been beaten by someone posing as a cop and had been tracked as a result of their information system. It would take a while for that fear to wear off. Steve placed her hand in his.

"What did you find out about DiSantis? Has he turned up?" Steve asked, giving her hand a squeeze.

"No sign of him," Rick answered, before deliberately

taking a long pull on his beer. "His home is locked up and his car is gone. On a positive note, he did ask a neighbor to take in his mail."

"So, he just took off?" Gib asked. Hair that was normally tied off, hung loose tonight. He pushed it behind his ears.

"It looks that way," Rick said around a mouth full of food.

"Is he running?" Josie's voice was strained, her pitch abnormally high.

"Don't know but the fact that he left without notifying his business would lead me to think so. The question is where."

"I've dug up a couple of possibilities," Don volunteered.

"Shoot," Steve told the hacker.

"Not surprisingly, since he's a realtor, he owns several properties. One of them happens to be a little bit south of here."

"How far south?" Steve's blood started to hum. They were getting close. He could sense it like he'd sensed the enemy in the mountains of Afghanistan. It was only a matter of time before the pieces started falling into place.

"He's got a condo on Fort Myers Beach. A place just north of a state park called Lovers Key."

Two birds in the same neighborhood. McClaren and DiSantis. The players were moving into place. "I assume you have the address?" Steve asked.

"Yes… And the unit number but it's in a gated community, Steve. You don't get in unless you live there or a guest of one of the residents. I also have the landline number for the residence. I tried it but its voice mailbox is full."

"Text me the address," Steve said. Turning to Rick, he asked "Can you do anything?"

"It's one thing to do a welfare check at his home," Rick replied, knowing where Steve was heading. "It's another entirely to start knocking on the doors of every property he owns. He hasn't committed a crime that we're aware of so the authorities have no reason to be chasing him down. If we suspect he's there and in danger or involved in something illegal, I'll make the call. But right now, Steve, I just can't do it."

"I'll take a drive down there tomorrow," Steve said.

"I'll go with you," Josie cheerfully volunteered.

"No, you won't," Steve rebuked her.

Josie slowly, almost eerily, rose to her feet and turned to face Steve. Her hands fisted on her hips, she stared down at the man who had just held one of those hands. "Don't you dare take that tone with me," she hissed at him.

"Now, Josie, calm down." Her fierce stance had him leaning back. He could feel the heat of her anger.

Gib let out a snort that had Steve snapping his head in that direction. "What the hell is so funny?"

"You are. The last thing you say to a woman you've just pissed off is 'calm down.'"

Gib would know and a quick look at Josie confirmed that he was right. Josie's eyes were spitting fire. If it were anatomically possible, they'd be shooting darts.

"Josie, listen." He tried to reason with her. "You recently, and vigorously, pointed out that you were a target. You need to stay here where we can keep you safe." Now he sounded condescending.

"And look how that's worked out. I've been attacked by some jackass in the garden and shot at while trying to take a shower. Personally, I'd rather be a moving target than a sitting duck."

"Steve, think about it," Rick suggested. "Her leaving here could work to our advantage."

"How?" Gib asked, casting a worried look toward Josie.

"If there's anyone out there," Steve explained, his training kicking in, "they'd follow her. We'd spot them if they did." His initial response to her suggestion had been a knee-jerk reaction induced by fear. Instinctively, he wanted her hidden and safe. But she wasn't hidden and, therefore, would not be completely safe.

"Moving her is a risk," Rick added "but since they already know where she is, it's a calculated risk."

"But you're taking her to another target's location," Gib argued.

"Possible location," Steve pointed out. "We don't know if DiSantis is headed this way. He could have taken off for Timbuktu." Steve remembered how angry Gib had gotten when it was suggested they use Cat as bait to catch the sniper last year. Always ready to defend a lady in distress.

"I wish you'd all stop talking about me like I'm not in the room," Josie said.

"Alright, Josie, but you're going to have to listen to me. Whatever I tell you to do, you do it, for your own protection. Do we have an agreement?"

JOSIE's left hand gripped the armrest of the Mustang until her knuckles turned white. Her left hand grasped the edge of the leather seat she was buckled into. Closing her eyes was out of the question. She might miss the accident. Steve drove the car like a professional stunt driver in a Jason Bourne movie—navigating the dense, seasonal traffic and highway construction deftly as they made their way south on Estero Boulevard. She'd forgotten Steve's penchant for speed and his annoyance at sitting still in traffic.

Kevin was two cars behind them. At least, she assumed he was there. She'd been told that had been the plan but she'd been too terrified to take her eyes off the road to look behind them and confirm it. Don was staying on the island, watching for any unusual activity or anyone who might be a bit too curious about the residents that had just exited the Copeland home. Rick was at the station on standby, if needed. Josie had no idea what Gib was up to. She hadn't asked and no one had elaborated on his duties for the day, if any. He'd been absent from the planning session this morning.

When Steve was forced to stop at a traffic signal, Josie loosened her grip and glanced over at him. His jaw was set, his fingers flexed as he gripped the steering wheel. His eyes darted from the rearview mirror to the side mirror before shifting to the road again. No car went unnoticed. Guilt added torque to the already tightened muscles in Josie's neck. His protective instincts had been in overdrive since they left the house an hour before.

It wasn't until this morning as the men huddled around the dining room table over coffee that Josie discovered that what she'd assumed was a simple drive to the beach was anything but simple to these men. She sat on the couch searching for information about Lovers Key and the residences and businesses surrounding it but she'd found it difficult to concentrate as the men debated different scenarios and responses to them. They were concerned about the route due to road construction. Contingencies were planned. The longer the men plotted, the more the coffee in Josie's stomach soured.

By mid-morning, satisfied with the plan the men had put in place, Steve told Josie it was time to leave. Her elation at escaping the confines of the building she'd been shackled to for the last week had turned to dread. Was she putting herself and the men at risk by her desire to go with Steve? She'd been briefly tempted to withdraw her suggestion. But they'd worked to pull this off and thought it might hasten an end to the nightmare. She wasn't backing down. Hell, this drive was nothing compared to what she'd been through since she received the email. She'd been beaten, grabbed, and shot at. She could do this.

As Steve turned left into the condominium complex, three tall buildings came into view. The one furthest from the entrance was Lovers Key Resort. Her earlier search had revealed that the resort was not a hotel but condominium units that could be reserved for a day, a week or longer. The other two buildings consisted of private units. No doubt a number of owners rented them out on a seasonal basis. DiSantis' condo was in the high rise closest to the resort. In addition to the resort and the two private condo buildings, the complex consisted of a parking garage and a single restaurant and bar, Flippers.

Steve slowed as he passed the building where DiSantis's condo was located, then pulled into the parking lot of Flippers, an open-air restaurant situated between the two towers. The view through the window of the Mustang took Josie's breath away. The northern part of Fort Myers Beach had been crowded with hotels, motels, and restaurants and the massive number of people that went with them. The construction project underway on the two-lane road leading south made it congested and noisy. The waters of the Gulf of Mexico had been hidden by the buildings that stretched along the single route south.

But once they'd turned into Lovers Key Resort, the hustle and bustle of Estero Boulevard gave way to the beauty of Florida's estuaries. The resort sat adjacent to a state park. Looking past the pool, Estero Bay was dotted with mangroves of varying size. A variety of boats bobbed in the turquoise blue water. Some headed toward the Gulf of

Mexico, others were stationary, having found their place to relax or fish for the day. Kayakers in colorful vessels glided along. This tiny morsel of land was perfectly situated between the busy, touristy world of Fort Myers Beach and the natural beauty of Lovers Key. The best of both worlds for those who lived here. Dinner and a show? Turn right. Solitude and nature? Turn left.

"Now, to figure out a way to get up there," Steve said, interrupting Josie's thoughts. "We could buzz his unit and hope that he answers…"

Steve's comment brought Josie back to the reason for the trip and it wasn't to enjoy the scenery. Steve was gazing up at the Grand Island Beach condominiums which sat on the other side of a parking garage next to Flippers. She knew the DiSantis condo was on the fifth floor. Josie looked up as well but then dropped her gaze to the entrance of the building. From where she was sitting, she could just make out a young woman standing near the entrance holding a clipboard. Next to her was a large potted plant. A real estate sign had been shoved into the pot in front of the plant. "How about we go shopping for a waterfront condo?"

"What?"

Josie pointed through the windshield. "Someone is having an 'open house'. It should get us past security." Steve leaned toward Josie so he could see clearer.

His eyes brightened. "Perfect," he said, firmly planting a kiss on her lips. Steve sent a text to Kevin who had parked a little deeper into the complex.

"Okay. Let's go find out what these babies are selling for," he said as he opened the passenger door.

35

Steve's first priority was to get Josie safely into the building. There was no reason to believe anyone would have anticipated their arrival, but the past week had been filled with surprises. He didn't like surprises. Steve knew Kevin would be watching and remain on alert but there were a lot of units in the three buildings that comprised the complex. Any one of them could have a sniper on their balcony. If he voiced his concern, Josie would accuse him of being paranoid. But you didn't survive a war zone without being somewhat paranoid. Not being suspicious got you killed.

Steve hustled Josie toward the front doors where a perky young brunette waited for her next possible client.

"Are you here for the open house?" she asked.

"Yes, ma'am, we are," Steve answered smoothly, letting the southern drawl he'd developed from years of being stationed at Fort Bragg run free. "My wife and I were just talking about buying a place near here so we could come and go as the mood strikes. Saw your sign when we pulled in here for a drink." He indicated the bar now behind them. "Figured it was a good omen." Steve ignored Josie as she rolled her eyes. Fortunately, Josie was standing next to the agent who wasn't in any position to notice Josie's expression.

"Always cheaper than renting or staying at hotels and in this area, an excellent investment." The agent—Jayne, according to the name on her badge—handed them a copy of the MLS listing then buzzed them through the front entrance. "Take the elevator to the tenth floor. Heather is in unit 1003 and will be happy to show you around."

Josie jabbed Steve in the ribs as soon as the door closed behind them. "Why you little old sweet talker, you."

"I can be charming."

"Don't I know it?" she quipped stepping into the elevator. "You had me on my back three days after we met."

Steve grinned as he pushed the button for the fifth floor. He had set a different sort of speed record where Josie was concerned. Logic said he should have taken things slower but he didn't regret a minute of their lovemaking.

As soon as the elevator doors opened, Steve was once again on alert. Holding his arm out to stop Josie's exit, he checked the hallway. Satisfied they were alone, they followed the signs until they found 513—DiSantis's unit, according to Don.

"What's our story?" Josie asked while they waited for someone to answer Steve's knock.

"No story. Just the truth, assuming he's here. We want to know what he can tell us about Deets. It will all depend on what he says and how he acts." Steve banged on the door again. "He may not have headed this way. Don said he had several properties. He could be at any one of them for all we know."

"We can't stand out in this hallway too long," Josie said. "Miss Sunshine downstairs would have called her counterpart to tell her to expect us. If we don't show, security will most likely be the next call she makes."

Steve knocked one last time. "If he doesn't answer, we'll have to regroup." They'd talked this morning about covering this place if DiSantis wasn't here but they were spread extremely thin. There were a few other friends on leave they could call for reinforcements but getting them here quickly would be an issue. It was something they'd have to address if the man didn't answer.

DISCOURAGED by their lack of results, Josie turned toward the bank of elevators. As she did, an elderly man stepped out of the unit next door. Steve pushed Josie behind him.

"It's alright, son. I'm harmless," he said, smiling at Steve. "You two friends of Mr. DiSantis?" he asked.

"Yes, we are," Josie replied, as she stepped out from behind Steve's large frame. The man looked to be in his seventies. His thick white, wavy hair stood out against his tanned skin. His blue eyes twinkled with mischief. The charm of his smile rivaled Gib's.

"He left a little while ago," the neighbor volunteered. "If I wasn't headed out, I'd offer to let you wait at my place."

"That's very sweet of you," Josie responded. She was instantly endeared to the older man. How many trusting, kind souls were there left in this world? "We'll text him. Let him know we're here," she adlibbed.

"I don't know how long he will be but if you want to wait, Flippers, the bar here, makes one hell of a drink," he said with a knowing smile.

Josie easily returned the smile. This man was Gib in fifty years. "Thank you. We just might do that, Mr...?"

"O'Sullivan. Neil O'Sullivan at your service, ma'am." He tipped his head

"Well, I hope we meet again, Mr. O'Sullivan. You've been very helpful."

They rode down with him in the elevator, gathering what information they could in casual conversation about O'Sullivan's neighbor. As they exited on the first floor, Steve thanked the man, shaking his hand. O'Sullivan was so charming that instead of taking his extended hand, Josie gave him a kiss on the cheek. He was beaming as he turned to leave.

"Such a sweet man," Josie commented as they watched him depart.

As they passed the agent who had greeted them, Steve apologized and told her business had come up but they would try to return before the open house had ended. Josie took the card the agent offered as Steve rushed her toward the parking lot.

INSTEAD OF HEADING for the Mustang, Steve steered her toward Kevin's truck. "What's up?" Kevin asked as he jumped out to open the rear door for Josie. Steve followed her into the vehicle then waited for Kevin to get back behind the wheel.

"DiSantis arrived yesterday according to his neighbor. He's out right now, though." Steve looked around the lot. "We can't sit out here all night and wait for him to come back."

"We need a room," Josie said.

Kevin stifled a laugh. "Can't you two wait until we're back at the compound?"

"She's right," Steve responded, "for surveillance." He

turned to Josie. "You said this place reserves rooms like any hotel?" he asked, indicating the building behind them.

"It's a resort. A bit pricey but their website showed they do reserve rooms by the night."

"I'll see if they have anything available. Kevin, let me have your credit card and ID." The two men didn't look very much alike but did share some similar features. If the desk clerk was like most, though, he wouldn't look all that closely at the ID, assuming he'd look at it at all. Steve didn't want to take the chance that they'd trace him through his credit card again. Steve jumped out of the Tacoma as soon as Kevin handed over the ID and credit card then headed toward the entrance of the resort.

Inside the building, a sign directed people to the lobby on the second floor. Unusual, but the reasoning became clear as the doors opened to reveal the main lobby. A panoramic view of the waterways that separated the estuaries from the Gulf of Mexico greeted each guest as they approached the reception desk. Clerks stood with their back to the mangroves that dotted the sparkling water between the island and the mainland. Seagulls and pelicans, along with a few other birds he couldn't name, darted over the waters looking for dinner. As nice as this view was, what Steve wanted was a room with a view of the building next door.

Surprisingly, even with tourist season heating up, there were still rooms available. Steve managed to obtain one with a view of DiSantis' condo. Steve headed toward the elevators to check out the room and make sure it gave them the view they needed. When he reached the sixth floor, he pulled out his phone and called Rick. He was going to need some equipment. The naked eye would not be sufficient to spy on their neighbor, the small restaurant, and a parking garage separated the two buildings. None of them traveled with binoculars stuffed in their glovebox.

After inspecting the room and checking out the sixth floor, Steve returned to the parking lot. Josie turned to him as soon as he slid into the rear seat of Adam's truck. She was bouncing on her seat waiting for him to say something. Patience was not one of her virtues.

"Well?" she asked.

"I've got us a room. It has a good line of sight to DiSantis's condo." He told them, as he returned Kevin's identification to him. "I'm taking Josie with me. Rick is trying to round up some surveillance equipment. I don't know when he'll get here but he'll be texting us before he leaves Sanibel." Steve reached for the door's handle. "This place has security, so you may have to make yourself scarce. Use your own judgement but one option would be to check out the bar," Steve said, pointing to the *"Flippers"* sign. "Text me and let me know where I can find you but stay close. I want eyes on this entrance first and foremost. If you can find a spot that has a view of both condo entrances, even better."

Steve turned to Josie, "When I give you the word, get out and head straight to the door. Don't stop and make it quick." Steve made another visual check of the area.

Kevin climbed out of the driver's seat to provide cover, if needed. "Ready? Go." Steve jumped out of the truck and shoved Josie in front of him as she slid from the vehicle. Fortunately, she moved like a gazelle. He followed on her heels, his eyes scanning the area as they moved across the lot. When she reached the door, he was glued to her back.

As soon as they'd entered the condo, Josie had excused

herself to use the restroom. When she'd exited the bathroom, which was just off the foyer, Steve was on the other side of the unit, his imposing frame leaning against the sliding glass doors to the balcony. He looked…uncomfortable.

"Josie?"

"Yes?" she answered, hesitantly.

"We need to talk."

His tone was thoughtful. Not somber but definitely not light.

"About what?" Was this about them? Their future? She'd thought she'd made her feelings clear but she hadn't actually answered when he'd asked if she would stay with him. Had he changed his mind? She *was* trouble. She couldn't blame him if he walked away. It would serve her right to be put in the same position as she'd left him in.

"We have two choices."

"We do?" *God, just say it.*

"We can either stay here and keep an eye on DiSantis's place or I can have one of the guys take over the watch."

"What?"

"Do you want to stay here or return to the compound? Do you have a preference? Kevin or Don can take over here. I need to let one of them know. Kevin's downstairs so it would be a simple switch."

"That's it? That's what you wanted to discuss?" She grabbed a throw pillow and hurled it at him. He had her stressing out about concluding "the conversation" and all he'd wanted was her opinion on where to spend the night?

"What the hell?" Steve managed to block the flying object with this body before it sailed over the railing of the balcony. "What did you think I was talking about?" he asked.

"Us. I thought you wanted to talk about us."

"Why?"

Why *had* she thought that?

"You seemed nervous. Did I imagine that? I thought this was something serious."

He walked into the living room, threw the pillow onto the couch then took Josie's slender fingers into his hands. His thumbs rubbed gentle circles on the back of her hands as he looked into her eyes.

"I was trying to include you in a decision that concerned you. I haven't been very good at that, have I?" he said awkwardly.

"I wasn't very good at a lot of things," she responded.

"Josie, we're not going to work through our problems in a few short days. Particularly not while we're in the middle of this mess but I'd like the chance to try," Steve confessed. "Are you?"

Josie nodded unable to answer, as she reached to brush a tear from her cheek, Steve caught the droplet on the tip of his finger and touched it to his lips. The gesture was the most tender and meaningful action he could have taken.

"I wish this qualified as an argument and we had time for make-up sex," Steve smiled, changing the tone. He didn't need a blubbering woman with him on stake-out. "I've been away from the balcony too long." Steve grinned as he took her by the shoulders and set Josie back a few steps before heading towards the balcony. "What's your answer?" Steve asked over his shoulder quickly.

"About sex?" she joked.

"Unfortunately, the sex will have to wait," he grinned. "Do we stay here or call in replacements?"

"Let's stay. It's a beautiful view. I've yet to see a sunset since I've arrived," she said joining him on the balcony. She'd been a virtual prisoner in the house since the attack in the garden. Now she could see the sparkling water for miles.

This evening, the sun would slip below the water's edge and into the Gulf of Mexico. She wanted to stay and share the spectacle with Steve.

"This isn't a vacation. We're on stakeout," he reminded her.

Josie straightened her shoulders and saluted with a solemn face. "Yes, sir, Lieutenant." Inside, she was beaming. They were going to make this work.

$$\sim$$

.

While they waited for the delivery of equipment and the return of DiSantis, Josie and Steve sat on the balcony as the afternoon sun warmed the air. Steve talked about his family. He approached the subject carefully, gauging her response. She brightened when he related some of the trouble he'd gotten into when he was young. He found himself telling more stories about some of his stupid shit he did in high school just to hear her laughter. When he asked if she had any happy memories from her childhood, her forehead creased and a shadow creeped over her face as she thought about the question. She didn't back down, though, or change the subject this time. She came up with a few happy memories but those had involved people outside her immediate family. Her lack of fond memories went a long way to explaining her fears.

During their conversation, Steve rarely took his eyes away from the parking garage while Josie continually watched DiSantis's condo even though the naked eye was virtually useless. While he knew the make and model of the car DiSantis drove, the Mercedes SUV wouldn't be uncommon for this upscale area. Josie's chances of seeing

DiSantis in his condo from their location were even smaller. It was mid-afternoon when Steve received the text he'd been waiting for: *The equipment is on its way.*

A knock on the door sounded thirty minutes later. Steve left Josie on the balcony. Kevin had texted that the package was on its way up. Still Steve had his weapon in hand as he looked through the peephole. A familiar, crystal-blue eye stared back at him. Steve wrenched open the door.

His former commander strode into the room, tossing a duffel bag at Steve. Steve caught it, then quickly set it on the floor so he could greet his friend as Colt shut and secured the door.

"Colt," he said, a little surprised. "When did you get back and how did Rick rope you into being the errand boy?"

"Got back late this morning and walked into a full-blown scavenger hunt."

"Looks like they were successful." Steve indicated to the green duffel he'd just set down.

"Some of that equipment is on loan from the Sanibel PD so make sure Rick gets it back," Colt informed him. "And don't ask me where Gib got the rest of the stuff."

"How was your honeymoon?" Steve asked, as he led him deeper into the unit.

"It was a honeymoon, Steve, what do you think?"

Yeah, dumb question. Although, Josie and Steve had never had one, Steve didn't expect the couple saw much of the Southernmost City.

"So," Colt said, "Are you going to introduce me to Josie?"

JOSIE KNEW how much Steve respected Colt. The entire team

spoke well of their former commander. She was, frankly, intimidated by the legend. She'd intentionally stayed focused on the windows of their target condo, but now could no longer appear to be oblivious to the men in the living room.

Colt was instantly recognizable from the bedside photos. The man was tall, with shaggy black hair. He wore a bright Hawaiian style shirt and a pair of old jeans. As she reached out to the hand he'd offered, she was stunned by the color of his eyes. She had never encountered such an unusual shade of blue. Suddenly, her extended hand turned into a hook as Colt reeled her into an embrace. Locked against the tall man's chest, Josie eyed Steve, hoping for rescue. Steve smiled back at her. He was enjoying the scene.

"Where's Cat?" Steve asked.

Colt let Josie go. "Home. Unpacking."

"I'm sorry for any trouble I've caused," Josie said, moving to Steve's side.

"It's no problem, Josie. A little excitement keeps us on our toes," Colt laughed.

Steve placed the duffel bag next to the coffee table and began to unload its contents. Josie knew from the conversation they'd had while waiting for the package to arrive, the items Steve had requested. She could easily identify the binoculars. Then Steve pulled out something similar to the binoculars but with only one lens. Josie guessed that they were the night vision goggles, or NVG as Steve called them. A mini version of a satellite dish with a hand grip connected to a pair of head phones was the next item out of the bag. That had to be the parabolic microphone. Steve had wanted to be able to listen into any conversation from DiSantis's condo. Since it would be impossible to find and place a bug on short notice, he'd added the microphone to his wish list of items he'd given Rick.

Steve frowned as he scrutinized the item. He slipped on the headphones, headed to the balcony, pointing the dish in the direction of the restaurant below. After a good thirty seconds, Steve yanked the headphones off. "This isn't going to do it, Colt. Not powerful enough."

"I suspected as much but the guys did the best they could. Gib snatched that mic from God knows where. If he could have done better, I'm sure it would be in there."

"I didn't give them much time. We'll work with what we have. It's more than I started with."

"Gib threw a change of clothes for both of you since you might be stuck here for the night."

"Tell him thanks," Josie smiled.

"He's always happy to please a lady." Colt's expression turned serious. The corners of his mouth skewed as his intense blue eyes flicked from Steve to Josie now sitting across from him in the small living room.

"Is Josie coming back with me or staying here?" he asked.

"I'm staying," Josie answered without hesitation. Apparently, that was all Colt needed to hear.

"I know better than to argue with a woman," Colt said, rising to his full height. Josie strained her neck to look up at him. She guessed he was at least six-foot four.

"The hell you do," Steve laughed, getting to his feet, as well. "You and Cat make a sport out of it."

"Cat and I don't argue. We have spats. We like making up." Colt winked at Josie.

Josie's face reddened. *Make-up sex.* Had their sex lives become fodder for jokes?

"Gib talks too much," Steve said, smiling.

"He does, indeed," Colt answered, without argument. "If you guys are sure you're good here..."

"No one followed us. There's no reason for anyone to

suspect we're here. I checked-in under Kevin's name. It would take some time to make that connection, if they could do it at all. Whoever is behind this knows Josie was at the Copeland's so it's a good bet she safer here than back on Sanibel."

"Sounds good to me. You need anything else?" Colt asked.

"Nope," Steve said, slapping Colt on the shoulder. "Go take care of that wife of yours."

"I need to. Gib's practically sitting on her. Cat wants back in the garden. I don't want her out there under the circumstances. Not until we get a handle on this."

"The two of you should have stayed away a bit longer," Steve said. His brow wrinkled as he walked Colt to the door.

"Cat's stubborn but not stupid. We'll be fine. Just take care of Josie."

Steve turned both locks behind Colt.

Josie had walked out onto the balcony as the men were talking. She twisted a thick strand of hair into a knot. Cat was being kept from her garden. Josie knew from Gib how much the place meant to her. Of course, she'd want to check it out on her return and Josie was responsible for keeping her out of it.

"I feel like a jerk," she said as Steve joined her.

"Why?" Steve asked.

"I don't want to return to that place, Steve. I've interfered enough in their lives. What if Cat gets caught in the middle of this because of me? I've already made a mess of your friends' lives."

"Colt's not going to let anything happen to Cat. I can guarantee that," Steve said, brushing her hair behind her ear.

"How can you be sure?" she demanded.

"Because I know Colt and how he feels about Cat. It's the

same way I feel about you. Besides there are no less than three sets of eyes on her at this moment or Colt wouldn't have made the trip. He and Cat do like to scrap. It's entertaining as hell as long as her hissing isn't directed at you. We'll miss the show this time, but there will be others."

"It isn't funny, Steve. I don't want to be a burden to your friends anymore."

"First of all, they're *our* friends. Second, this mystery is about to come to an end. I can smell it. We're close. But if you want to stay here or somewhere else if this lead doesn't pan out then we can talk about it. Fair?"

He was asking for her input again. Neither of them was now assuming they knew what was better for the other. All the hurt they'd put each other through was because they hadn't talked. She felt unencumbered. Big word but it fit. "Fair," she agreed, smiling. "Just make sure those bastards know I'm gone from Cat's place so she's safe."

36

C at had stuffed a small lunch-size cooler bag inside the duffle which was filled with sandwiches, cookies, and chips. A note lay on top of the food. *"Take care of her. See you soon, Love, Cat."* Her sentiment and thoughtfulness was appreciated. It saved them the trouble of worrying about dinner.

Steve had given the binoculars to Josie while he fiddled with the parabolic mic. No adjustments or tweaks made it any stronger. He set it aside just as a dark Mercedes SUV stopped at the gate to the parking garage next door. The driver reached out and inserted a key card, opening the gate. The car fit the description of DiSantis's vehicle. As soon as Steve put his hand out, Josie slapped the binoculars into it. Another car waited at the gate after the SUV entered the garage. A few minutes later, a man fitting DiSantis's description walked out of the garage and inserted his key card, allowing the second vehicle to enter. The driver of that vehicle wasn't visible.

Steve trained the binoculars on DiSantis's condo and waited. A short time later, movement was visible in the fifth-floor unit. DiSantis approached the built-in bar Steve had spotted earlier through the binoculars. The man pulled two high-ball glasses from the cabinet and poured a hefty dose of amber liquid into each of them. A second man joined him as they gazed out on the water through their sliding glass door. Were they too nervous to step out onto the balcony?

Steve zoomed in on the second man. If he wasn't mistaken, DiSantis's guest was Joe Scagliotti. Steve grabbed his phone from the table and called Troy. He was still on bodyguard duty with McClaren.

"Do you still have Scagliotti's cell number?" Steve asked.

"Why? You need it?"

"Text it to me. But before you do, call him."

"He hasn't answered any of my other calls. Why would he answer this one?" Troy asked him.

"I don't care if he does. Just call him," Steve told Troy then he disconnected. He raised the binoculars again. Within minutes the second man reached into his pocket, pulled out his phone and studied it. Bingo.

Steve sent a group text with the news that Scagliotti and DiSantis where together.

"What next?" Josie asked.

"Watch and wait. Three people on that list are in the same neighborhood. Something is about to happen and happen soon." He was sure of it.

Josie had gotten her view of the setting sun as activity in the condo consisted of talking and drinking when the occupants where in sight. The lights had gone on in DiSantis' unit which made the pair easier to watch. The men's body language was telling. Their movements were agitated. Hands flew as they talked. Neither of them stood still. Then both disappeared from view and within seconds the lights to the unit went out. They were on the move.

248

Steve sprung out of his chair, grabbing his keys and his phone. "Josie, promise me you'll stay put. I need to follow them."

"They could be going out for dinner."

"Could be, but I'm not losing sight of them. Stay put for me, baby."

Steve called Kevin as he raced toward the door. They both needed to be ready in the event the men split up.

Moments later, Steve hit the stairwell. He didn't have time to wait for an elevator that might stop at every floor. His feet flew, springing from step to step. Using the railing, he launched himself around each turn. As he stepped out on the ground floor, he took one short second to ease his breathing so he wouldn't be noticed then double-timed it to his car. The Mustang's engine was purring before the SUV exited the garage. It was followed by Scagliotti's sedan. *Damn it.*

He didn't like it but he and Kevin had discussed the possibility as soon as Steve had confirmed that Scagliotti had joined DiSantis. Kevin slid in behind Scagliotti, who'd turned right heading north through Fort Myers Beach. Steve hung back then fell in behind DiSantis who headed the opposite direction—south through Lovers Key State Park.

The stretch of highway was not as dense as Fort Myers Beach but still busy. Steve trailed the man carefully. The circuitous route DiSantis was taking was either packed with other vehicles or had wide open side streets. Neither made tailing easy. Hopefully, in the darkness, DiSantis wouldn't spot Steve's unique vehicle. DiSantis turned north on U.S. 41, then finally to a road that was familiar to Steve. McClaren's home was a short distance away. The hairs rose on the back of his neck. This wasn't a coincidence.

About two miles after the turn onto the six-lane highway,

his phone rang. "What?" Steve asked, hitting the speaker button.

"McClaren just got a call from Scagliotti." Troy told Steve. "He wants to see McClaren. Says he's on his way."

"So is DiSantis. Hold tight until you hear from me."

Steve called Kevin. "Where's Scagliotti?"

"He just pulled into a convenience store parking lot. He's sitting in his car. My guess is he's waiting for someone."

"Where are you?"

"Next to the entrance to Pelican Landing. If Scagliotti moves, I'll let you know."

"I don't think he's going anywhere. Not yet, at least." Scagliotti and DiSantis were headed for a rendezvous. The question was why all the subterfuge? He damn sure was going to find out.

As soon as DiSantis slipped into the parking space next to Scagliotti, Steve blocked them both in with his Mustang. Kevin, who was parked at the other end of the lot so he could keep his eye on Scagliotti, exited his vehicle as soon as he saw Steve's car. Kevin and Steve approached the drivers' door cautiously. Steve's bigger worry was that they would bolt.

The targets had stayed in their cars. Steve asked the men to put their hands where they could see them. They had both complied but not before shooting each other worried looks. Their fingers trembled as they draped their hands across the steering wheel. Kevin and Steve then opened each driver's doors in what must have appeared as a choreographed move.

"Get out of your cars and put your hands against the doors," Steve told them.

Kevin sent Steve a wry smile. So what if it sounded like a bad line from an old gangster movie? Steve wasn't taking any chances. Too many people had already died.

"Step out of your vehicles, please," Steve repeated with authority.

"Are you the police?" Scagliotti asked, his hands visibility shaking as he leaned against the door to his Audi.

"Did Deets send you?" DiSantis asked, sliding out of his SUV.

"Hands where we can see them," Steve told them. "And no to both questions."

Kevin and Steve patted down their targets. If anyone noticed, Steve hoped they'd think it was police business and keep their noses out of it.

"We're the ones you've been talking to regarding Esteban and the Middle Keys Camp," Steve told them when the pat down was finished.

"Now you want to tell us why you two are sitting outside the entrance to Tony McClaren's subdivision? When we interviewed you, you stated that you barely knew each other and that you hadn't been in contact with anyone from the camp since that summer."

"You're not connected to Deets?" DiSantis questioned Steve a second time. Sweat beaded on his forehead despite the cool November night.

"And I told you, no. What has this got to do with Deets or McClaren? I assume that's why you're here."

"We just wanted to talk to McClaren. We hoped the three of us could figure out the best way to deal with Deets," Scagliotti admitted.

"One more time," Steve said, with more steel in in voice. "What has Deets got to do with this?"

"We think he had something to do with the disappearance of that girl," DiSantis confessed.

"Why would you think that?" Kevin asked. He'd taken a stand near the front of the vehicles so he could keep a bead on both men.

"Do we have to discuss this here? Out in the open?" DiSantis looked around nervously.

Steve checked the lot. No one lingered but it was busy and wide open. He should have moved them sooner. "If you two gentlemen will step to the front of your vehicles, my friend here will check your cars. Then we'll escort you to your destination."

Kevin quickly searched the vehicles for weapons while Steve kept his eyes on them. Kevin removed a small hand gun from each and tucked them in the waistband of his jeans.

The men returned to their respective vehicles and followed Steve into the upscale subdivision. Kevin brought up the rear. He'd called Troy while Kevin was searching the cars and told him of their impending arrival and to alert the security gate. It looked like they were going to have a party.

KEVIN PARKED in the street in front of McClaren's place. He immediately jumped out of his truck and motioned both DiSantis and Scagliotti into the driveway of McClaren's house. Steve parked in the street, blocking both vehicles in. Kevin reached Scagliotti's car just as Steve reached DiSantis's SUV. They opened the doors and motioned the men up the winding pathway toward the front door of the sprawling home.

Troy opened the door as they approached. McClaren stood in the middle of his massive living room, visibly anxious as he studied his former campmates. Understandable. They'd all lived normal lives since that summer—until this past week. Now they were caught in the middle of a nightmare.

Steve quickly took in the main room. Troy was no doubt responsible for the drawn blinds. A hurricane shutter had been lowered over the large window facing the rear of the property. Hurricane shutters had also been placed over the large sliding door to the patio. Troy knew how to secure the space. Steve didn't look any further.

"Mr. McClaren. Do you remember Joe Scagliotti and Peter DiSantis?" Steve asked.

No one shook hands. The older men nodded in a simple acknowledgement as they seated themselves in the massive room. The tension was palpable.

DiSantis was shorter and wider than Scagliotti. Both had thinning hair and tanned skinned, not unusual for full-time residents of Florida. While they were both about the same age, Scagliotti looked ten years younger than DiSantis—and a lot more nervous.

"What is it you wanted with me?" McClaren asked the two men, breaking the silence. He gestured toward the empty couch. His former campmates sat but both remained on the edge of the cushions.

"To put our heads together," DiSantis told him. "See what you remembered about the camp. The news of Esteban's and Roemer's deaths made me nervous. We were all together that summer."

"Why me? I wasn't part of your group." McClaren added.

"You were there that day," DiSantis said. "And we were both questioned recently about whether we knew you."

"A man was asking questions. We didn't know who he was," Scagliotti cautiously looked toward the three large men, who were now standing behind McClaren. He'd taken a seat across from them. "I'm assuming it was one of you?"

"You told Troy you hadn't spoken since that summer. Was that a lie?" Steve asked.

"No. That was the truth. I found Peter on Facebook after your guy called. Messaged him then we spoke on the phone."

"You still haven't explained why you're here," Steve pressed.

"Because we were afraid to go to the police," DiSantis blurted out.

"Why?" Steve turned to the stocky, perspiring man.

The old saying "the cat's got your tongue" came to mind. DiSantis had looked like he'd swallowed his.

Steve turned to Scagliotti. "Why were you afraid of the police?" he asked, mentally leaping hurdles. He knew where this was going. "Did you talk to Deets?" he added.

Even with their tans, the color visibly drained from both the men's faces. That answered Steve's question. "What did he say?"

"To keep our mouths shut about that summer," Scagliotti answered

"Was it you who talked to him?" Steve asked him.

"Look, I don't know if this is a good idea," the man responded, as he glanced at the front door.

"Do you plan on winding up like Roemer and Esteban? They hadn't spoken with anyone and look what happened to them. Take a guess how long your life span will be if Deets finds out you've talked to us. The man has ways of finding things out." Steve paused to let that sink in. "Do you believe he had something to do with Carr's disappearance?"

"Personally? I think he killed her," Scagliotti said.

"Why?" Steve asked.

"I didn't put it together until this week," the marina owner answered, sheepishly. "He'd left the cabin the night Ruth Carr disappeared. The rest of us figured he was scoring again. He'd already screwed half the girls at camp and bragged about it. Carr was a looker but she didn't give him the time of day. The few times I saw her, she seemed distant. He said she was snotty."

"And you didn't share this information with anyone?" The question was rhetorical. Steve's hands tightened into fists as he fought the urge to beat the crap out of both of them. They had a budding sexual predator for a roommate. They either didn't recognize one or turned their heads. More than likely the second. Too many men and boys chose ignorance or accepted the depraved comments of others, writing it off as locker room talk. Would Ruth Carr be alive today if either of these men had spoken up? They'd never know.

"We were fifteen years old at the time." Scagliotti explained. "We all thought he was just talking trash. Now he's a State Attorney. We can't go to the authorities with our suspicions. No one would take our word against his."

"We're working with the authorities now. Are you willing to talk with them?" Steve asked.

"Do we have a choice?" DiSantis asked. "If we don't, we're dead anyway."

"Deets is pissed," Scagliotti stated, wringing his hands. "He's being blackmailed—or has been."

"He told you that?" Steve was staring at the man, astounded that Deets would make that kind of revelation.

"No. But he warned me not to try it. Said no one else was going to put the 'squeeze' on him and get away with it. He told me twice to keep my mouth shut. 'Dead men tell no tales.' Those were his exact words," Scagliotti told them.

"You do realize he can find your condo as easily as we did, don't you?" Steve was talking to DiSantis now.

"I'd hoped it might take him a while. I have several properties. We wanted to put our heads together with McClaren."

"I didn't share a cabin with your group at camp," McClaren said. "What made you think I could help?"

"Your name is on that list. He told us so," DiSantis said indicating Troy. "We're tied together. Like it or not."

"We didn't know who you guys were working for," DiSantis said turning to Steve. "We didn't know who to trust."

SINCE TROY WAS ALREADY STATIONED at McClaren's and the home had been secured, they agreed that Scagliotti and DiSantis would stay there. Keeping the men together, would make things easier on the team. With Cat now at home, Colt would want someone with her at all times. With the attack on Josie in the garden, Colt wouldn't be taking any chances. He'd be her shadow but if for some reason that wasn't possible then he'd need back-up. Don would remain on Sanibel and continue to untangle threads that led back to Deets while he helped to watch over Cat. Gib and Rick would also serve as back-up there, when needed. Troy assured them he didn't need relief but agreed to call if he did. Kevin would return to Lovers Key to provide back-up for Steve.

As soon as the logistics regarding the team were solidified, Steve was in his Mustang and breaking speed limits to get to Josie. He didn't like leaving her alone even though he was confident their location wasn't known—yet. It was unlikely that they'd look for Kevin's trail but not impossible. His gut told him the shit was about to hit the fan—and soon. He wanted to be with Josie when it did.

His phone, which he'd tossed on the passenger seat when

he got in the car, began to play "Night Moves." Josie's ringtone.

"You okay?" he answered.

"Are you on your way?"

"Yes. Why?"

"Because I just received an email from Deets."

37

"Shit! What did he want? You haven't responded, have you?"

"You think I'm crazy? How the hell did he get my personal email address? I use my business address for everyone but a few."

"Josie, they were able to track you to Sanibel while you were totally off the grid. Getting your email address would be child's play."

Steve couldn't unleash his anger or fear for Josie. Could they have found her again? He pushed his car to its limits which wasn't much once he'd turned onto Estero Boulevard. It was packed with tourists hopping from one drinking establishment to another. Then there was the tangle of construction. He gripped the wheel harder, willing the roads to open up so he could pass through.

"True." He'd already forgotten the statement that promoted her remark.

"What did he want?" Why had the jerk contacted Josie?

"A meeting."

"Did he say why?"

"To quote him, 'to make me an offer I couldn't refuse.' I thought they only said that in the movies."

"Scagliotti believes Deets is being blackmailed."

"Okay. Now that makes sense. And he thinks I'm the blackmailer. Why?"

"You know about Ruth Carr. I'd say he's convinced you know more about what happened. Scagliotti and DiSantis believe he killed Carr."

"How would he know what I know? And why are those two just now mentioning it?"

His phone vibrated with her outrage. The conversation itself could have waited, but he wanted to keep Josie on the phone until he got back to the resort. He couldn't let her know how freaked he was by the email from Deets so he kept the conversation rolling as he maneuvered through traffic. "They didn't make the connection until all this hit the fan." He related the details of the meeting at McClaren's, adding information that wasn't necessary to their conversation to keep her talking. Relief flooded through his limbs as he turned into the resort.

Josie was standing in the foyer as he came through the door. She threw herself into Steve's arms the minute he latched the door behind him. "What are we going to do?" she asked.

We. In spite of all that was happening, he zeroed in on the "we" part of her question. She wasn't asking what she or he would do but what they would do—together. He brushed her cheek with the back of his fingers. This time, everything between them would be alright.

"*We* are going to end this. Then, we're going to start over."

With Josie at his side, Steve headed back out to his spot on the balcony, which was still shrouded in darkness. He called Colt and he read off the email Josie had received from her phone.

"Go ahead with the meet," Colt said. "Josie could wear a wire."

"That's crazy."

"Put him on speaker," Josie told him, her eyes going cold.

"Hang on, Colt," he said, taking Josie's hand to lead her back inside. It wouldn't be good if the conversation was overheard by someone on another balcony nearby. Steve left the slider open to let in the cool November night air and walked Josie deeper into the unit. "Why would you suggest that we set up a meet between Josie and Deets? He's a State Attorney. He'd suspect Josie of wearing a wire right off the bat."

Colt paused at the other end of the line. Josie jumped in. "I don't need to wear a wire if we already have one in place."

"What do you mean?" Steve asked.

"We pick a small place. Find a way to direct him to a certain table. I'm sure Rick or Gib can find some sort of electronic device indiscreet enough to plant under the table to record."

As he stared at her dumbfounded, she explained, "I'm a journalist, Steve. While I don't muck around in the dirt with the tabloid journalists, I do know how it's done."

"That still doesn't explain why he won't suspect you of wearing a wire," Steve pointed out.

"Because I'll be wearing a very tiny swimsuit," she said slowly, speaking toward the phone that now lay on the breakfast bar.

"The hell you will." When Steve's eyes snapped to hers. Josie's eyes were sparkling with amusement.

"What did you have in mind, Josie?" Colt asked, once he'd stopped laughing.

THE OUTLINE of an idea had formed in Josie's head while they were talking. She'd know in a minute if it was crazy. Steve was going to believe she was unhinged, regardless.

"Well, since Deets is anxious to see me and we're already here, we could meet at that Flippers place downstairs. It's small, open and from what I can tell from here, there's not a seat in the bar that can't be watched from one angle or another." She faced Steve. "I assume you or Kevin will check it out first. You'll make it safe."

Steve was still watching her intently but had remained silent, so she plunged on. "Deets is not known in this part of the state so he shouldn't be worried about being recognized. With the restaurant next to the pool it will give me the excuse for wearing a bathing suit, if I need it to show I'm not wired," she teased.

"You won't need it," Steve growled.

Josie stopped baiting Steve. "Deets may fly here," she conjectured, "but he wouldn't want to leave a trail." A thought dawned on her. "He's not a private pilot, is he?"

"I didn't see any record of that in Don's dossier on him," Colt said.

"Then my bet is he'll drive down. That will give us time to get everything ready. More time if I wait to respond." Josie looked over at Steve. Muscles taut, eyes focused, he was gearing up for a fight.

"It could work," Colt agreed.

"I don't like it," Steve snarled.

"Why am I not surprised?" Josie countered, patting his cheek.

"You wouldn't like it very much if we were setting Cat out as bait," Steve said into the phone. "You *didn't* like it much this past summer."

"Steve is right. If this guy is responsible for the deaths and disappearances of the people connected to that list, we don't want him anywhere near you."

"If he's the man behind all this, I can't run from him forever. He'll find me sooner or later if he's not stopped." And if he was the one behind this shit, then Josie wanted him to pay for whatever happened to Ruth Carr and possibly stop it from happening again.

"Steve," Josie implored him. "We can't play this cat and mouse game forever."

"She's right, Colt," Steve huffed. "If Deets is the one cleaning house, Josie won't be safe until he's taken down. Neither will the men at McClaren's. He has too much power. Too long a reach."

"And if we're wrong?" Colt asked.

"Then we've wasted time," Steve answered, "but you don't believe that any more than I do. If Deets comes the length of this state to talk to Josie, it's not so Josie can do a 'feel good' story on him."

"Okay," Colt said. The breath he expelled was audible. "If we're going to do this, let's do it right. Let's nail the bastard."

JOSIE LEFT Steve to work out the details with Colt. It might have been her idea for the sting but she was still scared as hell. Fighting the need to brush the imaginary ants from her skin, she took refuge in the bedroom away from Steve's watchful eyes. She could be facing a killer tomorrow. How the hell was she going to pull that off?

Suffocating with fear, Josie opened the sliding door to the bedroom's balcony to let in some fresh air. Melodies from the bar below now drifted in on a breeze. It was late. The chatter was low. The music was clear. What would it be like to be normal again? To wander downstairs for a drink or dance with Steve in the moonlight.

"Josie?"

Had her thoughts magically conjured the man up?

"What are you doing?" he asked, softly.

"Wishing. I imagine there are stars out there I could wish upon," she said, poking at the sheers that still covered the window. She'd known better than to venture out on the balcony alone. No point in frightening Steve.

"What were you wishing for?"

"Do you really want to know?"

"Yes, Josie. We agreed. No more secrets," he said. He reached for her hand.

"To dance."

"Dance?"

She smiled at his look of shock. Not what he'd been expecting. "Can you hear that?" she asked, cocking her head toward the open slider. Ed Sheeran's "Thinking Out Loud" floated into the room. "I want to dance in the moonlight with the man I love."

FOR AN INSTANT, Steve thought she was joking but the anticipation he saw in her eyes told him she was sincere. *Dance?* He'd never been much of a dancer.

Sure, they both loved music. It wasn't uncommon for

them to have something playing in the background when they were home, in the car, or making love. But dancing? They had never danced together. If he'd given her the wedding she deserved they would have had a wedding dance. He owed her that. At the very least, he owed her that dance.

He opened the slider fully and guided her out onto the balcony. As she suspected, stars dotted the clear, crisp night sky. His large arms circled her waist. Pulling her to his chest he began to sway to the rhythm of the love song.

38

The next morning, they were out of bed and dressed in time to see the sunrise. Last evening's slow dance had evolved into an all-night, horizontal tango. Hands, arms, and legs had encircled each other as they inched their way across the surface of the king size bed. Sleep was fleeting and secondary. They'd been hungry for each other and edgy about the day to come.

Savoring a steaming cup of coffee, Josie waited with Steve for the team to arrive.

It was amazing how quickly the plans had gelled. Rick had worked with the Lee County Sheriff's office as well as the owners of the resort and bar to gain permission for the surveillance and use of their property. The group's suspicions that Deets was behind two murders and possibly a third, were just that—suspicions.

Rick was well respected in the law enforcement community. In addition, he had the full support of his chief, who had an interesting and stellar background that Rick said he wasn't free to discuss. Between the two men, cooperation from other agencies was secured. No sitting State Attorney would be brought in for questioning simply on theories. Any questioning would lead nowhere and show their hand. But if Deets believed that Josie was a blackmailer, then the meeting might get them the proof they needed. The Sheriff's Office would be sending a plainclothes detective to observe. There had been no argument from anyone. This was their jurisdiction.

Rick had also notified the Florida Department of Law Enforcement. If a State Attorney was involved in a felony, they would eventually be taking the lead in the investigation. FDLE had been less than excited about the plan but they'd also had previous dealings with Rick and, as a result, trusted his judgment. They were waiting cautiously for the outcome of the meeting.

Gib arrived at the crack of dawn bitching about the ungodly hour while making Josie smile. She poured him some coffee while he and Steve retrieved items from a small canvas bag he'd brought with him.

Josie was handed a throw-away cell for her to use when it came time to contact Deets. Gib produced a pair of earwigs from the bag, similar to the devices she and her coworkers had used to communicate back when she'd worked retail in college. Josie immediately thought of Victoria's Secret. She wouldn't be surprised to hear that Gib knew the sales clerks there.

Josie couldn't place the other items Gib pulled out but guessed they were the microphone and recording device Rick had procured from the Lee County Sheriff's Office. Unlike the parabolic mic, this one was tiny so Steve should have no problem hiding it underneath the railing next to the table reserved for their special guest.

Troy, Kevin, and Don arrived shortly after Gib to review the details of the plan with Steve. Troy had been relieved from security at McClaren's by an off-duty officer and friend of Rick's. Troy would be a lone sunbather by the pool, allowing for a view of the front of the resort, the parking area, and the bar. He was dressed the part in swim trunks, shades and, a very tight t-shirt. He wouldn't be alone long once the ladies at the resort spotted him.

Kevin and Don were playing the part of buddies having spent the morning fishing. They would arrive at Flippers around lunch and then sip beers the rest of the afternoon telling fish tales. Once Josie arrived, one of them would attempt to record the meeting surreptitiously. It was unclear how they'd manage that, but Josie kept the question to herself. Text messages would be used to keep in touch. There'd be no reason for Deets to consider it unusual that other patrons were on their phones.

Colt and Rick were remaining on Sanibel. Gib thought it was hysterical that Colt couldn't join in the fun because of Cat. The woman had been obsessed with becoming part of the sting. "She'd have figured out a way, too, if Colt wasn't sitting on her," Gib said with a twinkle in his eye.

Rick was hanging back out of respect for the jurisdiction of others. Gib would be keeping them informed via group text. He'd volunteered to be the conduit for Steve and report to the others. His long blond hair, which he normally wore tied at the base of his neck, would easily hide the earpiece if he left his thick mane loose.

The bartender and other staff would be made aware of the operation. They were long time, trusted employees. The owner had vouched for them. His concern had been for their safety. Rick had assured him they would not be in harm's way.

Since Steve had already met Deets, he could not openly play a part in the scenario. The resort owners had agreed to add him to the general maintenance staff for the day. He would be keeping the area close to the bar spotless and wearing the other earwig.

Per Steve's instructions, Josie emailed Deets at 9:00 a.m. and set the time of the meet for three o'clock that afternoon at Flippers. She relayed the pre-paid cell number to Deets in her responding email and instructed him that all future communications would be conducted using that number. It should take him between five and six hours of straight driving to get there.

Fortunately for Josie, Gib stuck around after the others took off to play their roles. He had a few hours before he needed to take up the part of what he'd deemed as "a bar fly." The man liked to talk and didn't give Josie time to dwell on what was to come.

THE DOCK STEVE was cleaning ran the length of the resort and restaurant. It had several places for watercraft to tie up so boaters could stop and enjoy a drink or a meal. Flippers, however, was not at dock level. The restaurant sat several feet above the platform, providing patrons with a breathtaking view of Estero Bay. Still, from his position, Steve could easily see Kevin and Don sitting by the railing as they nursed beers. He didn't have a view of Gib from this position at the bar but the lady's man would periodically check in with Steve to tell him all was quiet or complain about missing an opportunity to hit on a "hot chick". Troy was eye level with Steve, "relaxing" by the pool. Now, if their villain in this scene would finally arrive.

Shortly before the appointed time, a dark sedan pulled into one of the empty spaces near the bar. The driver didn't opt for the valet parking that was offered for guests. Steve locked onto the vehicle still maintaining his guise of scrubbing the dock. It matched the description of Deets's car. Sure enough, the door of the Cadillac opened to reveal the man Steve had met in Jacksonville. The State Attorney's eyes darted over the landscape then focused on his destination: the stairs leading to the bar.

The State Attorney moved out of Steve's field of vision but Kevin, Don and Gib should have the man in sight. The assumption was confirmed a moment later via Steve's earpiece. "The asshole has landed," Gib reported in a hushed voice.

Steve gathered his bucket and cleaning supplies then made his way along the dock, setting up closer to the bar where he would have a clear view of Deets. With the exception of the table they'd designated for Deets, all the tables had been made to appear to be in use or recently vacated. It worked flawlessly.

After briefly looking the place over, Deets settled at the predetermined spot and pulled out his phone. He glanced at the screen then placed it face down on the table as a server approached. After his order was taken, Deets took out a second phone. A burner, probably. He quickly sent a text message. Josie would be receiving it within seconds.

GIB HAD TEXTED Josie the minute Deets had entered the bar. Still, she jumped when the cell phone purchased solely for conversations with Deets pinged. A tiny electrical storm erupted as nerves danced over her skin. *Get it under control, girl.* She was supposed to be a confident, greedy blackmailer when she sat down with the man. He'd have the upper hand if he thought she was a frightened rabbit.

C. F. FRANCIS

Wiping her sweating palms on her jeans, Josie grabbed the phone and opened the text message. *"Waiting at the designated location."* Damn, the man was careful. No mention of where he was or their names. Why, if he was so cautious, did he want to meet with her face-to-face?

She'd know soon enough.

Josie grabbed the cell phone Gib had picked up for her personal use shortly after she'd arrived on Sanibel and tucked it into the back pocket of her jeans. The burner which had been purchased solely for communications with Deets, was in her hand. The elevator ride to the ground floor was mercifully quick. It wasn't unusual, she'd been briefed, for guests to stop by the front desk to pick up towels on their way to the pool but right now making small talk with tourists would be a distraction she didn't need. And, since she was channeling her inner bitch, it wouldn't be a very pleasant experience for the guests.

She and Steve had tossed around several tracks to get Deets to reveal his part in this Rubik's Cube of a puzzle. She needed to approach the meeting as she would an interview for a story and still let him believe she was willing to make a profit for her silence. Easier said than done.

Josie needed to ask questions that might lead him to divulge information that would incriminate him. She was supposed to have information Deets was willing to pay to keep buried—or give him a reason to bury her. *Don't go there.* After Gib left this morning, she once again reviewed the data she had on Deets and the camp. She needed to lure him out with bait. She was on another fishing expedition. This time, however, it wasn't with a net. She was going to need a very big hook.

Of course, if the man was accommodating enough to offer Josie a payoff to keep her mouth shut about a crime he'd committed, FDLE would have their case on a silver platter. But Deets was a prosecutor. He'd be very careful how he worded any offer. Then again, research had shown him to be arrogant, which sometimes made people stupid.

Josie straightened her spine and threw back her shoulders as the elevator doors opened. She could do this. This bastard, in a convoluted way, had led her back to Steve. As a result, she had a second chance. A chance Josie had no intention of squandering. Josie recognized the mistakes she'd made and the misconceptions that she had held. But now she saw them clearly and in seeing them, she would be able to maneuver past them. But she and Steve weren't going anywhere until this threat was no longer hovering over them. So, she would succeed.

Josie turned toward the front entrance. Her route would take her past the glass door that led to the pool where Troy would be watching for her. The plan was for Troy to text Gib, informing him of her imminent arrival as she headed outside.

"Josie, wait."

Josie stopped then smiled as the voice registered.

"Erica?" she whirled around, the smile freezing on her face as her eyes made contact with the semi-automatic pistol pointed at her chest. "What the hell?"

"Move!"

"What? Why?" Her knees began shaking so hard she could almost hear them clacking together.

"You managed to fuck up one of my plans. I'm not going to let you screw with my current one."

It took a second but then the light came on in Josie's attic. "*You're* the one blackmailing Deets?"

"We don't have time to discuss this here." Erica motioned with her gun. "Move!"

39

Steve watched Deets. He kept looking at his phone. He was getting nervous.

Josie should have made it to the bar by now. This was the beginning of the end of this whole nightmare. No way in hell she'd delay or bail.

Steve yanked his own phone from his pocket and dialed Troy. "Have you seen her?" he asked.

"No. She hasn't passed the door yet."

"Find her," Steve barked. "She should be out by now." He hit the talk button on his radio.

"Josie's missing," he said to Gib. "Alert the others."

He was halfway through the entrance to the resort when a familiar and gut-wrenching sound reverberated down the narrow hallway. A gunshot.

He prayed Troy was the one doing the shooting as he sprinted past the elevators and out the rear door. As soon as he did, he saw Troy standing at the seawall. He turned as Steve came out the rear door. His right hand still held his gun but his left arm hung limp. Blood covered the sleeve of his t-shirt and ran down his arm.

The engine of a boat revved, drawing Steve's attention. The small craft had just cleared a mangrove and was pulling further away from the seawall.

Troy lifted his gun hand and pointed toward the boat. "Josie's in there. I couldn't get a clear shot. She has Josie."

"Who has Josie?" Steve asked, reaching Troy's side.

"Whoever is piloting that boat. Slim, red-haired woman. She had a bead on me the minute I rounded the building," Troy said.

"Erica?" They'd all reviewed Erica's Facebook posts. She was a beautiful woman with long red hair. None of them figured she was alive.

"Looked like her," Troy winced when Steve pressed his palm over the gouge in his shoulder.

"Was Josie hurt?"

"I don't know," Troy admitted. "She was already in the boat when I came around the building. Josie was fighting, though. She threw her weight at the woman, ruining her shot at me."

Gib came barreling out from between two parked cars, a cell phone in his hand.

"Where's Deets?" Steve asked, snatching the phone from Gib. It was Josie's. *Shit*.

"Don and Kevin have him out front. He tried to take off the minute he heard the shot." Gib took off his shirt and traded places with Steve, pressing the material against Troy's bicep. "Where's Josie?"

"Out there," Steve said, indicating the water. He was done talking. "Call nine-one-one," he yelled over his shoulder at Gib as he bolted toward the front of the building. He was damn well going to find out what was going on and where Erica was taking Josie.

Erica. He didn't doubt Troy's conclusion for a minute.

What were the chances there were two redheaded women involved in this clusterfuck? It had to be Erica. But why?

They were going to need help and need it fast. Steve punched Rick's number as he approached the trio standing near the front entrance.

Deets stood tall and defiant. Don had one hand on the man's shoulder. His other hand circled the attorney's upper arm. The older man wouldn't make a scene trying to break free of Don's grip. Deets was a politician, after all.

"Call in the troops," Steve said as soon as Rick answered. "Notify the Coast Guard and whatever other authorities have jurisdiction down here. Land and water. Erica has Josie. We need all the help we can get."

As soon as Troy and Gib caught up, Steve handed his phone off to Troy. "Give Rick a description of the woman and the boat," he told him.

"Remember me?" Steve asked their guest. The question dripped with loathing.

"What the hell do you want?" Deets snarled as soon as he recognized Steve.

"Get him upstairs," Steve said, addressing Kevin and Don. "We need to talk with him in private."

"I'm not going anywhere," Deets stated defiantly.

Steve's mouth came within an inch of Deets's ear. "You'll get your ass upstairs quietly or I'll use your balls for fish bait." The words came out clearly and thick with promise. The man's eyes widened but his feet moved.

Troy was already holding the door to the entrance open. Steve indicated to Don to go ahead. The police and paramedics were pulling into the complex. Steve wanted Deets out of sight until he got answers.

"Rick, Colt and Cat are on their way," Troy told him, dropping Steve's phone into his hand.

"What happened to Gib?" Steve asked.

"Taking another look around."

Not a bad idea. It wasn't likely that Troy had been mistaken, but you didn't take chances. They needed eyes on street level. Steve nodded toward the incoming EMT and Sheriff's units.

"Go," he said to Troy. "Get that shoulder looked at and buy us some time, if you can."

For all Gib's wishing, their best chance to find Josie lay with the man who was being forced onto the elevator. The trip to the sixth floor was made in silence. Don led them down the hallway and unlocked the door with the key card Steve passed to him. Kevin, who'd kept a tight grip on Deets's shoulder, shoved him inside. When Steve ordered their "guest" to sit, he stood defiantly. Fine. The gloves were off.

"Where's Josie?"

"I don't know who you're talking about."

"The woman you we're going to meet."

"It's none of your damn business. I like to keep my private life private and off the front page of the local paper. She didn't show. It has nothing to do with any conspiracy theory you've dreamed up." Deets started to walk past Steve as if that answer finished their business.

Steve shoved him back. "That 'woman' you were going to meet happens to be my wife." Steve took little pleasure as Deets's tanned skin turned a sickly gray. He'd just given the man who'd threatened to fillet his family jewels a reason to follow through with that threat.

"I DIDN'T MEAN it in that sense," Deets backpedaled, quickly. "It was just a business meeting."

"Right now, I want to know where Erica took my Josie." Steve demanded.

"Erica?"

"Yes. Erica. What does she want with Josie? Where did they go?"

Deets didn't answer but his pallor changed as quickly as a chameleon's. It was now an angry red. *Erica*. The name had been the trigger. "I didn't know Erica was here. I've been looking for the bitch for weeks."

Hunting would be more like it which would explain the flag on Erica's name and the thread that led Deets to Josie.

"Why?

Deets didn't answer.

"Why are you looking for Erica and what's it got to do with my wife?" Steve was trained in interrogation. Anger was not the way to approach this yet he could not contain it. He quickly had him in an arm lock and pushed him toward the balcony. "We're six floors up. Just imagine the damage a fall like that would do," Steve threatened.

"You wouldn't dare. It's murder!" The older man struggled against Steve's hold, twisting in his grasp as he looked to the two large men who'd remained at the balcony's entrance. His eyes were wide. "You can't let him do this," he pleaded but neither Kevin or Don moved to help him.

"If one hair on her head is harmed," Steve warned him, "I won't give a rat's ass what happens to me. Where the hell is she?"

"I don't know," Deets begged. "I came here to reason with Boussard. To pay her off, if that's what it took. Kill the story."

"Kill the story or kill Josie? Like you did Esteban and Roemer?" Steve pulled Deets off the railing and shoved him up against the balcony wall, his forearm pressing against the man's chest. Steve stared down into the bastard's fixed, wide eyes. In spite of the cooler weather, Steve could smell the perspiration on his skin. *Good*.

"I didn't kill those men," he protested.

"No. You had somebody do it for you." Steve pressed him further against the wall but Deets remained silent.

"What about Ruth Carr? What happened to her? Is she dead?"

Again, the man didn't respond. Silence was often a tool used by those who didn't possess the talent to lie convincingly.

"When did the blackmailing start?" Steve shoved him a little harder into the wall.

"What blackmailing?"

Steve quickly flipped Deets's position and had him in another arm lock. Anger vibrated through every muscle of Steve's body as he crushed Deets into the wall. He'd break the man's arm, if he had to.

"Okay. Okay," Deets answered. "Let me breathe." Steve let up the pressure on the man's back so he could fill his lungs.

"After Erica sent your wife that email with the information about the camp. That's when it started. Erica wouldn't dare blackmail me. It has to be your wife."

Josie wasn't blackmailing anyone but the timing cleared Steve's head. The last piece of the puzzle had been revealed. Erica was behind this elaborate plan to terrorize Josie. From friending Josie on Facebook, to the email and text. Why and where had she taken Josie?

"Where would Erica go?" Steve tried again, although he now believed Deets had been duped as well. Erica had orchestrated events to make Deets believe that Josie was given information and was now using it to extort payments from him. Erica had to be the blackmailer but why would she lead Deets to Josie? "If anything happens to Josie," Steve promised, "you won't live to regret it. Where are they?"

"Back off, Steve."

Steve pivoted as Rick stormed into the unit, followed by Colt and Cat. They must have had sirens blazing to get here so quickly. Didn't matter. Steve would willingly go to jail if it meant saving Josie's life.

Sensing an ally, Deets turned to Rick. "Call the police. I'm being held against my will. I want these men arrested."

"I *am* the police," Rick responded, flashing his badge so quickly Deets wouldn't have time to examine it and realize Rick had no authority here. "Now, if you'd answer this gentleman's question."

"I can't."

"Can't or won't?" Steve snarled from behind him.

"I don't know! I have no idea what Erica's doing here." Deets pleaded with Rick. He took another step away from Steve. "I can't be held here against my will."

"The woman you came to meet is missing. You're staying put until we find her," Rick stated firmly so there would be no question.

"Have at him," Steve told Rick, giving Deets a shove in his direction. "Erica's behind this. My guess is he's been played," Steve stated in disgust. The questioning was going nowhere.

Frustrated and angry, he headed toward the door. He might as well join Gib in his search of the grounds while Rick and Colt took a shot at him. Looking would be better than beating his head against a brick wall or beating the shit out of this asshole. Although that would give him a great deal of satisfaction, it wouldn't find Josie.

"Where's her phone?" Colt asked.

"There," Steve pointed to the breakfast bar and the phone that Gib found on the ground.

"She had two," Colt reminded them, snatching up the phone. He tapped the screen. "This is the one she used to communicate with Deets. Where's the other one?"

Steve disappeared into the bedroom. As he ransacked the duffle bag packed with their clothes. Kevin and Colt checked the rest of the unit while Don's fingers flew over the keyboard on his phone. They couldn't call Josie. If she had it, they wouldn't want Erica to know.

"Don, see if you can get a fix on her," Steve shouted as he raced toward the door.

"Already on it," Don shouted.

40

The boat's hull slapped against the chop of Estero Bay as the resort faded from view. The jarring movement intensified the pain in Josie's shoulder. Blood stained her blouse where Erica had rammed the butt of her gun against Josie's clavicle. If the grinding sensation was any indication, she suspected her collarbone was broken.

The second Troy had cleared the building, Erica had taken aim. Josie had recognized the stance. She'd spent time at the firing range with Steve. *"Aim for the central mass,"* he'd told her, repeatedly. Erica had been aiming to kill. Josie'd had no choice. She'd thrown her full weight against Erica as the trigger was pulled. She was immediately slammed to the deck by the blow from Erica. Hopefully, the damage had been worth the effort and Troy wasn't hurt.

Erica had hauled Josie into the seat next to the captain's chair ignoring her cries of pain. Now the crisp November air stung Josie's face. Her eyes teared as the boat sped across the Bay she'd admired just yesterday. The tears had more to do with the searing pain in her shoulder than the biting wind.

Bile rose from her stomach as it protested the pain and the rocking of the boat.

The sound of the Yamaha engines grew louder as Erica kicked them up another notch, clearing a bridge and heading toward open waters. Josie pressed her left hand against her collarbone hoping to minimize the painful movements. It had little effect.

"What the hell, Erica? What the fuck is going on?" Josie screamed to be heard.

"Retribution!" Erica yelled. Her lips curved in an evil grin. "It's due."

"Retribution for what?" Josie croaked. Her voice was getting raw from the shouting, not to mention the acid that rose from her stomach. "Can you slow this thing down?"

Instead, Erica pushed the small boat's engine to its max. Were they breaking any laws? Was it silly to pray they'd be spotted and stopped by a Wildlife Officer or the Coast Guard?

They passed another boat. Erica waved casually. Just another boater out for the afternoon. Josie considered waving her bloody hand in a plea for help. Her hesitation cost her. Erica pointed the pistol at Josie. "Don't try it."

Why had Josie hesitated? This was a one-way trip. She may have missed her only chance for help.

This *was* a one-way trip. The break in her heart surpassed the pain in her shoulder. She wouldn't see Steve again. *God.* Had she told him she loved him? She couldn't remember if she'd said the words. Last night they'd made love. There was no other word to describe the tenderness—the joining as one. They'd had last night, and their first dance. Steve had held her awkwardly as they swayed to the music. The man couldn't dance worth a lick but he'd given her what she'd needed. To be held and loved.

Don't give up on us, Josie. The silent order in Steve's

voice rose from deep inside her. Was she giving up? Not on them but on her chances of surviving?

She'd once stopped fighting for Steve. That had been a major mistake. She wouldn't make another one.

"Erica!" Josie screamed to get her former friend to look at her. "What did I do?" Could she reason with this woman she no longer recognized?

Erica's head snapped in Josie's direction. Rage emanated from her, its power sucking the air from Josie's lungs.

"You didn't go," Erica spat. "You wouldn't go. You wouldn't go that night like you promised." Erica was screeching. Not just to be heard over the noise of the engine but in sheer anger.

"What night?" Josie asked, her breath ragged.

"Our last semester together. The keg party. You said you'd go then decided to study instead."

The mist in Josie's mind cleared. The night of Erica's accident.

The night Erica had almost died.

Josie had stayed home to study for a test the following day instead of going to the party. Erica had been livid. The viciousness of her anger was as strong as a blow. She'd gone on a verbal tirade until Josie'd finally had enough. She'd told her friend to go get drunk, high, or laid—whatever the hell she wanted. Erica had stormed out. Josie had never had the opportunity to apologize. After the accident, Erica hadn't wanted visitors. Then she was gone.

"If you'd been driving I wouldn't have been hurt," Erica accused her. She'd been badly injured when the accelerator on her car stuck. Erica had lost control and slammed into a tree. She'd spent weeks in the hospital with broken bones and internal injuries.

"Why am I responsible for what went wrong with your

car?" Josie countered, while eyeing their surroundings. They passed the last of the small mangrove islands and were headed out to open water.

"There was nothing wrong with my car," Erica sneered, easing back on the throttle now that there were no other boaters in sight. "I was drunk, high—both."

"You couldn't have been drunk. You would have been charged." No charges had been filed against Erica, not that Josie knew about. Certainly, word on campus would have reached her.

"I was charged after I was released from the hospital. I got the prosecutor to drop the case." A smile crept over Erica's face. The rage and hate had been replaced by evil. The woman in front of Josie could kill. And kill without remorse. Was this the real Erica? Was this the girl she'd known since middle school?

Sure, before college their time together had been limited. They'd kept in touch but what did you really learn about a person from their emails? Josie'd sensed a difference when they were reunited in college but she'd thought she was the one who had changed—had matured more.

"That was my first lesson in the power of research," Erica said. She kept one hand on the wheel as the shoreline began to disappear. Her left hand rested on the gun in her lap pointing in Josie's direction. "It's been a very lucrative business ever since. It's how I stumbled onto Aaron. Then you managed to fuck that up too."

Erica's moods fluctuated so quickly from anger, bragging, and rage that Josie had a hard time keeping up. It was as if three different people were assailing Josie. There was something twisted in Erica, something Josie wasn't capable of understanding. There'd be no reasoning with her but damned if Josie was going to die without knowing why.

"Why is any of this my fault? You drove drunk. Not me. I didn't know who the hell Deets was until you sent me that damn list. What the hell is going on? Why are you ready to dump me in the Gulf now because of something that happened ten years ago?"

Erica slammed the throttle into neutral causing the small boat to rock violently. The pain of hitting the bulkhead almost caused Josie to black out. She blinked more tears away. When she opened her eyes, Erica was looming over her. The gun pointed at Josie's abdomen. "I might just shoot you in the womb before I dump you in the water. It would only be fair."

"Fair?" The boat was no longer moving forward but the wake created by the sudden stop of the engines along with the chop of the water jostled Josie. She reached out to steady herself. The action sent a searing pain through her arm. She had to catch her breath before continuing. "Why would that be fair? You've gone to a lot of trouble to get me out here. Tell me what horrible crime did I commit to deserve this?"

"They literally had to put me back together after that accident. Not all the pieces fit. Now I can't have children! It's your fault that I'll *never* have kids." The words spit out like venom. With the boat stationary, Erica turned and sat coiled in her seat. The gun was no longer laying passively in her lap but was pointed dead center at Josie.

"Why wait until now to come after me?"

"Aaron. I didn't give a damn about having a couple of rug rats to trip over—not until I met Aaron. He was my golden ticket." Her lips had thinned and her grip tightened on the gun as she said the name.

"What a sleaze bag," Erica continued. "I discovered he has a hidden taste for young girls. I couldn't have asked for a better mark but he was different. Ambitious. Very ambitious. He had Washington in his sights. He had the money to win."

Erica's eyes sparkled like a child getting her first look at the Magic Kingdom.

"Imagine the secrets I could unearth and the money I could make," Erica said, wistfully. "We struck a bargain. He needed a wife on his arm during his run for Congress. I wanted the connections he could give me."

"But he'd seen the scars. The bastard did research on me. Got my fucking hospital records! He kicked me to the curb as soon as he got the report. What good was a wife, he said, if he wouldn't have kids to parade in front of the press?"

"But you knew about his history," Josie said. "You knew about Ruth Carr."

"And others. He knew about my blackmailing. He could make good on his threats to put me in jail if I spoke a word about him or his past."

"*You* manipulated Deets to believe I was the blackmailer so that he'd come after me?"

"Bingo! Sweet, wasn't it? You both needed to pay and he paid handsomely. Along with the other cash I've accumulated, I'll have enough now to lay low and reinvent myself. Meanwhile, you'll be feeding the fishes." Erica gazed at the now quiet waters. "Are there sharks out here?" she asked. "I didn't have time to research that. After I saw his email to you, I had to get my ass down here in a hurry."

Josie hadn't given any thought to how Erica had located her but now it made sense. Somehow, she'd found a way to monitor Deets's emails. No wonder Erica thought she owned the man. How could he make such a stupid mistake?

"Did you kill those men?" she asked. "Esteban and Roemer?"

"Why would I kill them? They could help bring Aaron down. They were my ace in the hole until he turned on me. Knowing Aaron, he has some ex-cons going after those he knew at camp. Won't be many left for a reunion after he gets done. That bastard is bat-shit crazy."

Takes one to know one.

Erica looked over the horizon. The sun would set in a few hours. Darkness came early in November. Josie didn't have much time left.

"You know?" Erica smiled. "Aaron's going to be pissed that you didn't show."

The woman was insane. She had a gun pointed at Josie with no qualms about pulling the trigger yet she was enjoying the idea of Deets being pissed because Josie missed her appointment with him. She was indirectly responsible for the death of two men by exposing their names on a list she'd sent to Josie.

Erica had no idea that Deets had walked into a trap. Would that change Erica's plans? Why the hell did she care about Erica's plans?

Except how those plans might affect Steve. He'd be looking for Josie. Troy had definitely seen her on the boat. Every minute she stayed on board increased her chances of being found. Once she was in the water, even if she managed to stay afloat and assuming Erica didn't shoot her first—she'd be the needle in a haystack. The Gulf of Mexico was one hell of a haystack.

"Did he think I could lead him to you?" Josie asked to keep the conversation going.

"You didn't know where I was. You did a pretty good disappearing act yourself. If he hadn't contacted you for a meet, I wouldn't have found you. At least, not so fast."

"Why is he just now cleaning house?"

"Doesn't matter to you anymore. It's time for your swim," Erica grinned. "I want to be off these waters before sunset. It was nice catching up with you, though." With the barrel of the gun pointed at Josie, Erica motioned for her to stand. Josie didn't move.

"Get up," Erica ordered. "You can sit there where you'll be an easy target or you can get your ass into the water where you might have a chance."

The boat rocked as Josie awkwardly made her way over the rear seats and onto the first tier of the swim deck. Stumbling, she instinctively grasped the seat to steady herself. *Shit!* Her shoulder screamed and her knees buckled. Josie rolled to the second tier of the deck.

Erica was laughing as she leaned over the seat and pointed the gun at Josie's abdomen again. "I was just kidding." An unholy grin returned to her face. "You don't deserve a chance."

Josie didn't hesitate. She rolled off the platform and into the water.

41

Steve flew down the stairs. By the time he blasted through the exit door and into the sunlight, Don had already sent out a group text with the GPS coordinates to Josie's phone. Rick would relay the information to the Coast Guard and local authorities but Steve couldn't sit quietly and wait. He headed toward the docks. He needed a boat.

"That boat," he said when he spotted a sleek, white-and-red cigarette boat speeding toward the resort. Envy turned to relief as he recognized Gib at the helm.

Steve leaped off the wall and onto the foredeck as soon as the boat was close enough for him to make the distance. "Where'd you get this thing?" The question was automatic. Steve didn't care if Gib owned or stole it—as long as it could help him find Josie.

"Does it matter?" Gib shouted over the rumbling of the powerful engines. "I assume you have her location?"

"Got it. You know your way around these waters?"

"Good enough. Give me the coordinates."

Conversation ceased as they got underway. Steve shot Gib a quick, suspicious glance. This obviously wasn't Gib's first experience with a cigarette boat. Steve had been on a few go-fast boats but never one this powerful. The thousand or so horsepower straining to break free of the massive engines had the vessel humming. So was Steve. As fast as the boat was moving it still wasn't fast enough.

He had to find Josie.

Gib deftly handled the wheel, skirting mangroves and other boaters. Steve knew they were breaking wake zone limits in addition to committing a few other offenses the Florida Fish and Wildlife Department would frown upon. Belatedly, Steve texted Rick to let him know they were on the move so Rick could let the respective authorities know they were "friendlies." Hopefully, they'd back off if Gib and Steve were reported—assuming any agency in the area had a vessel that could catch this powerhouse.

"What happened with Deets?" Gib shouted after a few minutes.

"Rick's got him. Erica is the one behind this entire clusterfuck."

"Why?"

"No idea."

"Would she hurt Josie?"

"I'm sure of it. This has revenge written all over it!"

"Again, why?"

"We'll ask Erica when we catch them."

A small dot appeared on the horizon. With one hand, Gib pulled a pair of binoculars out of the storage compartment next to the Captain's chair and held them out for Steve. He didn't ask why the boat was equipped with field glasses or how Gib would know where they were stashed. Instead, he raised the glasses and focused on the boat off in the distance, bobbing in the water. A red head was racing from side to side of the small craft, searching the water around the boat.

C. F. FRANCIS

"It's gone!" Gib shouted in alarm.

"No, it's not. It's right there!" Steve yelled.

"Not the boat, Josie's signal. It's gone." Gib pointed to his phone which he'd slid under a strap on the console. "Don just texted."

"Punch it." Steve braced himself against the passenger seat as the bow of the boat shot out of the water then impacted the surface again. The roar of a go-fast boat going full throttle alerted the pilot of the smaller boat. Erica stopped her search and started the engines, slamming the throttle to full speed.

"I only see one," Gib shouted to Steve as they gained on the craft.

Steve looked through the field glasses to confirm what his naked eyes had already told him. Only Erica could be seen on the other boat. Where was Josie?

"What do you want to do?" Gib shouted.

What had happened to Josie? What had Erica done to her? She'd been looking at the water. Why?

Steve's stomach dropped like a stone as the answer hit him. "Head to the area where we spotted her."

"We'll lose her out here. We have no way to track Erica."

"Josie's signal disappeared when that boat came into view. She's in the water," he said.

Gib didn't ask any additional questions as he steered in the direction the boat had been sitting idle. Steve planted both feet solidly to the deck as he used the field glasses to scan the surface of the water in front of them.

"To the right," Steve pointed. "There. She's over there!"

He ached to dive in but the boat would get to her faster than he could swim the distance. He kicked off his shoes and tore off his shirt as they pulled closer to the struggling body in the water. The wake from the boat would overpower Josie if he didn't get to her fast enough. She was desperately fighting to keep her head above the water. The minute Gib powered down, Steve power dived.

JOSIE'S LUNGS were screaming as she kicked toward the sunlight. She'd rolled into the water as Erica had started shooting. She'd swam deep, away from the hail of bullets. But she'd been down too long.

Desperate for air, she kicked harder toward the light. Her right arm hung useless at her side except for the pain that reminded her she was still alive. Her left hand clawed for the surface as if it were solid and grasping it would be enough to pull her above it. She broke through the salty barrier and threw her head back, gulping air until her lungs were satisfied.

Erica was gone. It had no longer mattered as Josie had made her way out of the darkness. Her choice had been simple: stay under or be shot. One she had the chance of surviving. The other, none.

Her relief at catching a breath was fleeting, though. Her legs were tired and weighted by her wet jeans. Moving them was a herculean effort—one she could not sustain. With only one useful arm, treading water became impossible. She attempted to float on her back but a wave overwhelmed her and sent her sinking below the surface again.

Her mind told her legs to kick but her feet barely fluttered. Panic crept in. She reached for the surface, forgetting her injured arm. The pain was the shot of adrenaline she needed. She struggled toward the light, hoping it wasn't the proverbial light at the end of the tunnel.

You didn't struggle to get to the "other side", did you?

The sun on the horizon is what blinded her as she broke through the surface. Gasping, she filled her lungs with air then was sucked under once again.

She had no strength left to fight the pull. She thrashed about but sank deeper into the sea. Her lungs screamed for air as she floundered about. She drifted down. The light above her faded as she surrendered herself to the waters of the Gulf.

STEVE'S HEAD broke the surface but he couldn't see Josie. He suppressed the snap of panic and muscled his way through the choppy water in the direction he'd last seen her.

Her head popped up in front of him then quickly sank beneath the waves created by the wake of Erica's boat. His heart sank with her. *Come on Josie. Don't give up.*

As if answering his prayer, she rose to the surface once again. With one powerful stroke, he was there. But she'd disappeared beneath the waves.

He filled his lungs with air then he dove under the surface, ignoring the sting of the saltwater in his eyes. She flailed about in panic, though her right arm hung limp. Her body had reached its limit.

But he'd reached her.

He encircled one arm around her chest, gripping tight. Using his free arm and the strength of his legs he propelled them up.

As soon as they broke the surface, Josie choked and gasped for air. Steve gave her abdomen a quick squeeze, forcing a cough out of her. She winced in pain, but it didn't matter.

She was breathing.

"You're okay, baby. You're okay," Steve said, reassuring

her as much as himself. "I've got you." And he wasn't letting her go again.

She was gasping for breath but she was conscious. When she'd slipped below the surface, he'd been terrified at the possibility he'd be hauling a lifeless body out of the water.

Instead, the woman he loved was alive and in his arms.

A life preserver slapped the surface next to them. Steve looped his free arm through the floatation device and let Gib pull them both toward the safety of the boat.

"It was Erica." Josie told Steve as she gasped for air. "Erica was behind everything."

Gib had lifted Josie from the water. It had killed Steve to hear her yelp in pain as Gib hefted her over the side of the boat. But there'd been no choice. The boat was a pleasure vessel not equipped for rescues and Steve wasn't waiting for the Coast Guard to arrive to get Josie out of the water.

"I know, baby. We'll deal with her later. Right now, I need to check your wound. Were you shot?" Steve asked as he dropped to his knees in front of Josie but he was already gently removing the wet blouse.

"No. She hit me with the butt of her gun," Josie answered between chattering teeth. Her chest continued to rise and fall like bellows.

Steve took the belt from his waist and looped it around Josie's neck then carefully slipped her right arm into it. He picked up the floatation device that Gib had used to pull them to safety and yanked at the cord.

"I need a knife!" Steve yelled to Gib over the sound of the engines that had just kicked in. Gib pointed to a compartment next to Josie. In addition to a first aid kit, Steve found a large, sharp knife in the cubbyhole. It easily sliced through the nylon. He secured Josie's arm against her chest then pressed gauze pads to the jagged cut. Finally, he grabbed the shirt he'd discarded before diving into the water. He carefully pulled it over her head, slipping her left arm through the sleeve, leaving her right arm bound against her to keep it immobile.

"Are you hurt anywhere else?" Steve asked, as he did a quick inspection of her.

"No but I just can't stop shaking." Her teeth continued to chatter.

"Adrenaline," Steve explained. The temperature of the Gulf wasn't cold enough this time of year for her to be experiencing hypothermia considering the short time she'd been in the water. He was more concerned about the exposure of her open wound to the water and any water that might have gotten into her lungs.

"Hang on baby, we're almost there," he reassured, as he carefully pulled Josie into his arms, sharing the heat from his body. He pressed her head to his chest. *God.* He'd come so close to losing her today. He touched his lips to the top of her hair and thanked every deity out there for the woman he now held in his arms.

42

Once back at the resort, Josie was swept away by waiting paramedics. Steve followed in her wake, ignoring calls from the authorities that they had questions for him. They could catch up with him at the hospital. He'd hopped into the back of the EMS unit over the objections of the EMTs. One stern look from Steve had quieted their objections. He had no intention of leaving her side.

Steve recognized the hospital as it was the same one Cat had spent some time in last summer. The hospital emergency room was bustling when they arrived but not so much that Josie wasn't immediately rolled into a cubicle. By the time she was transferred from the EMS gurney to the hospital bed, the room was full of emergency room technicians checking her vital signs and asking questions. An ER physician followed, looked at her wound and reviewed Josie's vitals. He disappeared and two nurses appeared. They removed the makeshift sling Steve had contrived then helped Josie into a hospital gown. They'd no sooner finished when two techs arrived to take her to radiology. Steve was impressed with the organization and choreography of the staff.

When the room was vacated of all but him, Steve dropped his head in his hands. He could have lost Josie today. The hospital staff could have been rushing her to emergency surgery from which she might not return. The thought weighed on his shoulders, pushing him further into the chair.

Then a voice brought him back to the present. "Is Josie okay?" Rick asked. Steve looked up to see both Rick and Colt had entered the room. Both expressions serious and concerned. He nodded. "She's fine. She's in radiology. I was thinking how bad it could have been," Steve admitted. "I don't know how you got through this last year, Colt."

"You get through it. She'll get you through it. Our strength lies in them."

Steve got to his feet. He took Colt's hand and pressed his shoulder to his friend's, slapping him on the back as he did. "Thanks, man."

"How's Troy?" Steve asked.

"Patched up and in the lobby along with the rest of the gang. Anxiously waiting on an update on Josie."

Steve looked at Colt, a slight grin on his face. "I'm surprised Cat didn't follow you in."

"She would have, except for the two Sheriff's deputies blocking her way."

"They're just outside," Rick informed him. "You managed to evade them at the resort but you both need to make a statement now."

Steve rubbed his hand across the back of his neck. He really didn't want to relive it but a statement would eventually be required. And he wanted to see both Deets and Erica put away. "What happened to Deets?" Steve asked recalling he'd left the bastard with Rick and Colt.

"Enjoying the hospitality of the Florida Department of

Law Enforcement at this moment." Rick filled him in on the details.

"And Erica?" Steve asked.

"No sign of her or the boat. The Coast Guard got a report of a boat that had been rented and not returned. The rental place was worried. The woman matches Erica's description although the name on the identification was different."

Rick looked back over his shoulder toward the door. Steve got the message. "Send the cops in. Let's get this over with."

Rick stayed while Colt returned to the waiting room to sit with Cat and the others. The tight space was filled again when the two deputies entered. With the exception of the time Steve had played the part of custodian at the resort, one of the team was with him at all times. He wasn't concerned that their stories wouldn't mesh.

Before the cops were done interviewing Steve, Josie was rolled back into the room. She looked tired and pale. "Can we do this later?" Steve asked the two cops, keeping an eye on Josie.

"I'm okay, Steve." Josie smiled softly. "I'm stuck here for a while yet. Might as well use the time." She turned to the two officers crowded into the tight space. "I'm guessing you have some questions for me?"

"Yes, ma'am," the younger and leaner of the two answered. "We'll try not to wear you out." They introduced themselves and then began asking questions.

Steve hadn't asked Josie anything about her ordeal after he and Gib had fished her out of the water. His main concern had been about her physical condition.

Now, Steve's hands fisted and muscles tensed as he listened to Josie describe the details of what she had gone through. Her encounter with Erica came straight out of a

Stephen King novel. It killed him when she broke down repeating Erica's claim that Josie was to blame for everything that had happened including the deaths of two men all because she'd ducked out of a party in college. Josie was tired and hurting and, therefore, emotional. Regardless of the reason, Steve wanted the interview to stop.

"I think we're done for now," Steve interrupted from the corner of the room he'd been occupying.

"No. I want to finish," Josie said, then wiped her eyes and took several jagged, deep breaths before continuing.

Steve almost wished she hadn't when she detailed how Erica had pointed the gun at her stomach which forced Josie to plunge herself into the Gulf of Mexico. Steve couldn't remain on the sidelines any longer. He strode across the small space and planted himself on the edge of the bed, grasping Josie's hand tightly. He needed her touch—to feel the warmth of her hand in his hand. She was alive. It was a mantra he'd found himself repeating several times since finding her in the water.

The questions finally ended. Rick stayed long enough to kiss Josie on the cheek, slap Steve on the back and warn them both that there would be more questions once the authorities had a chance to conclude their interview with Deets.

"How are you holding up?" Steve asked Josie when they were finally alone.

"Sore but okay. I'd feel like a million bucks if I could get this salt out of my hair," she joked.

Steve didn't smile. He found nothing about today funny. He brought her hand to his mouth and kissed it. He was grateful her trembling had stopped. Her nerves were settling. He was anxious to get the doctor's assessment of her condition and, then, hopefully, get out of there.

"No one has told me what happened to Deets. Did he take off when I didn't show?" Josie asked.

"Deets is in custody. He tried to slip away but Don and Kevin changed his mind. The Florida Department of Law Enforcement arrived after a call from Rick and took him to their Sarasota regional office for questioning. He's admitted to paying blackmail and that was enough to take him into custody while the other charges are being investigated.

"And Erica?" Josie asked. Her voice trembled once again but not from a chill. Erica had once been Josie's friend.

Steve squeezed her hand. "We notified Fish & Wildlife and the Coast Guard but there's been no sign of her." Steve felt nothing but rage toward her old friend but Josie's face reflected sadness so he kept his temper in check. "She could be anywhere." Another doctor arrived at that time, thankfully ending the conversation.

Dr. Ruiz was a squat, jovial man who was "on call" for orthopedic injuries. After introductions, he pulled up the scans of Josie's clavicle on his laptop. Gone were the days of slapping a large piece of film against a flat white light box, Steve thought. As suspected, Josie's collar bone was broken but, fortunately, the break was clean. She would be relegated to a sling until the bone healed.

A physician's assistant arrived while the doctor was still there and announced that x-rays showed her lungs were clear. She would be given prescriptions for antibiotics and pain.

Finally, a nurse came to dress her wound, give her the prescriptions and discharge instructions.

THE SUN WAS RISING as Steve helped Josie out of the passenger seat of his Mustang. Someone had grabbed the duffel bag from the resort room and delivered it to the ER so Josie had a change of clothes. She was once again barefoot, however, so Steve gently carried her through the garden and into the home next door to Cat and Colt's.

He settled her on the bed, gave her one of the prescribed pain pills and sat with her until she fell asleep.

While the events of the last week could not be classified as a mission, every man on the team had treated them as one. Steve wanted a report from each team member. Colt and Rick did, as well. Individually, and as a team, they had led a multitude of missions over the years. Habits developed on foreign soil were not easily forgotten at home. Sometimes those habits could haunt a man but sometimes they could be put to good use. This was one of those times.

Was Josie safe now? Were they free to plan the rest of their lives together? The debriefing scheduled for later when everyone could be present would provide answers.

Steve managed a short rest which helped to clear his head. Josie had slept a large part of the day away. Her body had needed the time to regenerate. Due to the limited use of her arm, Steve helped her to freshen up. He didn't rush the process, relishing every opportunity to touch her. He even washed her hair.

The aroma of charbroiled meat greeted them as the pair climbed the stairs to Colt's unit. Steve kept his arm securely anchored around Josie's waist. He was reluctant to break contact. It would be a long time before the sight of her struggling in the water would fade.

As they reached the upper deck, Colt was there, flipping hamburgers on a large grill. A man's toy, Steve thought. "Cat's letting you cook?" Steve chuckled.

"I've graduated since you were here this past summer,"

Colt proclaimed. His lack of cooking skills was legendary among the group.

"Just don't poison us." Steve smiled as he ushered Josie through the door.

Inside the kitchen, Cat and Gib, were preparing plates of sandwich fixings and side dishes. Voices rumbled from the living room. Steve started steering Josie toward the living room but she insisted on staying to talk with Gib and Cat while they worked. She'd become friends with Gib and was intrigued by Cat. He wanted her to rest.

Josie settled herself at the small kitchen table as a concession.

Steve was ready to argue with her when a large hand grabbed him by the shoulder and yanked him out of the way.

Troy, one arm bulged beneath his t-shirt due to the thick bandage. He took Josie's left hand in his. He then bent over and lifted her hand to his lips. He kissed the back of it as if she were the queen and he a gallant knight pledging his loyalty to her. "I owe you an apology and my thanks," he said. "Steve is lucky to have you."

Gib flourished a paper napkin in Josie's direction. "Women," he said rolling his eyes then winking at Steve. "They cry at the drop of a hat."

Troy pulled Steve into a brotherly hug then returned to the men gathered in the main room.

Steve followed Troy as far as the doorway before turning to face the kitchen again and leaned his substantial weight against the jamb. He watched as Josie talked and laughed with Gib and Cat. Such a simple act, chatting with friends but one that he was profoundly grateful she was there to do. A darkness settled over him as he imagined the kitchen with only Cat and Gib in the room.

Steve was aware the minute Colt had joined him. His

former commander had the moves of a predatory animal, but Steve had always been able to sense that he was near. Without turning around, Steve said, "I don't know how you did it."

"Did what?" Colt asked.

"How you stayed calm this past summer when Cat came so close to dying at the hands of that nutcase?" The terror of this past summer still stuck with Steve.

"Where are you getting the idea I was calm?" Colt asked with a smirk. "I was a fuckin' train wreck. It was you, Rick, Gib, the others…" Colt's voice caught in his throat. "You all kept me focused and sane. And if I couldn't keep it together then I would've lost Cat. She was the biggest motivator. That little spitfire is my world. I suspect yours is sitting at that table."

Colt had been a sniper when they served together and Steve had never known Colt to miss his mark. He hadn't missed it this time. Josie was his world. The axis was a bit tilted but, looking at the beautiful, feisty, intelligent woman he'd fallen for, he knew they both had the strength to make it right.

THE JOURNALIST in Josie was eager to hear everyone's report. This was a story that needed to be written. One she would write with first-hand knowledge. When word got out that Deets was in custody—and that wouldn't take long—every news organization would be on it. Initially, Josie would be the story. She wasn't naïve enough to think otherwise. But as the story faded from the headlines, she'd have the opportunity to tell the full story of a man without a soul who preyed upon women. Josie thought of the massive number of missing girls and young women. How many, if any, was Deets connected to?

The investigation of Deets was just beginning. Once she had the corroborated facts, she'd write her news story, one that could only be written from her point of view, freelancing it to whatever publication wanted to run it. Then, Josie would dig deep and write a book, telling the story of Ruth Carr, of girls and women like her. She'd write about boys and men who listened to friends talk "trash" about women and think it was okay. A book that would give value to the women's lives and shine a spotlight on abuse, power, and harassment.

Josie had missed a lot since being kidnapped by Erica and awakening from her drug induced nap. Steve had told her that Rick also had additional information to share.

Three of the men from the list, McClaren, Scagliotti and DiSantis were present. Cat had sent word through Rick inviting them to this gathering. Josie had been introduced to them and knew how each was connected to Deets. Steve had filled her in on the way home from the hospital. She liked McClaren immediately but the jury was still out on the other two who, at the age of fifteen, thought their roommate was "just talking trash."

The words grated on Josie since Steve had related the story. Had they matured and learned? They'd been respectful, concerned, and polite. She'd find out what sort of men they'd become when she interviewed them in depth. She was looking forward to it.

Josie's foot was tapping against the hardwood floor, but she could do nothing to stop it as she waited for everyone to fill up their plates and filter into the living room. Her food remained untouched. Steve had offered to feed her. Fortunately, he was able to read her expression at the suggestion.

She'd figure out how to eat left handed when she didn't have an audience.

"Well? Is anyone going to start this show?" she asked after everyone was seated. "What happened to Deets? What about Erica?"

Steve took the plate from her lap and set it on the coffee table then gripped her hand. "There's been no word on Erica. She hasn't been spotted since she left you in the water. There's a warrant out for her arrest."

"For what?"

"Jeezus, Josie, let's start with kidnapping, assault, attempted murder and blackmail."

Josie's shoulders slumped. "I know, Steve. She was my friend."

"She could still come after you," Steve warned her.

"I don't think she will. She admitted she's been black-mailing people for years," Josie added. "She has the financial means to run. Her intricate plan proves she's not stupid. I don't think we'll hear from her again." *At least, any time soon.*

Steve clasped her chin with his long fingers and turned her face to his. "It'll be okay, Josie. We'll deal with whatever comes our way."

They still had issues to sort out but they seemed minor now. They'd sort them out together. What couple had a perfect life? How boring would that be? She understood that she had a partner. One that would support and love her. Her heart was no longer sealed for fear of being hurt. It was now open, freely accepting and giving affection.

"So," she said then took a deep breath. "What are the charges against Deets?"

"Your attempted murder, for starters," Rick said.

God. Had she forgotten that little detail? "You can connect him to that?"

"And more. FDLE has already uncovered a few felons who have reasons to make deals. It looks like Deets was trading softer charges or probation in exchange for felons he could tap at a later date to do dirty work for him. We have enough evidence to arrest him for the attempt on your life and the assault at your place in St. Augustine. I suspect we'll also be able to tie him to the murder of the man who posed as Detective Watson. Those threads are a little thinner but we're early in the investigation."

"What about Roemer?" Josie asked.

"Deets has offered limited information on the death of Roemer," Rick told them.

"He's a prosecutor, for God's sakes. Why would he do that?" Josie asked. "Seriously. Why would he do that?"

"Because he knows they're going to figure it out eventually," Colt explained. "He's bargaining for a deal. Leaking little bits of information to the investigators in exchange for concessions. He knows the drill better than most. Knows how to play the game."

"Did he kill Ruth Carr?" Josie asked.

"I wouldn't be surprised," Rick told her. "He's holding back information on Carr, right now. He's *suggested* he may have information that could lead investigators to her remains. He's jockeying for a big deal. FDLE won't bite until they know the extent of his crimes."

"I never liked that son of a bitch," McClaren chimed in. "I hope they throw away the key."

"I can't imagine he'd last long in prison," Cat jumped in. "Not with his background." Cat had once worked for the State's Attorneys General Office. She'd know.

"That's why he's talking," Rick elaborated. "We're

hoping that Ruth Carr was his only victim although I wouldn't bet on it. Erica told you he had a sick interest in young girls. FDLE is looking at cases of missing girls and whether he was anywhere near the area at the time."

"What about Esteban?" Josie asked.

Colt, Steve, and Rick exchanged knowing glances. "What?" Josie asked. Was she the only one there who didn't understand the silent communication?

"He claims he had nothing to do with Esteban's death. I agree," Rick said.

"It was unconnected?"

"It appears so," Steve acknowledged.

"Just like that? How can you be so sure?"

Josie didn't miss the hand-off from Steve to Rick. Her eyes danced from one to the other as Steve rested against the cushions and Rick placed his arms on his knees.

"I got a call earlier tonight from the FBI. Special Agent Hernandez, to be specific," Rick told those present.

You could have heard a pin drop in the room. Josie looked from person to person. There was definitely some significance to the news.

"Oh, shit." Cat swore. Colt swept Cat onto his lap, wrapping his arms protectively around her.

"Okay," Josie admitted. "What am I missing?"

"State authorities have been instructed by the FBI to drop the investigation into Esteban's death. Hernandez was the agent in charge of the Gravestone investigation this past summer," Rick told her.

"Gravestone?"

"A murder-for-hire organization. They're the reason we were here this past summer."

"And they believe this Gravestone was involved in Esteban's death?"

"The FBI didn't come out and say that. Hernandez told me to let it drop, which is odd because it is out of my jurisdiction anyway. I couldn't officially investigate his death even if I wanted to."

"He's baiting us," Colt stated from between clenched teeth.

Josie turned to look at Colt. His turquoise eyes turned stormy as he held Cat tightly.

"Could be," Rick responded to Colt's assumption. "I pushed but was repeatedly told to back off at every turn. Hernandez hung up on me. Really, he should have never called me in the first place. My bet is that he was giving us a carrot on a stick."

"I'm not following," Josie told them.

"We have a score to settle with Gravestone and Hernandez knows it," Colt explained. "He's been hunting them for a long time and he's not afraid to accept unofficial help."

"I thought you'd stopped looking for them." Cat squirmed until she could look at her husband's face. "You told me Williamson hadn't lasted a week in custody before they got to him. The man that wanted me killed is dead. Gravestone has no reason to come after me now."

"But I have more than enough reason to go after them. They tried to kill you, Kitten. That gives me every right to bury them, if I can."

"Colt…" Josie heard the warning in her tone.

"We'll talk about this later," he said, laying a kiss softly on her hair.

"Damn straight we will." Cat's voice didn't reciprocate the gentleness of her husband's touch.

The couple was fascinating. Cat was clearly not happy with Colt but it looked like she knew how to pick her battles, or at least, pick the time for them. Colt acted as though he'd won the skirmish, but Josie was betting there would be some fireworks after the place cleared out.

Other members of the group were still watching the newlyweds in anticipation. Josie held her tongue.

After a few moments of silence, Gib broke the spell. "Well, boys, no show tonight."

The room filled with laughter.

"I don't get the joke," Josie said, looking at Steve.

"You remember the Fourth of July fireworks at Fort Bragg?"

Josie smiled. She'd just been picturing them.

"Well, they don't hold a candle to Cat when her temper flares. It can be quite entertaining," he added.

Despite the glare Cat was giving him, or because of it, Steve laughed.

STEVE HAD EXCUSED both himself and Josie shortly after filling everyone in. Josie was dragging. Dark circles formed under her eyes and this time from exhaustion instead of a beating. Watching her wince at every move hurt him more than he'd let on. She was going to take her prescriptions and get into bed. Steve guided her down the stairs.

"Josie?"

"Yeah?" she answered

"How come you could remember your password for your Cloud?" The question had popped into his head several times over the last week but something always prevented him from asking. "You write down all your passwords."

"It wasn't one I'd ever forget." Josie let out a little sigh of relief as their feet touched solid ground.

"Why not?" She was intentionally drawing this out to tease him. "What is it, Josie?"

"1959Impala," she smiled.

The car that she'd been taking pictures of when Steve had first laid eyes on her.

"Now that you know, I'll have to change it," she grumbled but Steve didn't miss the small smirk.

"No, you don't. My lips are sealed," he said before sealing his lips over hers.

Steve held her hand as they headed toward the future home of Sanctuary Gardens.

"We can't stay here forever, Steve," Josie pointed out.

"Cat won't kick us out anytime soon."

"What about the place in Fort Bragg?"

"That was a rental, Josie. I gave it up when you left."

"Where do we go from here? I doubt they'll want me back at the condo in St. Augustine—not after Sykes got finished with the place. I guess I should head back there, though, and see what I can salvage."

"We'll go together as soon as you're in better shape."

"And then what?"

"Do you like it here?" Steve asked her.

"What's not to like?" Josie asked "Well, except for the assault, kidnapping and being shot at part."

"McClaren made me an offer tonight," Steve admitted.

"I saw the two of you talking. Looked rather serious."

"He asked me to take on the job as head of security for his import business. Their security is lacking and he knows it. Rent-a-cops, mostly," Steve told her, opening the door to the house.

"And you agreed?" Josie asked as she followed him toward the bedroom. She was so ready for that pill.

"No," Steve answered quickly. "It was a nice offer but

I'm done taking orders. That part of my life is behind me now. I made him a counter offer."

"And what was that?"

"I want to try my hand at running my own business. To be the one on top for a change. I asked if he would like to be the first client of Island Security and Investigations."

Josie's eyes sparkled in the moonlight at his remark. "On top, huh?"

"In this case, yes," he answered, laughing.

"And what about me? What about my job?" she asked, taking a serious tone as she dropped to the edge of the mattress.

"Can't you work from here? You once told me a freelance journalist could work from anywhere."

Josie didn't have the heart or the energy to hide behind her stern face. She'd planned on telling Steve she'd follow him anywhere, even back to Fort Bragg, if that was what he wanted.

"Yes, Steve, I can work from here. From Fort Bragg. From West Africa, if need be. The only place I need to be is at your side."

Steve clasped Josie's head between his hands and kissed her long and deep. As long as she was with him, she was home.

EPILOGUE

J osie leaned against the balcony railing looking down at the sparkling pool and the man doing laps at seven o'clock in the morning. She and Steve had been given a week long stay at the Gardens Hotel as a wedding gift from the team. Cat had explained to her that this place was special. She'd freely admitted it was where she and Colt had first made love. Like Josie and Steve, they'd also spent their honeymoon here.

Their second wedding had taken place on the beach at Lovers Key State Park. The reception had been at Flippers. Their nightmare had ended there and, Josie explained, it was only right that their happily-ever-after would begin there, as well.

As soon as Josie had healed, Steve hadn't wasted any time finding a minister–one he'd thoroughly checked out. Cat had volunteered to marry the two since her notary license was still valid and notaries could officiate at weddings in the State of Florida. But Josie had wanted her as her maid of honor. They'd become good friends over the past eight weeks. Colt had stood at Steve's side. Gib, of course, took photos. Josie hadn't seen them yet but she hoped he'd captured the sheer joy in their faces as he'd done at Colt and Cat's wedding.

Before the ceremony, Josie had given Steve back the wedding band she'd stashed in her cosmetic bag so he could place it on her finger once again. Steve had hugged the breath out of her when she'd admitted that she'd worn it around her neck until her arrival on the island. He, in turn, surprised her by adding a band of rainbow-colored semi-precious stones to the wedding ring.

"You deserve an engagement ring," he'd whispered. She'd fought the tears as he slipped it on her finger next to the wedding band. When he'd pulled a man's wedding ring from his other pocket and asked her to slip it on his finger, she'd lost the battle and let the tears fall.

Now she watched this man, her husband, hoist his broad chest out of the pool. As he reached for a towel, the owner of the property came over to speak to him. Kate's easy smile and extended hand didn't bother Josie. Steve loved her. She knew that with all her heart. She'd been a fool to doubt him but even fools could learn. She would never forget the lesson.

Kate had made a point to introduce herself when they'd checked in. She'd worked with both Colt and Gib, who'd done the photography for the hotel's publications and she knew Cat from the couple's previous stays. She was a gracious hostess, ensuring Steve and Josie privacy but making sure they had everything they needed.

She was also a potential client. Turned out that Steve had a knack for business. He trolled for clients with every conversation. Kate was well connected in the Lower Keys and Steve wasn't planning to limit his clientele to a specific geographic area. He had already started the process of getting his private investigator's license. In the meantime, his start-up was advising companies on how they could beef up their current security. He had plans to hire staff as the business grew. Troy had indicated an interest in working with Steve once he left the army. Steve would be glad to have someone he trusted working with him but that was in the future.

They were still staying at Sanctuary Gardens but were looking for a permanent home nearby. Cat had decided she had more space than she needed for an office and offered to share the property with Steve for his business. Sanctuary Gardens and Island Security and Investigations would both be opening their offices very soon.

Kate saw Josie up on the balcony and waved at her. Steve turned as she did. When he'd spotted Josie, his desire was immediately telegraphed across the distance. Josie blushed. And from the grin on Kate's face, it showed.

Josie didn't turn away, though. There was no embarrassment in wanting her husband—or him wanting her. She looked at the man she loved, happier than she could remember ever being.

STEVE EXCUSED himself from their host, as he headed for the stairs and his wife. *His wife*. Josie had been in his heart since the day he'd met her. Foolish or not, it was true. The letter from the Clerk's office had not changed that—would have never changed that. But now, they were legally man and wife. Their fears might never be fully abandoned but they had both opened their hearts and souls to each other. They'd talked. They'd laughed. They'd cried. Neither of them felt the need to hide their feelings from each other anymore. It was a slow and, sometimes, painful journey. But they were making it together.

Josie had not taken her eyes off of Steve. She was

wrapped in a complimentary guest robe the hotel provided. What was she wearing underneath? He was hungry after his workout and Kate had mentioned the breakfast buffet was being readied.

But life was short. Before breakfast, he wanted dessert.

ACKNOWLEDGMENTS

To my family and friends Amy, Barbara, Anne and Carrie… for your support and assistance with this project. Thank you all.

I may not have completed this novel without the support and encouragement of my new friend and Romance Writers of America RITA nominee, Sarah Andre. Thank you for picking me up when I was down and for your guiding hand.

Anya Kagan, Touchstone Editing…Thank you for your patience and tutoring. This work is far from perfect but it's better because of your guidance.

Thank you, Shannon Sykes of SilverGirl Designs for the awesome cover, marketing materials, editorial assistance but, most of all, for your support.

Mario & Kim, real heroes who are always happy to answer my questions about anything Special Forces. If something is off, it is my mistake alone. Thank you for your service to our country. It is an honor to know you. (And no, Mario, you can't kill off a hero to make things more interesting – it's a romance novel.)

And, finally, a tip of the hat to Ed Sheeran, for his beautiful love song "Thinking Out Loud" which is featured in one love scene and inspired them all.

ABOUT THE AUTHOR

C. F. Francis is a native Floridian who loves mystery, suspense and romance. Her favorite pastimes are reading, shelling and traveling. Her diverse background includes working in law, insurance, tourism and a stint with the Florida Legislature's Organized Crime Committee. She is honored to have friends who have served in the Special Forces and Military Intelligence, who have generously shared their expertise when asked. Ms. Francis lives in Southwest Florida near the areas where her novels take place.

If you enjoyed this story, please consider leaving a review on Goodreads or your retailer's site.

www.cffrancis.com
cffrancis@earthlink.net

ALSO BY C. F. FRANCIS

Sanctuary Island

Excerpt…

Colt jolted awake, instinctively reaching for the Glock he'd placed on the nightstand before crawling into bed with Cat. Thunder rattled the windows and he relaxed his grip on the gun. It was just a storm. A nasty one from the sound of the rain beating against the glass. The power had gone out, making the room black as pitch. He checked the display on his cell phone—just after four in the morning. Surprisingly, he'd slept for several hours.

Lightning flashed, illuminating the small body curled up next to him. Without air conditioning the room had rapidly warmed. In an unconscious effort to keep cool, Cat had kicked the sheet away. As he'd imagined the night before, her t-shirt had worked its way above her hips. This time the vision revealed a pair of sexy black lace panties. With each flash of lightning he imagined sliding the delicate fabric lower until she was free of the dainty lace, then staring into those dark eyes as he filled her.

Instead of giving in to the carnal urge he slipped from the bed and went to the window, forcing his thoughts to the storm raging outside. This room, as with all the rooms on his side of the building, overlooked the drive that led to the private parking area in the rear. Just past the drive was his neighbor's extensive garden. As lightning danced across the sky it cast an eerie glow over their tropical wonderland. The rain was coming down in sheets. The fronds of the palm trees were being blown horizontally by the strong wind. The locals would call this a "palmetto pounder." Colt had yet to decide whether the term referred to the plant or the large, flying cockroach —both abundant in the area.

His eyes had adjusted quickly to the darkness and, as he glanced back at the bed, he could see Cat trembling in her sleep. He wasn't surprised she was having a nightmare—not after the past two days.

Leaving his post, he settled on the bed next to her and began to gently stroke her hair, shushing her softly as he did. If he had to wake her he would but she seemed to instantly calm at his touch, giving him an unusual sense of satisfaction. When, at last, her breathing steadied he reluctantly removed his hand and left the bed. Stepping into a pair of jeans, he returned to his position by the window. There would be no more sleep for him tonight and if he stayed in bed with Cat, her hair wouldn't be the only thing he'd be stroking.

He wanted to explore every inch of that sensuous, petite body. His desire for her bordered on primal but he also acknowledged that there was more to it than a sexual pull. She intrigued him. She was strong, smart, and independent as hell. She had worked her way into his heart at a speed that was both frightening and exhilarating—not unlike a roller coaster ride. If he wanted to ride this car to the end he would need to keep Cat safe. Then, as if on cue, the heavens lit up and Colt caught a glimpse of a man sliding around the corner to the back of the building.

Made in the USA
Columbia, SC
24 February 2019